WHEN THE ATTACK CAME, IT WAS SWIFT, HARD, AND DEADLY

The first sign of it was when one of Bullock's men fired a rifle at Finch. Then the horde of howling men charged into the three partners' camp.

Campbell had heard the shot, and he looked up quickly, a sliver of cold fear lancing into his bowels. He wasn't afraid for himself—it would take a hell of a lot more than a gunshot and some screams to scare him after what he had been through—but he was worried for Morning Sun and their almost-year-old child, a boy they had named Coyote Heart.

All that passed through his mind in less than an eye blink. Then he was up and racing toward his lodge. He fired his rifle from the hip, hitting one man—he thought it was Edgar Purdy—and then barreled into four others. All five went sprawling across the snow. Campbell lost his rifle in the collision, but he didn't care. It would be useless except as a club with four enemies so close.

By the same author

Mountain Country series:
Southwest Thunder
Winter Thunder
Mountain Thunder

Buckskins and Blood
The Frontiersman
Fire Along the Big Muddy
Buckskin Vengeance

Published by HarperPaperbacks

BUCKSKIN VENGEANCE

JOHN LEGG

HarperPaperbacks
A Division of HarperCollins*Publishers*

HarperPaperbacks   *A Division of* HarperCollins*Publishers*
10 East 53rd Street, New York, N.Y. 10022

Cover illustration by Tony Gabriele

First printing: February 1996

Printed in the United States of America

HarperPaperbacks and colophon are trademarks of HarperCollins*Publishers*

❖ 10 9 8 7 6 5 4 3 2 1

For the BU
graduate assistant
who put me on the path on which
I've been riding for so long now.
Your name has long since been forgotten,
though your contribution will
remain with me forever.
Thanks.

1

Alex Campbell clopped slowly past the scattered, crumbling adobe shacks on the fringes of Taos. He had never been here before, though he had heard great stories about the town. He thrust that thought out of his mind right away. It only made the simmering anger rise to a boil inside him, since with it came remembrances of his two partners, who had told many of the tales.

Campbell ignored the wary but half-friendly looks of the poor inhabitants of those shacks. Those impoverished folks presented neither danger nor promise to him. They were merely another part of the dusty landscape.

His Appaloosa was coated with a thick layer of dust—except on the lower legs, where the animal had splashed across Taos Creek. But the horse still had some life in him, which Campbell thought was more than he had. Campbell had been on the trail a long, long time now, and he was tired. Not weary of travel or hardship or any similar normality; it was the overwhelming tiredness of stunning failure, the exhaustion bred of deep loss.

Campbell was a tall, broad-shouldered, red-haired Scotsman. A big, ragged beard and mustache covered a fair portion of his face. His osnaberg shirt was stretched across his back, and was torn and tattered. It was covered with blood and dust, grease and mud. His buckskin pants were worn, missing most of their fringes, and seemed to be held together solely by dried grease, old blood, and smoke. His simple, center-stitched moccasins had holes in them, and his battered felt hat had seen better days.

Only his weapons were clean and well cared for. Campbell's .50-caliber Hawken flintlock rifle lay crossways across the pommel of his saddle. He had won the firearm from Ol' Gabe Bridger himself, and it had seen him through some mighty tough times. Two .50-caliber percussion pistols were stuck in the front of his wide leather belt. A sheathed knife rode in his belt on his right hip, hilt tilted slightly forward.

As he drew closer to the plaza, the houses were somewhat better made and more densely packed. The many businesses were bustling with activity—well, as much activity as such a sleepy place could muster—as were the vendors' stalls and carts.

In a sign of his dejection, Campbell paid little attention to the señoritas, most of whom had a cigarillo dangling from their lips and many of whom were openly interested in this big, fierce-looking Scotsman. Campbell also ignored the vaqueros and young caballeros who watched him with undisguised animosity as Campbell rode slowly down the dusty street, his string of horses and one mule behind him.

Campbell wasn't even really sure why he had come to Taos, other than the fact that he had tried everywhere else he could think of on his quest. He had found himself at a gratingly poor excuse of a rendezvous up on the Siskeedee-Agie, low on supplies, out of cash, and almost out of hope. He had eaten one horse several weeks back, and was contemplating starting on another. But by then he figured he was only a few days' ride from Taos, the nearest place to get supplies—and possibly find work. It was only late July as best he could estimate, and the fur brigades—if there were any this year—would not have left yet for the beaver grounds in the mountains. If any were going, he was sure he could sign up with one of them; most were always looking for a good hand.

Unless, that is, he found some information that pointed him to his long-sought quarry. In such a case, he would steal or beg whatever supplies he could and be off. The Mexicans wouldn't catch him, and the Americans wouldn't be interested in doing so. He was not worried about appropriating any goods from Mexican merchants in Taos should the need arise.

He stopped in front of a cantina just off the plaza. It looked an adequate enough place, especially considering the state of his purse. He dismounted, pulling his rifle with him. With one hand, he tied his horse to an iron ring attached to the wall of the adobe tavern. He hooked the rest of the animals, tied together, to another ring. The cantina door was open, and without hesitation Campbell entered.

Campbell stopped just inside the doorway and looked the place over. The cantina was much warmer and friendlier inside than it had appeared from the outside. Though it was still a few hours to dusk, the place was fairly busy. Most of the customers were men, though there were several women among them. Everyone seemed to be in good spirits. Most of the patrons glanced up at Campbell, but then went back to their food and drink.

He didn't see anyone he knew, so he marched inside and took a seat at one of the three empty tables. He pulled off his hat and tossed it on the table. He leaned his rifle against the edge of the table as he sat, his back toward one of the unfinished adobe walls.

A young woman, pretty, with deep, dark eyes, glossy hair, and bare feet, stopped by the table. She smiled with warmth and promise. "I am Rosalinda," she said rather boldly. "What can I get for you, señor?" she asked. Her voice was melodious, rich with invitation.

Campbell grimaced as he pulled out his few last coins and slapped them on the table. "How much food can I get for that?" he asked. His years in the mountains had done nothing to file the edges off his sturdy burr.

"Not much, I'm afraid, señor," the young woman said. Disappointment was evident in her voice. She had held out hope that this big American—to her he was an American if he was not Mexican or Indian—would be a good catch. She was disappointed to see that he was poorer than most of the men she knew in Taos.

"Well, then, lass," Campbell said tiredly, "bring me what it'll buy and I'll have to be satisfied with that." He smiled a little, though at the moment it was an effort for him.

"Sí, señor," Rosalinda said. As she began to sweep up the coins in a small brown hand, a handful of other coins suddenly clanged on the table.

Then a boisterous voice said from behind Rosalinda, "Hell, a man cain't eat on that little bit of specie. Now ye start a-bringin' food and Lightnin', and don't ye stop till I tell ye to. Ye got that, purty leetle señorita?"

"Sí, sí, señor," Rosalinda said, turning with bright eyes. She was smiling grandly. When she saw the short, whipcord thin man, she shrugged. He didn't have the breadth of shoulder or the rawboned power of the red-haired man, but if he was that free with his money, she would not mind him. She hurried off.

The other man slid into a seat across the table from Campbell. He was short of stature, but looked as tough as a buffalo bull. He was dressed much the same as Campbell, but his outfit was in considerably better shape than the Scotsman's.

"I be obliged to ye, laddie," Campbell said evenly, "whoe'er ye might be."

"Name's Christopher Carson," the small man replied almost arrogantly. "But folks jist call me Kit."

"I've heard of ye, Kit," Campbell said. "Ye have a grand reputation in the mountains, lad."

Carson nodded. He knew what his reputation was, and he figured he deserved it. He was a man short of height, but not short of self-esteem. "And you're Alex Campbell?" he questioned.

"Aye." Campbell might be feeling a mite tired and somewhat of a failure these days, but he was not lacking in pride.

"Seems ye got a mighty big name among the mountaineers yourself, ol' hoss. You're the one who beat Eagle Foot in that race up to rendezvous that time, ain't ye? And won Ol' Gabe's buffler dropper in the doin's?"

"Aye," Campbell said with a weak grin. He patted the rifle leaning against the table. "Still shoots plumb center, she does. Aye, that's a fact."

"So where's your two amigos?" Carson asked, still friendly. "From what I heared, ye three ol' farts was always together."

"They've gone under," Campbell growled. "Three years ago now." The pain was still evident in him—on his face, in his voice, in the way he held himself so tightly all of a sudden.

"What?" Carson said, eyes widening in surprise. "Ol' Caleb Finch and Ethan Sharp gone under? I cain't believe it."

Campbell nodded, not trusting his voice right now.

"Good goddamn," Carson spat. "I nary thought they'd go under in their prime. Hell. They didn't go peaceful in their sleep, did they? Or get et up by a griz?"

Campbell shook his head.

"They went under fightin'?"

"Aye."

"Well, if they had to go under, that's the way they'd want to do it. Hell, any of us would want to git rubbed out fightin' Blackfeets or somethin' instead of dyin' of ol' age. How'd it happen?"

"We were up . . ." Campbell started.

Then Rosalinda was there, setting down a bottle of Taos Lightning and two copper cups. She left and was back again in moments, carrying a large plate of tamales and another of tortillas. After several more trips, there were bowls of beans and chili peppers, spicy chicken and goat meat, hot from cooking—and from the chili peppers.

Hungry as he had ever been, Campbell dug into the food, chawing down tamales. He wrapped goat and chicken meat and peppers in flour tortillas and wolfed them down, too. In between, he spooned beans into his mouth, heedless of the spillage.

Carson ate more slowly, but just as heartily. Since he was in less of a hurry, he filled his and Campbell's cups with potent Taos Lightning. As he held his own cup up in sort of a salute, Carson said, "Best-tastin' awardenty ye can git. Made right here in town by some old reprobate." He chuckled, though his heart wasn't in it. "Tell ye the truth, Alex, this ol' chil' thinks the hoss who makes this brew has hisself a two-hunnert-year-old Apache squaw who pisses into his cookin' vat to give this goddamn stuff its flavor. And he probably tosses in a month-dead polecat, too."

Even Campbell had to smile a bit at that. He drank the harsh, foul brew anyway. It wasn't the worst thing he had ever drunk. He set the cup down and went back to eating.

Finally Campbell had had his fill. He sat back and let out a sigh. He hadn't eaten like that in a long, long time. He wished he had some tobacco left. A cigarillo or his pipe would be mighty soothing right about now.

As if by magic, a small tobacco pouch and a sheaf of corn husks landed on the table in front of him. He nodded thanks at Carson, pulled out a little corn husk and poured some tobacco into it. He rolled it, making sure it was sealed as best he could. Then he fired it up with the flame from the candle.

Drawing the smoke deep into his lungs, he suddenly began to feel a little better. Not that the pain of the loss of his partners lessened any, or the sense of failure that hung over him like a thunderhead. But he had started to think that maybe his quest was not quite over, that perhaps there were some other places to look for the men who had killed his partners and taken so much from him. He growled low in his throat, not knowing that he had done so.

Carson poured them more whiskey and called for another straw-wrapped bottle of it. When Rosalinda brought the fresh Taos Lightning and set it on the table, Carson said, "Go on and tell it now, ol' hoss. Ye might feel the better fer it."

"Shit, laddie," Campbell snarled, "I dunna want to feel the better for it."

Carson studied Campbell for some moments, taking in the fierce cast to the face under the wild beard, the hard, pale blue eyes, the determined squareness of the shoulders. "I believe ye, hoss," Carson said quietly, which was unusual for him. "And you've been huntin' them boys since?"

"Aye." The word was as flat and as barren as the Cimarron Cutoff of the Santa Fe Trail.

"Well then, maybe talkin' of it'll help clear your

mind for continuin' the hunt. Ye look some beaten
down, boy, and I expect ye ain't found them boys
what done it."

"Nae," Campbell said, clipping the word off
short and brutally.

"Mayhap ye jist ought to go out and kill ye the
first red demons ye can find—of the same tribe as
those what kilt Caleb and Ethan, of course. Hell, ye
wouldn't want to go killin' some friendly Injins."

"That wouldna do nae good, lad." Campbell
sighed. He pulled his pipe from the bandanna he
used as a hat band, filled it, and lit it. He leaned back
in his chair, stretching out his long, lean legs.
"Perhaps I better tell ye, lad. Who knows, ye might
have some knowledge of the men I'm after that'll set
me on their trail again."

"I know damn near ever' chil's ary set foot in
these mountains since I come out this way back in
'26. If what I think you're tellin' me is true, there's a
good chance I do know of 'em."

"What's your stake in all this, Kit?" Campbell
asked suddenly. "I figure ye knew Caleb and Ethan,
but they were nae close friends of yours."

Carson shrugged, but his voice took on a harsh
tone. "Any time one of the mountain boys gits
rubbed out, it becomes all our business, hoss. Ain't
no one in these mountains who's got the hair of the
bear on him gonna let nobody git away with some
shit like these doin's. Especially if they're ours, which
I figure these ass-wipin' shits are. Now tell me."

"Well, laddie, seeing as how ye put it so kindly, I
canna do anything but obey," Campbell said
sarcastically, his attempt at humor falling flat.

2

Campbell straightened up quickly but silently when he heard the sharp whistle of a mountain chickadee. It was an odd sound here in the midst of the fearsome, growling snowstorm that had been growing more harsh since shortly after the camp had woken that morning.

He looked down at Morning Sun, who still squatted in the snow, left arm cradling a pile of firewood, right arm frozen with another stick heading toward the pile. She looked a bit bewildered, but not afraid.

Campbell shrugged, then began a slow survey of the area, moving only his head. Bright plumes of vapor whispered out of his mouth and nose as he breathed quietly, the wind whipping them away. The air was bitter cold, though the cloud cover and the snow had warmed the day just a little. The thick flakes of snow sighed on their way to settling on the thick carpet already covering the ground, seeming to deaden the air a little.

The sound of the bird flitted through the trees,

wind, and snow, sounding even more eerie than before. Campbell craned his neck and spotted the quick flash of a hand signaling to him, then pointing to the northeast.

Campbell nodded at Ethan Sharp, one of his two partners. He had no idea where his other partner, Caleb Finch, was. Not that it mattered. He knew the cantankerous old mountain man was not far away and on the alert. Campbell knelt where he was, and winked at Morning Sun. That seemed to reassure her a little.

As he gently eased his rifle off his shoulder, he thought he heard horses coming toward the camp. He pulled the blanket case off his rifle and made sure the gun was primed and ready. Then he draped the gun case over the lock, both to keep the powder from getting damp from the snow and to make sure it didn't freeze. Then he waited.

It wasn't long before the sounds of mounted men became more clear. They weren't loud, but the clink of a tin cup, the snuffle of a horse, the clank of a bit were quite distinguishable.

But the group of travelers was well into the camp before they became visible. To Campbell, it seemed as if they appeared from nowhere. One moment there was a sheet of blowing snow; the next a man appeared, then another—until there were six of them. They stopped, looking around, suddenly aware that they were in a small, tight camp.

The winter camp in a wooded valley along Buffalo Fork was, as usual, comfortable. Ethan Sharp had a knack for picking good places for the three men and their families to winter.

Their lodges were set up amid the strong firs and pines, cutting down the wind a little and preventing at least some snow from getting through to them. Aspen logs tied to lodgepole pines with strips of rawhide formed a crude corral for the horses and mules. Before the snow really covered the open spots of the valley, Sharp, Finch, and Campbell had brought the animals out to let them graze on the fading grass. The men gathered cottonwood shoots and whatever other forage they could find, storing it under tautly stretched hides.

There was more than enough wood for their fires, and with the river only twenty yards away, they would have no dearth of water, even if it did freeze over. And there would always be plenty of snow to melt, if need be. Game was adequate, if not overly plentiful.

The men hunted often, and within a week of their arrival, drying strips of meat decorated every available tree branch. Trapping had not been neglected either, as the men ran their trap lines each day, and where drying meat was not hanging, there were willow hoops of curing beaver pelts.

The women had their work, too. They were in charge of the children, which was a job all to itself. In addition, they had to keep up the lodges, skin and tan the beaver pelts, butcher the elk and buffalo their men brought in, then cut the meat into strips and hang it out to dry and later make pemmican of it.

Then the winter had really hit, virtually stopping the trapping and, at times, keeping them confined to their buffalo-skin lodges.

Sharp and Finch had been in the mountains

nearly a decade when Campbell had stumbled into their camp. For some reason that even they did not know, the two mountain veterans had taken the young Scotsman under their wing.

In the almost three years the three had been together, they had fallen into an easy, comfortable relationship. Each knew what work had to be done, and they went about it without fuss or argument. They were generally jovial around each other, yet respectful of each man's privacy. Not that they were completely without friction. No three men who were so fiercely independent, so purposefully cantankerous, so self-assured, could live in such close proximity without a ruckus brewing up among them now and again.

For a few moments, Campbell thought the intruders were Indians, but the momentary glimpse of a thick beard when the wind pushed aside one man's hood convinced him that his initial assessment had been wrong. It had been hard to tell, what with the six men dressed in blanket capotes or buckskin coats.

Despite the fact that they were white men, Campbell didn't know them, and he was fairly sure he did not want them in his camp. He was certain it would bring nothing but trouble. One reason was because of Morning Sun and the wives of his two partners. Unless these newcomers had hidden their women in the woods out there somewhere, they had no women, which would assuredly cause trouble if they stayed more than a couple of days. Then there

JOHN LEGG / 14

were the practicalities. Campbell, Finch, and Sharp
had enough meat and such to get by, but to add six
more mouths to feed for any length of time would
see them all having starvin' times before spring
arrived. And it sure didn't appear that these men
had much in the way of supplies to offer.

Finch walked out to greet the new arrivals.
Finch was the nominal leader of the small
partnership, though no one seemed to know why.
Campbell often thought with humor that it was
because Finch was the most crotchety of the three.

Campbell noticed that Sharp hadn't moved, so
he stayed where he was, too, watching warily.

"I'm Caleb Finch. Welcome to our camp," Finch
said evenly to the newcomers. "You boys hungry?"

The man in front of the group shoved the hood
off his head. "Why, I expect me'n my boys here
could do with a bite," he drawled.

"And jist who might you and your boys be?"
Finch questioned. He had not changed the timbre of
his voice, but it was evident he would get an answer.

The leader of the new group hesitated just a bit,
then said, "Name's Lije Bullock. The other'ns is
Orval Creach . . . "

A long-legged, hatchet-faced man with a long,
hooked nose and a grizzled, patchy beard and
mustache nodded.

". . . Viktor Kleinholtz . . . "

"Yah," a hulking "Dutchman" growled. He had
a wide face fronted by a bulbous nose. Outsized
hands covered with thick mittens held the reins to
an ugly, mottled-color horse.

". . . Duff Doolin . . . "

A fairly young, freckle-faced Irishman grinned and nodded. "Top o' the day to ye," he said in a friendly voice.

". . . Delbert Harmon . . . "

Showing an unwarranted disdain for his hosts, a nondescript man of indeterminate age and size leaned over from his saddle and closed off a nostril, blowing snot out the other, then again with the other side.

". . . and Floyd Willsey."

The last was a solemn young man, wearing a pair of wire-rimmed spectacles. He looked almost lost.

"Welcome to our camp, boys," Finch said evenly. He was having his doubts about having invited these men to stay even for a meal. Then he sighed. It was not his way to turn away fellow mountaineers in the teeth of such a storm.

"*Our* camp?" Bullock questioned.

"That's what he said, hoss," Sharp said flatly. He stepped out from behind a tree and moved up alongside his partner. "I'm Ethan Sharp."

"Jist the two of ya?" Bullock asked.

Preparing to stand, Campbell didn't like the tone of Bullock's voice. It was somehow too calculating, as if he were plotting something. And that possibility was all too real, Campbell thought.

Indicating that Morning Sun should stay where she was for now, Campbell moved through the wind-whipped snow until he was on Finch's flank opposite Sharp. "Alex Campbell," he said.

"Pleased to make your 'quaintance, boys," Bullock said unctuously, doing little to ease the tension.

Finch nodded. "Well, light and tie. Meat's on the fire and you hosses is welcome to eat your fill." He said no more, but it was implicit in his tone and manner that the invitation was not an open one and should not be abused.

The visitors dismounted. Towing their horses, they followed Finch, Sharp, and Campbell to Finch's lodge. Bullock's men left their horses saddled and ground staked, and everyone crammed inside the tipi.

The men sat shoulder to shoulder around the fire, while the three women—Morning Sun; Many Bells, Sharp's woman; and Dancing Feather, Finch's wife—dished out stew and coffee.

As Bullock dug into the horn bowl of pemmican-based stew, he said, "How about you boys have your women go tend our horses there, Caleb." It came out sounding like an order.

"Ye laddies want your fuckin' horses tended, ye kin do it yersel's," Campbell snapped. He didn't care what Finch and Sharp planned to do about this, but he'd be damned if he'd allow Morning Sun to do such work for these men, not with the surly way they had been acting. He didn't figure, however, that his two partners would be any more willing to let their women do it than he was.

"Now that ain't near neighborly of you . . . Alex, was it?"

"Aye, my name's Alex. And I dunna care what ye think of my neighborliness, lad. My woman is nae gonna do that kind of work for the likes of ye."

"Them words come damn close to an insult, this ol' chil's thinkin'," Bullock said. He and his men had quickly grown sullen, and all of them looked about ready to draw their weapons

"Now let's not go gettin' nervous, boys," Sharp said calmly, no trace of rancor in his voice. "There ain't no need for us to have us a set-to."

"Vasn't us who started gettink troublesome," Kleinholtz snarled.

"Well now," Sharp said soothingly, "I don't know as if ol' Alex was bein' troublesome, it's just that, well, our women has themselves plenty to do as it is, what with our remuda, and the young'ns and all. You boys should be able to appreciate that."

Bullock nodded, though he still did not look pleased. "Reckon we can at that," he said.

"Still don't give that red-haired son of a . . ." Delbert Harmon started.

"Stow it, Del," Bullock snapped. "Them women belong to these here boys, and if they don't want to help us, then that's their doin's."

Finch spat a piece of fat into the fire, making the flames leap up for a second and sending small sparks skittering into the air. "We done give ye coons more help already than many a chil'd give ye," he said evenly but with a touch of flint. "You're in out of the storm and you're bein' fed. Ye best learn to take what comforts ye can find in life and be glad of 'em."

"Reckon you're right there, Caleb," Bullock said, trying to achieve a look and tone of amiability. "We should consider ourselves right goddamn fortunate, boys."

Finch and his two partners knew Bullock was

being sarcastic, but all felt it was time to let this thing die down.

"What brings ye to be out in this storm anyway?" Finch asked. He had gone back to eating but was keeping a wary eye on his visitors. "Ye should've had yourselves a winterin' place a long time ago."

"We did," Bullock said. "A good'n, too. Up in Absaroka country. Purtiest leetle valley you ary saw."

"What happened?" Sharp asked.

"Crows run us out."

"Crows?" Campbell asked, a little surprised.

Bullock shrugged. "Hell, if you been out in these mountains any time at all, you should know those critters. Warm and friendly as the spring sunshine one minute, hell's own demons the very next."

"That's a fact," Finch agreed. "Them Crows're about the most devious critters this chil' knows. I ain't ary seen no one pretend to be your friend better'n them, and then turn on ye so fast."

"Damn if they don't do just that," Bullock said, a strange gleam in his eyes.

Campbell noted that, but didn't know what to make of it. He hoped Finch and Sharp, with their considerably greater experience, might have some thoughts on it.

"Where're ye boys gonna head?" Finch asked after a short silence.

"No chance of us stayin' here?" Bullock asked, trying to sound contrite and somewhat humble.

"Ye can stay," Finch responded. He paused, then added, "Till this storm blows itself out."

Bullock nodded, biting back the strong rush of anger "Well, then, where kin we store our plunder and set our robes?"

"There's a heap of land hereabouts," Finch said quietly. "Ye can use what of it ye need. Jist keep away from our horses and lodges. Ye need a little meat, we can spare some, but not too much. There's game about, so ye can hunt."

Bullock nodded again, the sour look returning to his face. He rose and headed out, his men right on his heels.

3

When they awoke in the morning, the storm was still howling through the valley. That was bad enough, but when the three partners could take stock of their visitors, they found that eight more men had joined them. Finch called a hurried war council in his lodge.

"Ye boys got any solutions to this here little problem?" he asked bluntly. Pussyfooting around was not his way.

"Mayhap we ought to just kill 'em all in their sleep," Sharp said matter-of-factly. While he was the calmer and more reasoned of the two longtime friends, he was also practical and would do whatever seemed necessary—including the cold-blooded killing of more than a dozen men whom he and his partners were certain would cause trouble.

"I dunna like that idea, Ethan," Campbell said uneasily. "It dunna sit right wi' this chil'."

"Much as I hate to agree with such a faint-hearted bughumper as Alex there, I cain't say as I'm fond of that idee neither," Finch noted. He wondered why, though, since Bullock and his horde were not the kind of men who inspired faith and trust. He didn't believe a word any of them said.

"Didn't say I liked the idear," Sharp commented. "Jist offered it out as a suggestion. You got any better thoughts?"

"Cain't rightly say as I do, ye clap-drippin' ol' fart ye," Finch snarled. " 'Cept to say let it sit a day or two, and hope they cain't work up no mischief before the storm breaks."

"That's a damnfool notion, you piss-besotted idiot," Sharp snorted. "Goddamn, boy, we give 'em any time at all, they'll come up with somethin' sure as shit. You know that well as I do. Or you ought to. And when they do, we're gonna be at a hell of a disadvantage outnumbered as we are."

"Goddamn if ye ain't turned into a worrywart, Ethan," Finch said. "Christ, next thing me'n Alex know, you'll have took up doin' beadwork."

Sharp laughed. "That's jist wishful thinkin' on your part," he said, "since Dancin' Feather cain't do that work no good." He looked up and winked at Dancing Feather, letting her know he was only fooling.

The Nez Percé woman smiled back. She had been Caleb Finch's wife plenty long enough to know the ways of her man and his best friend. It had taken quite some time for her to begin to understand their bantering, but once she did, she had actually started to enjoy it.

"Hell, my woman shines at such doin's and ye full well know it. Or ye would if ye cleaned out the shit cloggin' your ears," Finch growled. He meant it, of course, but didn't like having been forced into saying it aloud.

"Ah, don't ye lads think we ought to be discussin' our wee problem 'stead of playin' such damn foolish games?"

"Damn if I ain't surrounded by faint-hearted worrywarts," Finch grumbled.

"Piss on you," Sharp said without rancor. "I still say we ought to jist mosey on over there after dark and make wolf bait out of those ol' coons," he added.

"They've nae done anythin' to us, Ethan," Campbell said uneasily. The thought of slaying twelve men in their sleep was no more palatable now than it had been when Sharp first broached it.

Sharp shrugged. "They will, though. I'd wager my year's catch, my lodge, all my plunder—and Many Bells—that they will. And I reckon it'll be soon, too. They don't strike me as the kind of critters to sit around when there's animals, plews, and women to be took."

"But how can ye be sure of that?" Campbell asked.

"Goddamn, boy, you saw the way those asswipes acted yesterday. Come in here and first thing they do is sass us, and then go tryin' to order our women about. Besides, boy, I don't git a good feelin' about 'em. I got a hunch they're troublemakers."

"Yer hunches've nae always been right," Campbell said reasonably.

Sharp shrugged. "This'n is," he commented simply as he reached to pour himself some coffee.

"What aboot ye, Caleb?" Campbell questioned.

Finch rubbed a callused paw over his chin. "I ain't so sure they're demons, like the Blackfoot. But I figure for sure they're the kind of critters that'll take advantage of every opportunity for deviltry that presents itself to 'em."

"So ye dunna think they'll kill the three of us and make off with all our possibles?"

Finch shrugged. "I cain't say that for certain, ye understand, but I think they'll sit and stew for a day or two—at least till the storm breaks—and then one night they'll try'n run off our remuda. I figure that if we rub out one or two of 'em then, they'll skedaddle for good."

"I think you got buffler shit where your brains used to be," Sharp snapped.

"If you're that worried, hoss, take Many Bells and the kids and ride on out," Finch said, sounding unconcerned. But he knew his longtime partner wouldn't be going anywhere.

"I tend to agree with Caleb, Ethan," Campbell said quietly. He had come to the mountains an untested young man, and though he had been out here but three years, he had taken his place among these old-timers because he had earned it. He felt no compunction now about voicing his opinion among these men, or any other group of men. He frequently deferred to Finch or Sharp, simply because they were older and wiser in the ways of the mountains, not because he felt inferior to them.

"There's somethin' else ye ain't thunk on, Ethan," Finch said. "It'll be nigh onto impossible for us to kill all of 'em in their sleep. They wake up, we're gonna be ass deep in angry critters. Then we might get rubbed out ourselves—over nothin'."

Sharp nodded. He still thought they would have a better chance by killing Bullock and his men in cold blood, and that it would head off serious problems. He only hoped that he was wrong. "Seems like I'm outnumbered on this'n," he said evenly. "So I expect I can do it your way."

Finch nodded. "Ye know, ol' friend, that at the first sign those fractious bastards're gonna pull somethin' we'll run 'em out."

"Well," Sharp drawled, "I was figurin' on doin' that no matter what you was gonna say about it."

Finch grinned a little, then looked at Campbell. "That suit ye, Alex?"

"Aye. But we'll have to keep a close eye on those laddies."

The storm continued for that day and the next, and through the next night. It abated only rarely, and at those times not for long. The snow might have piled up to huge levels, but the caterwauling winds spread any drifts around the camp and through the forest.

The members of Finch's small group rarely left the warmth and comfort of their lodges. When anyone did, he as often as not did so with a horsehair rope around his waist and tied to a tree next to the lodge. This way no one could get lost in the maelstrom of the snow and wind.

When Campbell, Finch, or Sharp went out, they generally tried to swing over near Bullock's poor encampment to see how they were faring—and to try to ferret out any possible plot against them.

But those men, too, seemed to be pretty well sequestered in their own camp. They had set up one tent and several canvas and log lean-tos. They huddled inside their poor shelters, freezing and half starving. Having arrived in the midst of the storm, they had had no chance to really gather firewood, and their food supplies were quite low. When they could, one or another of Bullock's men would head toward their hosts' wood supply and pilfer a few precious sticks of fuel.

None of this served to improve the spirits of Bullock and his men. They were a surly bunch at the best of times, and this particular little adventure only soured them all the more. They muttered among themselves as they cast covetous glances toward the warm, snug lodges so close by. They usually couldn't see the tipis through the snow, but they knew they were there. And they knew the men inside them were warm and well fed and enjoying the pleasures of their women. It was enough to drive men like Bullock, Kleinholtz, Creach, and all the others to contemplate mayhem.

Kleinholtz was among the most vocal proponents, and his word carried a considerable amount of weight with Bullock, who was and always had been the leader of this group.

Bullock surprised even himself when he said, "Let's jist wait and see what happens, boys."

"You gone frightened?" the hulking German asked suspiciously.

Bullock gave his old companion a look of utter disdain.

"If not that," asked Charlie Blanchard, one of the

late arrivals, "then what's got you thinkin' in such a way?"

"I jist think," Bullock replied slowly, "that it'd be unwise to take them boys on jist yet."

"Hell, we can take them," Creach said with a snort.

"No doubt about that, but them boys're old-timers in the mountains, and they ain't to be took too lightly. They'll get some of us, sure as a wolf shits after feedin'. Especially if we have to go into their lodges for 'em. And this ol' chil' don't want to be the one rubbed out by them—or by one of you ass pickers in a lodge."

He waited while the others mulled that over for a spell. Then he added, "Besides, we watch ourselves, and be good for a bit, I reckon we can lull them boys into thinkin' we mean 'em no harm. Once we do that, it'll be easy to take 'em without endangerin' ourselves."

"Dot zounds reasonable," Kleinholtz conceded. "As long as ve get to kill dem later."

The others were in full agreement.

The storm finally drained itself, and the still-powerful wind blew away its dregs by midmorning. The sun came out then, and cast a blinding white light over the valley. It brought no heat, though, as the temperature plummeted to below zero.

Campbell ventured out into the crystal-white world and instantly regretted it. The brightness of the sun glaring off the snow was like having fresh icicles jabbed into his eyes, and Campbell clamped his lids shut. He sucked in a quick breath of cold air, against the pain in his eyes, and then decided that had been a foolish idea, too. The frigid air raked his lungs like an eagle's talons.

Finally, he cracked his eyes open again, and found it almost as painful as the first time. Stumbling back into his lodge, he sighed in relief at the warmth and dimness.

"I tell ye that was foolish," Morning Sun said in English. She had learned to speak it fairly well in her three years with Campbell, though she still had a thick accent.

"I just had to get oot," Campbell answered sheepishly.

"You're too reckless," Morning Sun chided gently. "Here." She handed him a strip of beaver fur with two slits cut in it.

Campbell nodded and took it. He tied it around his face so he could peer through the slits. He went back outside. The glare was still intense, but the strip of fur across his face made it bearable and would keep him from going snow-blind.

Finch and Sharp, similarly protected, were outside now, too, heading toward the corral. Campbell hurried to catch up to them, his thick bearskin moccasins crunching on the ice-encrusted snow.

Finch and Campbell leaned their rifles against a tree and climbed into the corral to check the horses. Sharp stood, resting his back against a tree. With his rifle resting easily in the crook of his left arm, he stood watch.

It took a couple of hours for the two to

thoroughly check all the horses. One pony had died, and a mule had to be killed to end its suffering. The rest had withstood the worst of the storm surprisingly well. Campbell and Finch finally spread out a fair portion of hay and cottonwood shoots, which the horses took to eating with gusto.

About the time Campbell and Finch were finishing, Sharp called out softly, "Some of our guests're comin'."

His two partners hastened out of the corral and grabbed their rifles, tugging off the cases. They waited, watching as Bullock and Kleinholtz walked unhurriedly toward them. The two also had coverings over their eyes.

"Hope you boys fared well durin' the storm," Bullock said in almost friendly tones.

"We did," Finch responded easily. "And ye?"

"Didn't lose no one. No animals either," Bullock answered. "We was beginning to wonder there for a while, though." He laughed, though it rang false to the three partners. "I'm ashamed to admit, though, that we're gittin' mighty low on meat, and we was wonderin' if you was to have any you could spare."

Finch thought about it for a few seconds, then asked, "You and your boys got anything agin horse meat? Or mule meat?"

"Cain't say as I'd prefer it to buffler," Bullock allowed. "But in starvin' times, I've et a lot worse. You lost a couple animals?"

Finch nodded. "Weren't too bad, though." He rubbed a mittened hand across the lower half of his face. "Well, you're welcome to them. Why don't ye git a couple of your horses and bring 'em over here.

Ye can use 'em to haul the carcasses back to your camp."

"Obliged, Caleb. We'll be back directly."

Finch nodded.

Bullock and Kleinholtz started walking away, but then Bullock stopped and turned to look at the three partners. "You boys mind if we stay a few days longer?" he asked. "Jist till we git fit fer travelin' after the storm and our hardships." Seeing the looks of skepticism on his hosts' faces, he hastily added, "We won't be no bother. You won't even know we're here."

Finch reluctantly nodded. "No more'n a couple days, though."

"We'll be gone by day after tomorrow," Bullock said. "At worst the day after that."

Finch nodded again.

"You don't believe him, do you, Caleb?" Sharp asked as Bullock and Kleinholtz walked off.

"No," Finch said. "I'm still some suspicious of those critters, but I hope Bullock'll keep his word. If he does, there won't be no bloodshed. If there is, we're gonna be up shit creek."

4

When the attack came, it was swift, hard, and deadly. The first sign of it was when one of Bullock's men fired a rifle at Finch. Then the horde of howling men charged into the three partners' camp.

Campbell had heard the shot, and he looked up quickly, a sliver of cold fear lancing into his bowels. He wasn't afraid for himself—it would take a hell of a lot more than a gunshot and some screams to scare him after all he had been through—but he was worried for Morning Sun and their almost-year-old child, a boy they had named Coyote Heart.

All that passed through his mind in less than an eye blink. Then he was up and racing toward his lodge. He fired his rifle from the hip, hitting one man—he thought it was Edgar Purdy—and then barreled into four others. All five went sprawling across the snow. Campbell lost his rifle in the collision, but he didn't care. It would be useless except as a club with four enemies so close.

He managed to get to his feet, though it took some doing. The ice was treacherous and made every movement an adventure. Campbell jerked out a pistol, rammed back the hammer with the heel of his left hand, and fired, just as a man named Rudy Beck was about to grab him. The man slumped against him with a loud moan, then fell to the ice.

Campbell clubbed down another one—Will McCaw—with his pistol barrel and kicked McCaw in the stomach as he fell. With just a moment before the next man would be on him, he took a fast look around.

Sharp and Finch were fighting like wildcats, though Finch seemed to be favoring one shoulder, as if he were wounded. He saw a couple of bodies on the ground near his two partners. But then it was time to turn back to his own battlefield.

Two more of Bullock's men—Del Harmon and Jed Moss—had joined the two—Bob Hogg and Ty Hubbard—who were left standing. All four pounced on Campbell, whose feet slipped on the ice-covered snow; before he knew it, his back slammed on the hard ice, and four men were scrambling to hold him down.

But Campbell wasn't about to just give up. He cursed in English and Gaelic. His knees and elbows flew every which way. He bit, kicked, and punched. Several times he knocked one or two enemies off him, only to have them surge back into the brawl within moments.

This went on for what seemed like an hour to Campbell, before he decided he'd had more than enough of this scrabbling around on the cold ground. He managed to get himself turned over, so he could get his hands and feet under him, all the while enduring the blows his foes kept pouring on him. With a mighty shove, he pushed himself up, Harmon and Moss falling off him.

On his feet, Campbell kicked Moss in the face and elbowed Hubbard in the throat. He got his knife out, slashed Harmon across the face, and then plunged the blade into his chest.

Campbell fell to his knees when someone clubbed him on the nape of the neck with balled fists. He shook his head for a second to clear it and then shoved himself up again, doing so easily despite the fact that one foe was clinging to his back trying to wrestle him down. Campbell hooked his toe behind one of the man's ankles and jerked it forward.

The man's foot went out from under him, and he fell backward, carrying Campbell with him. Campbell had counted on that, and he dug an elbow into the man's side as they hit the ice.

Campbell pushed himself up quickly, stomping down hard on the man's kneecap and then on his chest. Just as he tromped on the man's throat, someone clubbed him on the back of the head with what Campbell assumed was a gun butt.

Not that he really had any time to think. He simply collapsed, half atop the man he had just injured. He was not out, not quite yet. He dimly saw a figure looming over him, a knife in his hand. As he tried to put up at least some resistance, he felt the knife punch into his chest, followed by the sticky wetness of his blood.

Then he lost consciousness.

. . .

Campbell came to slowly. He lay there for a few more minutes, trying to remember what had happened and why he was lying here alone. He wondered why it was so quiet, and an insistent feeling of gloom began to spread over him. None of this boded well.

He sat up cautiously. His limbs moved woodenly and his mind was fuzzy. His head throbbed and there was a fiery pain in his chest. Feeling half-frozen, he forced himself to his feet, pushing up from the cold, stiffening body of Bob Hogg, the man he had stomped just before he was taken out of the fight.

Standing, Campbell kicked the body and regretted it. The corpse was frozen and had settled into rigor mortis. He thought he had broken a couple of toes. "Fuck," he muttered. He had the sudden thought that perhaps his feet and hands had become frostbitten.

Pushing that thought out of his mind, he pulled open his blanket coat and looked inside. When he had been stabbed, he thought for certain that he was about to die, but here he was alive and almost well. He had to see, though, how bad the wound was.

"I'll be damned," he said, almost amused for a moment. The knife blade had somehow managed to go through two thicknesses of his coat—probably because of the way it was twisted when he had gone down after being clubbed—then hit his pipe, which rested in a piece of buckskin hanging around his neck. Finally the blade, its power much diminished, had hit his chest, but turned on the breastbone and slid across his left breast. The wound was not life-threatening and, while it was a little painful, Campbell knew it would not slow him down at all.

He finally turned, knowing that what he would find was not going to be pleasant. The camp was devoid of life—except for himself, of course—as far as he could tell from where he stood. All three lodges had been burned, and were now little more than blackened lodgepoles standing guard over smoldering ashes. His stomach lurched as the pain of what had occurred here hit him.

He lurched forward leadenly, the pain in his head almost forgotten. There was still plenty of light, though the sun would be going down soon. He stepped over Harmon's body, heading across the camp. He saw what he assumed were more bodies, and he had to find out if any of his group were among them.

He found the bodies of Will McCaw and Charlie Blanchard. Between them was Sharp's corpse. Sharp's face was frozen in a rictus of anger, and it was battered and mottled. Campbell knelt, not knowing what to say or do. He felt utterly useless. Through the tears that had sprung up unbidden in his eyes, he noted that Sharp had been shot at least three times, and that he had suffered a number of tomahawk blows. Frozen blood grimly decorated the body and the ice around it.

He stood after a few minutes, knowing that he had little time left before darkness and that if he was going to find out what had happened to the others, he would have to hurry.

It didn't take long to find Finch's body. It was in much the same condition as Sharp's had been. He had killed Wood Eckles and Duff Doolin, but from the frozen blood around the area, Campbell suspected that his friend had wounded at least a couple more foes.

His heart hardened with sadness and rage, Campbell stumbled around the rest of the camp, looking for any of the others of his group. Along the way, he retrieved his rifle and two pistols. He loaded them and then continued his search.

He was surprised, and rather relieved, when he found none of them. That meant they had been taken alive. Of course, Bullock and his men might very well have killed all of them within half a mile of the camp, but Campbell doubted it. At least the women, he figured. They would want the women to use and abuse. The children were another matter. Bullock's men would not tolerate children getting in the way of their pleasure. At the first sign of trouble from the youngsters, there was a good chance Bullock would have them killed. That chilled Campbell even further.

His explorations around the camp also showed him that Bullock's men had taken all the partners' furs, including the ones they had cached; all the mules and horses; plus most of their other supplies.

Campbell was mighty surprised when one of their mules wandered back into camp soon after. It looked mighty skittish, and Campbell figured the animal would be off like a shot if he tried to approach it now. He decided he would leave it be for the time being.

Campbell knew there were things that had to be done before he could begin to track the culprits. He wasn't sure he had the energy or desire to do any of them right now, though. The fact that darkness was just about on him convinced him to put off everything until tomorrow.

Since there was no food or anything else usable in his camp, he wandered dully over to where Bullock and his crew had camped. They had left the lean-tos up, and there was some firewood around, so at least he would be warm and somewhat protected if another storm blew in. First, he painfully dragged Finch's and Sharp's corpses to his "new" camp so animals would not get at them. He was a little surprised that scavengers hadn't ventured forth already, though he supposed the burning lodges and the still-strong man-scent had kept them away.

Then he poked around and found some fairly large chunks of horse and mule meat. That would do for the night, he figured.

Campbell painstakingly built up the fire, and spent a few minutes enjoying its heat. Then he tomahawked some chunks of frozen meat off and tossed them straight on the fire. He didn't have the time or patience for being fancified about his cooking right now.

He ate without enthusiasm, but with full knowledge that he needed the heat and life-giving energy it would provide. When he was finished, he lay down in the lean-to, shrugged as deep into his thick coat as he could, and promptly fell asleep.

The morning sun brought little warmth and no cheer. Reluctant to begin the tasks he had before him, he dawdled over more meat. He wished he had some coffee, thinking that would help invigorate him a little. But he didn't, and there was no prospect of getting any.

Finally he stood. Squaring his shoulders, he headed toward the forest. His two partners had to be buried, and Campbell was not about to tackle the ice, snow, and frozen ground out in the open. He thought he might be able to find a place under a tree where the ground was a little less frozen.

It took some searching and experimenting, but he finally found a spot he thought he could deal with. Without a shovel, he had to rely on his knife, tomahawk, and hands. He worked hard and steadily, allowing his straining muscles to keep his mind off what lay ahead.

By the time he thought he had a deep enough hole, he judged by the sun that it was nearly noon. Shaking from the exertion, he wobbled back toward his lean-to and cooked and ate more meat. That made him feel a bit better, and he went to his friends' bodies a few feet away.

"Sorry, auld hoss," he mumbled as he relieved Sharp of one of his pistols, a pouch of tobacco, and his shooting bag and powder horn. "But I need these things more than ye do. I hope ye ken that."

He bent and lifted the board-stiff corpse. Carrying it was an awkward endeavor, but he managed it. As gently as he could, he set the corpse down in the hole. He repeated this with Finch's body, after having relieved it of more tobacco, powder, and ball.

Once the two bodies were in the hole, Campbell retrieved their rifles and placed them in with his friends. "'Tis nae much of a send-off, lads," Campbell said, tears again leaping into his eyes, "but 'tis the best this chil' can do right now. And I'll tell ye, my friends, I'm nae much given to sermonizin' or the sayin' of prayers, so I'll nae waste my time, or yours, wi' it. But I will say this to ye, auld coons—I'll find the fuckin', haggis-eatin' bastards who did this to ye, and I'll make them pay with their miserable lives. Aye, damn right I will. That I promise ye. And more. I'll take their hair, like the Nez Percé do, so their spirits'll wander in nothingness for all eternity. I swear it on the head of Coyote Heart."

He filled in the hole, sadly, blindly scooping the dirt over his two dead friends. He wasted no time, but it still took him a while. Especially when he dragged up rocks and placed them on the grave to keep animals out. By the time he was finished, he was exhausted. Looking at the sun, he knew he did not have enough time to get on the trail.

Wearily, he headed toward the mule, which seemed to have become quite pacified. It had even wandered back into the corral, though all the logs had been knocked down. The mule allowed Campbell to come right up and pat its brawny neck. "Looks like ye and me have nae but each other, lad. We'll have to watch o'er each other now." He patted the animal a few more times, made sure there was a little fodder for it, and then replaced some of the logs. The mule could get out if it really wanted to, but Campbell had to at least try to keep it penned up some.

He went and ate again, mind almost numb. As

he chewed on the leathery meat, he stared into the gathering darkness, wondering where Morning Sun and Coyote Heart were, and if they were alive and well. And he wondered about the others—Many Bells, Dancing Feather, Spotted Calf, White Hawk, and Otter. True, they were not really his relatives, but they were nothing if not family. He would grieve for them hardly less than he would for his own wife and child—if grief was necessary. He hoped that it wasn't, of course, but his reason told him it was likely.

Worried, aching, sad, and beset by an overwhelming rage, Campbell at last lay down again. It took a while for sleep to come, but it finally did.

Sleep refreshed him a little, and in the cold light of the next morning, the rage that had been sitting inside his stomach like a lump of lead suddenly burst forth, charging upward and outward. Campbell roared out his fury, and then smiled grimly. "Aye, ye scabrous bastards have a demon on your trail now, and I'll nae give up till your bones are rottin' in some lonely valley."

Feeling renewed, he hustled around the camp, trying to salvage whatever supplies he could. There was not much, but he found an overlooked parfleche of pemmican, a few scraps of buffalo jerky, two blankets, a leather sack, and his saddle. He was surprised at the last, but he was glad he had it.

He headed for the corral, where he threw a piece of buffalo robe on the mule, followed by the saddle. He tied one blanket behind him and hung the leather satchel with the pemmican, mule and horse meat, and jerky over the saddle horn. With his two pistols in his belt and the one he had taken from Sharp shoved inside his coat, he mounted the mule, sliding his rifle through the loop on the pommel.

"All right there, mule, 'tis time ye and I was on the trail of those clap-ridden bastards."

5

Campbell moved on at a slow, steady pace, and kept on going once darkness was encroaching. He had planned to ride all night on the villains' trail, hoping to make up some of the time he had lost while unconscious and burying his friends. But a powerful snowstorm sprang up, and he decided it would be best to make camp.

He unsaddled and tended the mule, gathered firewood, cooked meat, and ate. Once again he wished he had some coffee. After he had eaten, he realized he was glad he had stopped for the night. He was still mighty tired and considerably underfed, and he felt it. A night of rest would do him a world of good, he figured.

The snow did not get too heavy overnight, just enough to cover him with a thick layer. It helped preserve his heat, and allowed him a night of mostly undisturbed sleep.

With a fairly large meal of meat under his belt and a decent night's sleep, Campbell was feeling pretty good—at least physically—in the morning.

Showing a bit more verve, he saddled the mule, kicked some snow over the fire, and pulled out.

Whatever trail Bullock and his men might have left was wiped out by the snowfall. Still, there was only one way to go, at least until they got to the big lake some miles southwest. Campbell was not about to worry about it right now, anyway. He wanted to find the women and children—if any of them were still alive—first. After he found them, dead or alive, he could seriously take off after Bullock's men. He had to set his priorities, even if he didn't like doing it. Nothing would sway him from his vow to his two dead partners, however. It might take him a little longer to track down Bullock and his men, but track them down he would.

Just after noon, Campbell heard something on the trail ahead. His heart began pounding hard in anticipation. He was fairly certain it was his quarry out there, and he could not believe his good fortune. He figured they had assumed he was dead, and so there was no reason to keep moving. They would most likely be enjoying themselves on their plundered meat and stolen women.

The latter thought made his sphincter clench in anger, and he fought to control it. He knew he had nothing to really worry about. If Bullock's men had taken their sport with Morning Sun, she would not have been a willing participant in her abasement.

Still, something about it all bothered him. Then it came to him—if the renegade band of mountain men was indeed out there, they were being mighty damn quiet. He realized then that it could only be a couple of people on the trail. All he could assume was that whoever was coming was affiliated with Bullock. Maybe they were heading back toward the camp to make sure no one was following them. Maybe they had just gotten tired of Bullock and the others. Perhaps the reverse, and Bullock had kicked them out of his camp.

Whichever, it was not going to be good for Campbell. If he was captured or killed, Morning Sun's and Coyote Heart's fates would be sealed.

Without another thought, he turned the mule and trotted through the widely spaced trees off the trail. As the aspens and firs bunched up, he stopped and dismounted. Pulling the mule along, he wove deeper into the forest. Finally he stopped and tied the mule off behind a good-size clump of beaked hazelnut. The shrub was mostly bare, but it would give him and the mule enough protection from observation. Unless whoever was coming on the trail rode up close to him—or the mule decided to bellow out a warning—he would not be visible from the trail.

Standing next to the mule, with one arm around the animal's neck, Campbell waited.

After a while, Campbell began to think that either he had just been hearing things where there was nothing, or whoever had been on the trail had turned around and headed back the way they had come.

But suddenly two figures came into view. They were on foot, and moving slowly, as if worn down by great labors. He watched for a few moments and then realized the two were women. A second later, he recognized one as Morning Sun, and his eyes widened in shock.

Campbell was about to burst out of the trees and charge toward his woman, but then he caught himself. He did not think it was likely that Morning Sun—and Many Bells, he recognized now—had been let go so that Bullock's men could follow them. But there was every chance they had escaped and an enraged Bullock had sent some men to recapture them and bring them back for punishment.

Making up his mind in an instant, he turned and walked off on a course roughly parallel to the trail—and heading the way Morning Sun had just come from. He tugged the mule behind. As he walked, he began angling toward the trail, so that he came to it about two hundred yards behind where he had seen the women.

He mounted the mule and followed the trail for almost half a mile, moving slowly, extra alert all the while. But he saw no one. Finally he stopped, and breathed a sigh of relief. With a hard grin, he turned the mule and trotted back up the trail.

As he neared the spot where he had first seen the two women, he slowed considerably, and then moved off the trail again. He didn't want to go racing up to the women from behind them. That would scare them to death. So he moved farther off the trail, where he figured he wouldn't be seen, and then picked up the speed again.

He estimated when he had passed them, and he rode on another quarter of a mile. Then, with his heart pounding hard in his chest, he turned and rode down the trail, looking forward to his pending reunion with Morning Sun. There was a touch of fear and worry mingled with the anticipation. He was not encouraged that he saw only Morning Sun and Many Bells. He wondered if the others were dead, or still captive. Or whether they had been injured and left on the side of the trail to die.

And what had happened to Morning Sun? Had she been abused? Tortured? And the children, where were they? He wasn't sure he would be able to stand it if he learned that Coyote Heart had been killed.

He stopped to get control of himself. He was letting his imagination run away with him, he knew, and that would not do anyone any good. With a few deep breaths, he was back to what passed for normal for him these days, and he moved on.

He spotted the women about the same moment they saw him. The two women reacted faster than he did. Within seconds of seeing him, they had dashed off the trail and into the trees. Campbell trotted forward, stopping when he reached the spot where the women had been when they disappeared.

"Morning Sun," he called softly in Nez Percé. "It's me. Alex. Come out now."

There was no reaction. "Now, lassie, ye should be comin' oot here now," he said, switching to English. "Aye, there be no reason for ye to be hidin' from your own Alex."

"He's dead," Morning Sun said in Nez Percé from somewhere in the trees. Her voice let the world know she had been crying. "I saw him lying there after those men had beaten him and stabbed him."

"Aye, they did all that to me, my lass. But it'd take more than that to put this auld chil' under. Aye. They canna kill auld Alex Campbell so easily as that." He smiled a little. "Now come on oot of there, Miss Fancy

Leggings," he added, calling her by the pet name for her that he had used only a half-dozen times.

In a heartbeat, Morning Sun was trotting out of the trees, carefully carrying a bundle. With a fierce, worried smile, Campbell pulled his right leg over the saddle horn and slid down the side of the mule. He landed on his feet just in time to sweep Morning Sun into his arms. He wanted to hug her with all his strength, but as soon as he made contact with her, he realized that the bundle she had was their son, so he controlled himself.

A few seconds later, Many Bells—Sharp's widow—walked up to them from the other side of the trail.

Both women looked worn down, exhausted, and strongly dispirited, though they didn't appear to have been physically assaulted too much. At least on the little flesh Campbell could see, there were no bruises, neither seemed to have any broken bones, and he had not noticed either of them limping.

Still, he had to ask. "Ye all right, Morning Sun?"

The woman nodded. Her pretty face was slack and dark rings circled her large almond eyes. But she managed a small smile.

"And Coyote Heart?" Campbell asked nervously.

Morning Sun's smiled widened a little, and she pulled the baby away from her chest and peeled his blanket back. Coyote Heart gurgled and kicked about a bit, oblivious to all that had happened to him and to his mother.

"And ye, Many Bells?"

"I'm all right," she answered in Nez Percé. She was sobbing and didn't seem able to stop herself.

Campbell could sympathize, considering she knew her man was dead. And it made Campbell wonder again about what had happened to the other children. He feared the worst.

"What happened, Morning Sun?" Campbell asked softly. Then he caught himself. "Nae, not now. There be time for that later, I suspect?" It was voiced as a question.

Morning Sun nodded sadly, confirming Campbell's fears. Dancing Feather and the rest of the children were dead.

Campbell shook his head. His anger resurfaced and he had to stand there, perfectly still, muscles rigid for a minute or so, until he had control over the rage. There would be time for that later, too. But first, there were things that had to be done.

With a sense of urgency, Campbell helped Morning Sun and Coyote Heart into the saddle, and then Many Bells behind them. Walking off with the mule's reins in hand, he headed for the spot where he had taken refuge before. It was the best spot he knew of nearby. But as he moved through the forest, away from the trail, he found a much better place to make camp.

At the foot of a craggy cliff was a roughly circular fortress of boulders that had tumbled down from the jagged mountain. Inside the fortress there was plenty of room for the three adults and one small child, as well as the mule. One huge semi-flat slab of stone lay across several others, making a roof over a fair portion of the haven.

Campbell nodded. This would do well, he figured. "I'll hunt meat for us," he said to Morning Sun in Nez Percé.

"That's too dangerous," she replied in kind. She was grieving for her friends, but she was still a sensible woman, another of the many traits that Campbell had come to admire in her.

"It's a risk I have to take, Morning Sun," he said quietly. "We need meat. We all need to regain our strength."

Morning Sun nodded, knowing it was the truth. "Watch yourself," she said, lovingly touching his cheek. "And don't be gone too long." She hesitated, shifting a little so that she was holding Coyote Heart on her hip. "I'm afraid, husband."

Campbell gathered Morning Sun into his arms and held her tightly, careful of his son on her hip. "We're fortunate," he said in English. "We have each other, and our son. The others . . . are . . ." He bit back his rage once more, cutting off the words. They did not need saying anyway.

"Aye, we're fortunate," Morning Sun said into Campbell's broad chest.

Finally Campbell pulled himself away from his wife. "Ye and Many Bells get a camp going. Build a fire under that rock across the others there. The stone'll help contain the smoke some so that . . ."

"And just who makes your camps all the time?" Morning Sun interjected, falling back into Nez Percé.

"Aye," Campbell said with a nod. " 'Tis ye. And I should nae be tellin' ye how to do it. Ye know those things far better than this laddie. I was nae thinkin'."

"You have many things on your mind, husband. Now go. Bring us meat, and return soon. Many Bells and I will do what we have to here."

Campbell nodded again. He kissed Morning

Sun lightly on the lips, then mounted the mule and
rode out. He turned deeper into the forest and rode
slowly for about ten minutes, then stopped and tied
the mule to a tree. He moved off a few feet and sat,
his back against a tree trunk. Then he waited.

It was not long before an elk wandered into
view. It was a buck, Campbell noted, and a fairly old
one. That meant the meat would be tough and not
nearly as tasty as a cow's, but at the moment
Campbell didn't care. He was worried about the
others and wanted to get back to the haven as
quickly as possible. Besides, he figured that after all
the horse and mule meat he had eaten, even stringy
old elk would taste pretty good.

He eased the hammer of his rifle back and
glanced to make sure it was primed. Then he
shifted so that he was up on one knee. A few
seconds and one loud gunshot later, the elk was
down. As Campbell reloaded his rifle, he hoped
that Bullock's men were not anywhere within
hearing range. He reassured himself with the
knowledge that even if they were, it would be next
to impossible for them to determine where the shot
came from. It had echoed off cliffs and scattered
through the trees and air. He stood, grabbed the
mule, and headed for the elk.

Campbell worked swiftly, heedless that he might
not be too careful with his butchering. He simply slit
the hide and peeled it off. Then he hacked off meat
and dropped the chunks on the hide. When he was
done, he wrapped up the meat and tied the hide
closed with rawhide thongs. Campbell tossed the
meat-laden hide onto the saddle and tied it down.

Wiping his hands and knife on his shirt and pants, he began walking back toward his camp.

He pulled the meat off the mule and set it near the fire. While Many Bells and Morning Sun unwrapped the meat and began cooking some of it, Campbell walked around the outside of the little fortress. Neither fire nor smoke could be seen coming from the camp, and Campbell nodded. Satisfied that they were as safe from observation as possible, Campbell went back into the rock circle. He unsaddled the mule and took care of it. By the time he was finished with that, the meat was done.

The three adults ate in silence, none wanting to really broach the subject of what had gone on. They washed down the elk meat—which wasn't as bad as Campbell had thought it would be—with water from Campbell's wood canteen.

Then the meal was over, and the issue could not be put off any longer. "Better tell me what happened, Morning Sun," Campbell said.

The woman nodded, but took several minutes before she began speaking.

6

Morning Sun told the story in a combination of English and Nez Percé. She stopped frequently, and her voice was usually fractured with pain and grief. Her tears ran unchecked throughout most of her narration, and she absentmindedly wiped them away.

But she never faltered, though she started slowly.

"When I first heard the attack," she began, "I ran for Coyote Heart. I thought maybe Crows were attacking—until I saw those other trappers. I ran away with Coyote Heart, and thought I was going to get away, but one of them caught up with me."

Morning Sun hadn't wanted to get too far from the camp. She had a lot of faith in her man, as well as in his two partners. She was certain they would prevail, even though they were so greatly outnumbered. So she wanted to get far enough away that if Bullock's men should defeat Campbell and his two friends, she could make her way back to her people. And, should her group win, as she expected, she didn't want to be so far away as to worry Campbell and the others.

So as soon as she thought she was at a reasonably safe distance, she ducked into a thatch of hazelnut bushes and squatted, Coyote Heart held close to her chest to keep him quiet. She could hear the gunfire and shouts, and she began to worry more and more. Then there was quiet, and her fears grew even stronger.

Morning Sun decided that she would make a run for it, trying to get back to her people. She was certain now that her man and friends were all dead. Getting back to her band of Nez Percé would be more difficult than anything she had ever done before, and it would take all her courage, training, and perseverance—as well as large portions of luck and help from the spirits.

She hadn't gotten more than fifty yards before one of Bullock's men ran her down. She could hear him charging up behind her, and she glanced over her shoulder. Knowing that she could not escape, she stopped and turned, standing almost defiantly.

The man slowed down and walked up to her. Then he slapped her hard across the face. The blow rocked her head and left a bright palm print, but she made no outcry. Nor did she say anything. She kept a good grip on Coyote Heart, praying she did not accidentally smother him against her blanket coat.

Orval Creach slapped Morning Sun twice more, venting some of his undeserved anger. Then he grabbed her by the yoke of her dress and shoved her forward. "Git," he ordered, voice deeper and smoother than Morning Sun had expected.

The woman moved, knowing Creach was right behind her. She wished she had gotten away, but she hadn't. And now that she was a captive of the renegade mountain men, she knew she would have to submit to anything they demanded if she and her child were to survive. The thought of giving in to these men, and she was certain she would be taken by them at the earliest time, sickened her, but she would be able to deal with it. She had been trained all her life to expect such treatment at the hands of other Indian tribes. As she looked at her situation now, she considered this band of white men just another tribe of enemies. She could expect no better treatment from them than she would get from the Blackfeet if they had captured her.

She vowed silently to do what she had to do. It didn't matter to her right now anyway. Her Alexander lay out there in their camp dead; growing cold already. Nothing that these men could do to her now meant anything. She would as soon be dead, too, joining Campbell in the Afterlife. But there was Coyote Heart to think about. She refused to die, if she could do anything to prevent it, for the boy's sake. And she was certain that these men would not hesitate an instant to kill her or Coyote Heart or any of the others if the thought crossed their minds.

Morning Sun also vowed to herself that if the renegades did kill her son, she would make their lives as unpleasant as she could—until they sent her to join her husband and child. That served to settle

her, and made it just a tiny bit easier to handle her
mourning for the time being. She would cry and
wail and express her grief in her people's way when
she got a chance to, if she ever did. If not, well, it
wouldn't matter much then.

The best that she thought she could hope for
was to be taken and traded to an enemy tribe
somewhere. If that happened, she would be made a
slave, most likely. From there, who knew? Perhaps
she would remain a slave; perhaps some warrior
would make her his wife. In either case, there was a
high likelihood that Coyote Heart would live, and
that was all she cared about.

Creach gave her a shove, and she slipped on the
ice, almost falling. She managed to catch herself and
cut off Coyote Heart's startled cry almost instantly.
She looked back over her shoulder, face not
reflecting the fear she felt inside.

"Git yo' ass over there wit' the others," Creach
growled.

Morning Sun said nothing, but she hurried over
to where Many Bells, Dancing Feather, and their
children sat on a blanket. The children looked
frightened, but the two women's faces were stoic.
Morning Sun took a seat on the blanket, which was
wet with melting ice and snow.

"Are you all right?" Morning Sun asked her two
friends in Nez Percé.

Both nodded. "Except for our grief," Dancing
Feather said bitterly.

"My Alexander is dead, too," Morning Sun
responded evenly. "And my grief cries out for relief.
But we have the children to concern us." She

explained her thinking to the others. It took only a minute or two.

While the women talked, they kept glancing at their captors. Bullock and his men were gathering supplies and loading them on horses and mules. They plundered the lodges, dragging out everything of use. What was not of use they left inside or tossed haphazardly about the camp.

"I will try to do as you do," Many Bells said to Morning Sun.

A moment later, a skeptical Dancing Feather nodded acceptance. "It won't be easy, though," she muttered.

"I didn't say it would be," Morning Sun retorted, though her voice remained soft. She didn't want to arouse any suspicions. "But it's what we must do. Our children must live, if that's possible."

"And if it isn't?" Dancing Feather asked. She looked ready to break down and start wailing. She and Caleb Finch had been together more than a decade, and she had come to love him more deeply than anyone or anything she had ever known. More than her child, White Hawk; more than her mother and father; more than her homeland. Now that he was gone, she cared not a whit for anyone or anything. All she wanted to do was get ahold of a knife somewhere and hurry her way to the Afterlife to join her man. Her child, she figured, if she thought about him at all, could fend for himself. Or the other women could take care of him. She didn't care.

Morning Sun shrugged. "Then nothing will matter, and we can all join our husbands."

"That's what I want," Dancing Feather said, coming close to whining.

"So do I," Many Bells added.

"I feel the same," Morning Sun said, trying to keep calm. "But we'll join them one day. And it's more important that our children should live. They will carry on in their fathers' place."

Dancing Feather did not look convinced, but she seemed a bit calmer.

"Now, see to White Hawk," Morning Sun ordered gently. "He's cold."

Dancing Feather pulled her eight-year-old son to her with a lack of enthusiasm, wrapping the boy's blanket coat more tightly around him.

Feeling almost shamed, Many Bells gathered in her two offspring—nine-year-old Spotted Calf and six-year-old Otter—and tried to give them some of her warmth. She loved Ethan Sharp as much as Dancing Feather did Finch, but she saw the wisdom in what Morning Sun had said. And she knew that Morning Sun grieved as deeply as either she or Dancing Feather. There was no questioning Morning Sun's love for her husband.

It took nearly another hour, but finally Bullock's men had ransacked the camp to their satisfaction. The women all tensed even more when Viktor Kleinholtz headed toward them.

"Where're you goin', Vik?" Floyd Willsey asked.

Kleinholtz pointed. "It's time to take mein pleasure," the big German answered.

"Vik!" Bullock snapped. "Git your ass back here. We ain't got time fer sich doin's."

Kleinholtz stopped and turned, surprised. "Vot in hell do you mean, ve got no time for such doinks? Ve're in no hurry."

"I want to get out of here."

"Are you vorried about somethink?"

"Nope. But we got all the supplies loaded and we didn't do all that fer nothin'. Besides, I got me the thought that Injuns're headin' this way. Hostile critters, too."

"Your hunches are buffler shit," Kleinholtz said with a sneer.

Bullock shrugged. "Some've been right. There's one more thing, too: The quicker we find some friendly Injuns, the faster we can git rid of a heap of these horses and other plunder we don't need. With the furs we'll git, plus these and what we cached before, we'll be doin' right well fer ourselves."

"Ve von't find any of them anytime soon," Kleinholtz responded. "It von't take long to take a little pleasure."

"That's a fact," Jed Moss said with a laugh. "Especially when it's you doin' the takin'."

The others also laughed, drawing a scowl from Kleinholtz. "Ve haff been vorking hard," the German said, "und deserve some pleasurable doinks."

"Oh, for Christ's sake, Vik, jist keep your dick in your trousers," Bullock snapped. "You'll have plenty of time to hump them Nay Percys. You ain't fucked no one in so long, a few more hours or days shouldn't make you no never mind, ol' hoss."

"But there is another reason, yah?" Kleinholtz insisted.

Bullock sighed in annoyance, then nodded. "I'm hopin' we can find Red Bear's village. We do that, I aim to see if he's interested in takin' these three bitches off our hands. They'll bring a damn good price. And I don't want 'em damaged."

"They haff children," Kleinholtz protested. "It's not like they vas untouched."

"I know that, Viktor," Bullock said somewhat soothingly. "But I've seen how you hump women, and you'd sure as shit damage 'em. Now let's git movin'."

Kleinholtz scowled but said nothing. He and Bullock had been partners a long time, well before the others joined their enterprise, and so he understood Bullock's thinking in this matter. Still, he did not appreciate being taken down in front of the other men like this. Then he shrugged, getting control of his temper. It had happened so often that its shock value to the others was long gone.

"The women and brats gonna ride or walk?" Moss asked.

"Well, what the hell do you think, ya goddamn moron?" Bullock countered scornfully. "We got us a passel of extra animals and we're in a hurry."

"Sorry, chief," Moss said sheepishly. "I just wasn't thinkin'."

"Shit, I would've been a heap more surprised if you ever did think." Bullock paused. "All right, boys, let's git them women and brats mounted. Give 'em mules, if we got any left. Horses if not."

Less than half an hour later the procession pulled out of the camp, leaving behind three brightly burning lodges, many bodies, and scattered plunder.

They rode slowly, not strung out too much. Creach rode out ahead, watching the trail. Bullock led the main part of the procession, followed by the horses and mules. Behind the animals rode the women and children, being watched by Ty Hubbard and Floyd Willsey. Bringing up the rear were Kleinholtz and Moss.

During that long afternoon, Otter began raising a fuss. The boy was only six, and didn't know what was happening to him. All he knew was that his father was not here and he was being taken he knew not where and his mother seemed terribly upset by everything that had occurred since this morning.

Frightened, Many Bells did what she could to try to comfort the boy. She even succeeded several times. But as the day wore on, Otter became inconsolable and more intractable. Hissing out her fear in sharp Nez Percé words, Many Bells tried desperately to stop the boy from complaining.

Kleinholtz grew annoyed after a while, and then called to Willsey. The solemn looking young man trotted back to ride alongside Kleinholtz's mottled horse.

"Shut dot brat up," Kleinholtz ordered.

"You sure?" Willsey squinted behind his spectacles.

"Yah." Kleinholtz knew that Willsey would have no problem with his small mission. Despite his bookish look, Floyd Willsey was a cold-blooded man, one who lacked any sense of conscience.

Willsey nodded seriously and trotted back up the line of horses. When he got to the one Otter was riding, he reached out and grabbed the boy's hair and jerked his head back a little bit.

Many Bells saw it and screamed, "No!" She had to, since she had no other way of protecting her son.

But her pained voice had no effect on Willsey, who casually slit the six-year-old's throat. He wiped his knife on the boy's coat while holding the jerking little corpse in place by the hair. Once his knife was sheathed, Willsey coaxed Otter's horse—now splattered with its rider's blood—off to the side. There he casually tugged the young corpse off the horse and dropped it in some brush alongside the thin trail. He trotted back to the line and put the horse in with the others. As he moved back to retake his spot in the column, he nodded his head at Many Bells. "Sorry, woman," he said, not meaning it at all.

Many Bells could not believe what had just happened. She was still numb from having seen her husband slain that morning, and now this. The cruelty was beyond her. She was a woman used to hardship and privation, of the terrors of enemy tribes. But never in her life had she encountered anything like this.

As she rode along for the rest of that afternoon, Many Bells kept looking to the side, expecting to see Otter riding there. It was just too hard for her to accept that he was dead.

7

Late in the afternoon, the snow began to fall; thick flakes clung to their blankets and seemed to weigh them down even more than their gloom. Bullock soon after called a halt for the night.

Morning Sun was exhausted, more from the tension of trying to keep Coyote Heart quiet than anything else. That and her grief. But she had succeeded so far in preserving her life and Coyote Heart's; that was all that mattered. Still, it had her shuffling as she moved through the trees—Coyote Heart hanging from her back in his cradleboard—gathering sticks for firewood.

Morning Sun suddenly stopped and stood stock still and silent in the soft soughing of the snowfall. The sound wasn't much, but it would mask an escape—if she were careful. Her heart pounded excitedly at the thought, but then she managed to calm herself. Now was not the time. Perhaps later, when the camp was asleep. Or maybe it would have to wait for another day. But she felt better for having had the thought. She went back to picking up sticks.

When she got back to the campsite, she began building a fire. With the snow, it was difficult, but she was well practiced and soon had a nice little blaze going. While she worked, she kept her eyes moving about the camp, watching Dancing Feather and Many Bells, as well as White Hawk and Spotted Calf. All were already beaten down by the hardships they had suffered that day. But they were making do and not causing trouble. Perhaps, Morning Sun thought, they might all survive this and then be traded off to some tribe where they could earn their way into being adopted. It wasn't ideal, but it was better than the alternatives she could think of.

She tried shaking off the feeling of doom, but it was impossible. Not when she had so recently lost her Alexander, and when she was in the clutches of men such as Bullock. Still, she had to try to do better to clear her thoughts; otherwise she would never be able to develop a plan for escaping, which she fully intended to do as soon as she figured the time was right. To do so, though, she would need her friends' help, so she wanted to keep an eye on them to make sure they were going to be all right when the time came.

Morning Sun mostly worried about Many Bells. She had taken the loss of her husband hard, and that grief was doubled when Otter had been killed that afternoon. Morning Sun hoped her friend would be able to overcome her grief enough to survive.

The men had shot two deer during the day, and as soon as she had a fire going, Morning Sun went to help Dancing Feather cut some meat out of one deer carcass.

The women set the meat cooking over the fires and began coffee. Only then did they take a few moments to care for their own simple needs, seeing to the children and such. But that time was short enough, and then they went to serve the men.

Being anywhere near Kleinholtz made the fine hairs on Morning Sun's forearms stand on end, but she gave no sign of her distaste as she set a chunk of deer meat on a "plate" of bark down next to the big German. She kept her face emotionally blank when Kleinholtz grabbed one of her buttocks and squeezed.

"Das goot," he said with a hoarse laugh.

The other men also laughed, nodding in agreement. Morning Sun made no move or sound.

"Hey, Lije," Kleinholtz roared, "Vhen vill ve haff our chance to fulfill ourselves vith these sqvaws?" There was a touch of annoyance in the voice.

"When I say so, and not a goddamn minute before," Bullock answered easily. "I figure the wait'll whet your appetite some."

"Mein appetite for screwink sqvaws is plenty vhet enough," Kleinholtz growled, bringing chuckles from the other men.

"You must learn patience, big friend," Bullock chided gently.

"Vhy?" Kleinholtz questioned, puzzled. "You haff never shown much patience. Nor haff any of us."

Bullock shrugged, unfazed. "I decided recently that the acquirance of patience might be of benefit to us all."

"What the fuck does that mean?" Jed Moss asked roughly.

"It means, you dumb bastard," Bullock said quietly, "that times is changin' and we got to change, too, or we'll be left to sit out here like hunnert-year-old buffler shit."

"How're things changin'?" the slow-witted Ty Hubbard asked.

"Unless you ain't been payin' no heed whatsoever, boy," Bullock said easily, "the beaver trade's changin'. Dyin' out, it is. Prime pickin's like the plews we took from them boys the other day ain't gonna be near so easy for us. We might have to change the way we do business, and that means we got to have more patience." He laughed. "Hell, we're gonna have to set and wait a while longer whilst these mountaineers go out and hunt our catch for us."

"Vhat's dot got to do vith humpin' sqvaws?" Kleinholtz asked.

Bullock shook his head in annoyance. Kleinholtz was a man Bullock trusted with his life, and he would want no one else at his side in a battle. But even he had to admit that the big German was stupid and had a mind that almost always was focused on one thing. Bullock figured it would be the end of Kleinholtz one day.

"Because, ol' hoss, we must learn patience for the other, and this is a good place to begin learning it, eh?"

"You vorry too much, Lije," Kleinholtz said, finally releasing Morning Sun's buttock. "But I vill haff mein fill of dot von—und the others, too—before we haff gone too many more days," he added, a threat evident in his words and tone.

Bullock was not concerned about the warning. "When the time's right, you can have 'em," he said soothingly. "Until I say so, though, y'all leave 'em alone, Viktor." He glared at his longtime friend and partner.

Kleinholtz gave an exaggerated sigh, then grinned. "You try mein patience, Lije. Yah." He dug into the meat as Morning Sun moved away from him.

Morning Sun was relieved, but she did not show that either. Once the men were served, she placed some meat for herself on some bark and poured a tin mug of coffee. She sat and ate slowly, trying to savor the deer meat and the hot liquid, but not able to enjoy it much.

She had been too disabled by grief before to really think, but something in Kleinholtz's words when he had held her moments ago had sent a chill through her. She understood now that what frightened her so much about these men was that none of them had a soul. Any one of them would kill the women with as little feeling as they would fornicate with them, with no more feeling than if they were skinning an elk. Not burying their own dead should have been her first clue to that.

Morning Sun forced herself to finish the meat and the coffee. She knew she needed the nourishment, both for herself and for her child. She wanted to be as ready as she could when she tried to escape. When she finished eating, she nursed Coyote Heart. When the child was done, she edged closer to one fire, but not so close as to be near the men, and she pulled her blanket around her and Coyote

Heart. Sitting on the ground and leaning against a log, she closed her eyes and tried to sleep.

But she could not, and she soon rose. Making up her mind, she moved a little away from the men, none of whom paid her any mind. She walked about in the snowy twilight, gathering more firewood. When she had made a decent pile of it, she built another fire.

"What the hell's that fahr fer, woman?" Orval Creach asked once the flames were going.

"For women," Morning Sun said, affecting an even stronger accent than she usually had. She didn't want these men to know she could speak and understand English as well as she did. "And children." She paused, hoping she was not pushing too far. "We have meat maybe? And coffee?" she asked hopefully, looking toward the group of men.

Bullock shrugged. "Sure, woman," he agreed. He didn't figure it could hurt anything, and if the women and children were well fed there was less chance they would cause trouble, which was a benefit. Since there was plenty, he could be magnanimous.

Within minutes, the three women and their children were gathered around their own little fire, a pot of coffee sitting on a flat rock and hunks of meat dangling over the flames from sticks propped up by stones.

Frequently glancing at the men to make sure none was approaching, Morning Sun spoke softly: "We should try to get away from here. Soon."

"How?" Dancing Feather asked.

Morning Sun shrugged. "I don't know. Just slip away once they're sleeping, maybe."

"They'll catch us," Many Bells warned.

"Maybe," Morning Sun said. "But maybe not. The snow will cover our tracks quickly, and they won't care that we're gone."

"They will. They want us to do everything for them."

"Not enough that they would waste much time looking for us, Many Bells," Morning Sun said firmly.

"I need time to think about this," Many Bells said.

Morning Sun was about to retort, but then she thought better of it. All three of them had been sorely pressed by the travel, and by their grief. A decision such as this was not to be made lightly, although she still thought it should be made quickly.

She sighed and settled back, cradling Coyote Heart against her chest. Her mind was made up. She would leave here as soon as she thought she could do so somewhat safely. Tonight if possible.

So exhausted was she that she nodded off almost instantly, though her slumber was less than peaceful. Each time the baby wriggled, Morning Sun woke and shifted, but then would drift back to sleep. Sounds from the men's camp disturbed her, too, and with each new noise, she again came awake, worried that the men were coming for her and the others.

Eventually, though, things quieted, and Morning Sun relaxed. Sleep came then, though she was still nervous. It seemed like a long time, however, before she woke.

She thought she was dreaming at first when she heard the crunching of moccasins on ice. She opened her eyes, a smile curling on her fleshy lips, as she waited to greet Campbell. Then she saw that it was really Kleinholtz tromping toward them. Morning Sun sucked in a breath and clutched Coyote Heart closely.

Kleinholtz ignored her; appeared to not even have seen her. He stopped and knelt where Many Bells lay with her daughter, Spotted Calf. Kleinholtz wrapped a large mitt around the girl's arm. "Come vith me," he rumbled, tugging her easily up.

"No, no," Spotted Calf said urgently, trying to jerk free of the man's grasp.

Kleinholtz pulled back his other hand, prepared to slap the girl, but he stopped when Morning Sun shouted, "No!" He glared in her direction.

"Please. No hit," Morning Sun said quietly. "She only girl. Not understand. Tell her what you want."

Kleinholtz scowled, but said in a voice everyone else supposed that he thought was calm and reasoned, "I yoost vant you to giff me a little help, yah?"

Spotted Calf looked with large round eyes at Kleinholtz, but quit tugging. Then she glanced at her mother.

"Go with him, daughter," Many Bells said wearily in Nez Percé. "It'll be better that way."

"I von't hurt you," Kleinholtz said in a supposedly soothing voice.

"Go," Many Bells whispered. She was so disheartened she was unable to argue even if she had had the energy to do so. She was certain, however, that resistance was futile, and would likely be fatal.

Spotted Calf nodded at her mother and then at Kleinholtz. The man rose but did not let go of the girl's arm. He turned and walked off. Without a word, Spotted Calf followed him. The two figures soon disappeared into the darkness and whispering snow.

"You did the right thing, Many Bells," Dancing Feather said softly.

"Yes," Morning Sun agreed, but in her heart she did not believe it. Her heart and soul were frozen with fear. She was certain that another disaster was imminent. The only reason she had argued for it was that she thought it might be a little easier for Many Bells to handle if Spotted Calf was killed out of her sight. Morning Sun wondered if Dancing Feather really felt the same.

Many Bells didn't answer, and Morning Sun knew that her friend was positive she would not see her daughter again. Many Bells and Morning Sun could hear Dancing Feather sobbing raggedly.

Morning Sun fell into an uneasy slumber again after a while, comforted only a little by the soft, steady whoosh of the snow. She thought she was having a nightmare when, some time later, she half-awoke when she heard a rapidly muffled scream. She stirred restlessly but settled down again when the sound was not repeated.

8

A piercing shriek tore the snowy night air, and Morning Sun sat bolt upright. Her heart raced and she looked around, frightened beyond belief.

The fire had burned down to embers, and it was difficult to make anything out in the snow-obscured darkness. Slowly, dim figures began to take shape. She could pick out Many Bells hunched over something. And then the large, bulky shadow of Viktor Kleinholtz moving away from their little camp. A small, quick-moving shadow darted out from the other side of the fire and jumped. It landed on Kleinholtz's back.

The German grabbed little White Hawk off his back and flung the boy to the ground. He turned and looked down.

White Hawk scrambled up. "I kill you," he snarled as fiercely as he could.

"Shit," Kleinholtz said with a sneer. He slapped White Hawk in the face, knocking him down again. "You are an annoyance, boy," he said, just before he stomped on the boy's chest, crushing the life out of him. With another sneer, this directed at the women, Kleinholtz kicked White Hawk once, then walked slowly away.

As Dancing Feather dashed toward her dying son, a frightened Morning Sun rose slowly. She slid Coyote Heart into the cradleboard and slung it across her back. She edged toward Many Bells, fear coursing through her veins. She knelt next to her friend, and gently grasped Many Bells's shoulders, straightening and pulling her back a little.

Morning Sun recoiled in horror and fell on her buttocks. Her mind was awhirl with what she saw. As a Nez Percé, born and raised in a land surrounded by fierce and often savage enemies, she knew she could someday face a vicious and horrible end. Not that she worried about such a thing; it was simply part of her life, as much a part of it as eating buffalo meat or facing bitterly cold winters. But never had she encountered something as bad as this.

She got back onto her knees and leaned forward, wanting to make sure that what she had seen was true. With trepidation, she looked. Even in the ever-so-faint light from the fire she could see the bloody mess that was Spotted Calf's midsection. And she could see the bruises on the girl's face and around her throat.

To Morning Sun's surprise, Spotted Calf lived. She had not much left in her, but she still breathed, and she whimpered in pain and in her wretched debasement.

Morning Sun sat there for some moments, her senses dulled by the shock of what she saw, of knowing that there were men capable of abusing a mere child in such a way, of the realization that her fate, and that of the rest of them, was to be the same as Spotted Calf's. It was just a matter of time as to when that fate would befall them all.

Finally rage started to build in her, overriding the grief that had been eroding her insides ever since Bullock's men had attacked her husband and his partners. The anger crept up in her as fire slowly licked at a twig until it consumed its entirety. She made up her mind that escape must be made now; there was no time to wait. They must act now if they were to survive.

Yet there was much to do before they could leave. And little time in which to accomplish it. She rose, filled with fury and determination. Leaving Many Bells there with her dying daughter, Morning Sun marched over to where Dancing Feather knelt sobbing over White Hawk. "There's little we can do for him now, Dancing Feather," she said in Nez Percé.

Dancing Feather either did not hear her or was not listening, so Morning Sun grabbed the woman's sleeve and tugged until her friend was looking at her. "We must leave here—now," Morning Sun said, more urgently but without raising her voice.

"No," Dancing Feather said. "There's no reason."

"I don't intend to die here at the hands of these savages," Morning Sun insisted. "Nor to have my child die."

"You still have Coyote Heart," Dancing Feather said, an edge of bitterness in her voice. "I have nothing. No husband, no child. . . ."

"You are young and strong," Morning Sun said quietly, rubbing Dancing Feather's shoulders a little. "We'll get back to the Nimipu, and you'll find another husband. Before long, there will be children for you."

"No," Dancing Feather said adamantly.

"I'm leaving," Morning Sun said. "If you want to come with me and save yourself, you must be ready." Without waiting for Dancing Feather's reaction, Morning Sun spun and headed back to Many Bells. Now that she was fully focused on what she planned to do, there was no hesitation. She grabbed Many Bells by the shoulders and pulled her up, then gently shoved her away from Spotted Calf. "Gather what food you can find," she said in a voice she hoped would cut through Many Bells's grief and shock.

Many Bells stood for a second, but then turned and stumbled off.

Reaching into the front of her dress, Morning Sun pulled the patch knife she had sheathed there, grateful that Campbell had made her wear it. Then she knelt next to Spotted Calf and felt the girl's neck. There was still a heartbeat, though it was faint and thready. "Man Above, I implore you to take this unfortunate child into your welcome embrace," Morning Sun prayed softly. "She has suffered much and deserves a Nimipu's rightful place in your world."

Steeling herself, Morning Sun suddenly plunged the knife into the freezing, naked girl's little heart. She thought she saw a smile flicker on Spotted Calf's face just before the light in her went out for good.

Maybe she had just hoped it, she thought as she cleaned off the knife in the snow and put it away. She was certain, though, that the wetness on her face—and on the little corpse—was not from the snow.

Turning, Morning Sun saw that Dancing Feather still knelt crouching over White Hawk's body. Many Bells sat at the fire, doing nothing, saying nothing. Morning Sun shook her head. Her friends had more reason for grief than she did, but if they all didn't do something now, that would no longer be the case. With determination, Morning Sun headed toward the men's camp.

Moving with the silence of a ghost, she grabbed a buckskin bag. Then she gathered what meat she could, stole a sack of coffee beans and a small leather pouch of sugar. All went into the bag. Then she grabbed a flask of gunpowder, a fire-making set, a horsehair rope, a large butchering knife, and three thick blankets. Laden down, she hurried back to her friends. Ignoring them, she ate the rest of the little meat that had been left over the fire and drained the coffeepot, which she added to her bag of supplies.

"Let's go," she said. Neither of her friends moved. "Dammit," she muttered in English, thinking for perhaps the thousandth time how useful some white men's words could be. She grabbed Many Bells's blanket coat, hauled her up, and shoved her forward. Then she did the same to Dancing Feather. Both finally moved, though not very swiftly.

Through cajolery, curses learned from Campbell, threats, force, and sheer determination, she kept

Many Bells and Dancing Feather on the trail. After
an hour, they even picked up speed. It was almost as
if they sensed they were out of danger for the time
being.

Still, it was not easy for Morning Sun to keep her
two companions going, especially loaded down as
she was with Coyote Heart in the cradleboard at her
back plus the sack of supplies, but she persevered,
ignoring the exhaustion that was her constant
companion. The rage that still simmered in her belly
and breast helped.

Morning Sun thought numerous times of having
one of her two friends carry the supplies. But Many
Bells and Dancing Feather were so overcome with
grief that they were of little use, so she just plunged
on, shoving, kicking, swearing, until her limbs had
as much life left in them as the branches of a long-
dead tree.

Progress was slow, but relatively steady, and
Morning Sun was grateful for the snowfall. It helped
mask any sounds they made, and it covered their
tracks quite quickly. On the other hand, the snow
was accumulating, making walking ever more
difficult. There was no wind to blow the snow away
from spots, so it layered itself evenly on the ice-
covered ground.

Sometime after midnight, as best as Morning
Sun could tell, Dancing Feather slipped and fell. She
yelped in surprise and pain, then lay there,
breathing heavily. Her waist was half twisted.

Morning Sun hurried to her and knelt. Even
Many Bells seemed to be somewhat broken from her
lethargy at the accident.

"Can you get up?" Morning Sun asked.

"I don't want to," Dancing Feather said tiredly. Her teeth chattered a little.

"Try."

Without enthusiasm, Dancing Feather made an effort. Then she fell back, emitting a short scream of pain.

Morning Sun ran her hands over Dancing Feather's body. When she got to the left hip, Dancing Feather started. Morning Sun probed more gently, then nodded. Glancing up at Many Bells, she said, "Her hip's broken."

Many Bells nodded, not caring too much. All it meant was that Dancing Feather could not go on any longer, something that Many Bells wished for herself.

Morning Sun covered Dancing Feather with one of the blankets and then pulled out a chunk of meat. It was frozen, but she gnawed at it while she sat. She hoped it would give her a little more strength as she wondered what to do next. It was plain that Dancing Feather could not go on. It was equally obvious that neither she nor Many Bells—nor both—could carry or even drag their injured friend. The only choice, really, was to leave Dancing Feather where she was, and Morning Sun was most reluctant to do that. So she continued to sit.

Dancing Feather herself, however, made the decision. She, too, knew there was only one option. At first she didn't care, but as she lay there in pain, she realized it would be foolish for them all to die here like this when so many had died already. Maybe her friends could salvage a life yet out of the despair. And she was happy that she would be joining her man and son soon.

"You must go on, my friends," she said softly in Nez Percé. Her voice betrayed no pain.

"We can't leave you here," Morning Sun said flatly.

"Yes, you can. Go. Get away from the white-eye demons," Dancing Feather insisted.

Morning Sun looked at Many Bells, who shrugged. She was too dispirited to care what happened. "Are you sure, Dancing Feather?" Morning Sun asked.

"Yes, go, before the spirits cloud my mind again."

Morning Sun squeezed Dancing Feather's hand and then stood. "Come, Many Bells," she said firmly.

Many Bells looked down and shook her head. "I can't," she said.

"Yes, you can," Morning Sun insisted.

"Go," Dancing Feather coaxed. "Soon I'll join my Caleb and White Hawk up there." She raised a hand and pointed feebly upward. "But you must get back to the People. They must know what happened to our warrior husbands and our children."

A small spark of life seemed to flicker in Many Bells's eyes, even in the darkness. She nodded a little and pushed herself wearily to her feet.

Heartbroken and feeling tremendously guilty, Morning Sun and Many Bells left their friend, shuffling through the foot-deep snow that showed no sign of letting up.

Several times in the next several hours, Many Bells began to balk. Morning Sun was forced to goad her and, twice, drag her by the hair until she was moving forward again. It all wore on Morning Sun, and she did not know how much longer she could keep going.

The next time Many Bells faltered, Morning Sun stopped. She was gasping for breath, and pains shot up and down both legs. She sat on a boulder and set the bag of supplies down. She took the cradleboard off her back and pulled Coyote Heart out. The baby was awake and smiling. "Quite the little adventurer, aren't you, Coyote Heart Campbell," Morning Sun said, managing a small smile of her own. She set the child to sucking as she sat and tried to relax, hoping to build up some strength.

When the baby was fed, Morning Sun gnawed on another chunk of meat. Many Bells had refused her offer of food. Morning Sun knew they could not sit here much longer. They had to make more progress, in case Bullock's men had decided to come after them. She thought that unlikely, but as far as she was concerned, there was no predicting the actions of white men. Or at least these white men.

She pushed up and put Coyote Heart back into his snug, plain cradleboard. Hefting the bag of supplies, she said, "Come on, Many Bells."

"Where're we going?" Many Bells asked listlessly.

"Back to our old camp first," Morning Sun said, realizing that that was the first time she had mentioned that. She had been going there all along, though not consciously. "Maybe we can find some things to use there. Then we can head back toward the People."

"Oh, what's the use?" Many Bells snapped. She

had lost everything, and could see no reason for continuing her suffering. She would have been happy to die right there.

"These men should pay for what they've done," Morning Sun said after a few moments' thought. "For killing our men and children. We'll ask Talks of War to call a war party and chase down these men."

"They'll be long gone by the time we get back to Tall Clouds's village," Many Bells muttered. "If we even get close to it."

"There is a great chance we might not make it," Morning Sun acknowledged. "But we must try so that our men and children can live at peace in the Spirit World."

"Let others worry of such things."

Morning Sun stopped herself before voicing the anger that had surged in her. She was glad she did, as she suddenly came up with an idea. "Let's press on for our old winter camp," she said almost eagerly. "It's not far. We can make it."

"Why?" Many Bells asked again.

"Because the bodies of our men are there."

"So?"

"So, if you were to die there, you would be with Ethan. Your spirits could mingle there before going to the Spirit Land."

Many Bells's head jerked up. That was not a perfect idea, but it was a lot better than just dying here. She nodded. "We'll go there. But no farther."

"Agreed." Morning Sun had no intention of keeping that promise if she could help it, but right now it got Many Bells moving again, and that was the most important thing.

9

"Then you found us," Morning Sun ended. Her voice, as it had been all along, was a dreary monotone of agony and despair. Even though she had come through mostly unscathed, her child was unharmed, and she had found her husband alive, she still felt crushed by all she and her friends had been through. The loss of Dancing Feather, Spotted Calf, White Hawk, and Otter was as disheartening as if they had been her own family members.

The rage Campbell had felt when this had first happened now seemed but a single tongue of flame compared with a roaring prairie fire. Fury tore through his body with the intensity of a rampaging herd of buffalo. The thought of what Kleinholtz had done to little Spotted Calf clawed at his warrior's heart like a starving wolf at an elk carcass. His hands knotted and clenched, as if they had a mind of their own and wished they had Kleinholtz's throat in their grasp right now.

The tempest of his emotions so completely filled his senses that it took Morning Sun four times

repeating her question before Campbell heard her:
"How did you come to be alive?" she asked in Nez
Percé.

"Ain't important," Campbell gargled, the words
strangled by the knotted muscles in his throat and
neck. His body was stiff and hard as iron, and his
jaw had begun to ache from clenching his teeth in an
effort to keep the fury from bursting out. He wanted
nothing more right now than to go after the six men
who had committed such a list of hideous crimes.
Every fiber of his being called out for him to just
jump on his mule and hunt down Bullock and his
heartless henchmen. He cared nothing that he was
so vastly outnumbered and outgunned. He would
kill each and every one of them before he went to
meet his Maker; he was absolutely certain of that.

But he could not leave the two women and the
child here. They had been through too much, had
suffered too much. They had no food, no one to
protect them from wild animals or hostile tribesmen.
No, they were too vulnerable. And he could not live
with the fact that they might now die after having
been reunited with him.

On the other hand, he could not take the three of
them with him. That, also, was far too dangerous,
and it would slow him down too much. While he
figured the renegades were not all that far ahead of
him, it might still take some time to track them
down. They had fresh horses and plenty of meat and
other supplies. He had only the mule to serve four
people. It could be days or weeks before he found
them.

The only other choice he had—the only sensible

choice—was to get Morning Sun, Coyote Heart, and Many Bells back to their village. They would be safe there, and taken care of. Then he could go after the devils who had done all this. He was sure he could get his father-in-law, Talks of War, to call a war party to go with him. He was not sure, however, that he wanted that. He wanted to take care of the renegade mountaineers on his own. But that could be decided later.

The trip back to Nez Percé country would take a considerable time, and that made him hesitate about undertaking the journey, even through he knew deep inside that it was the only reasonable thing to do. Still, the rage pounding through him as if it were a part of his blood made him unwilling to make such a decision.

Campbell looked at Morning Sun, who was feeding Coyote Heart, and a bit of his fury dribbled away. He loved them so dearly. That always came as a shock to him. He never thought he would be able to feel that strongly for a woman—or a child. But he did. He did not know how it had come about, only that it had and that he was happy about it. He was feeling guilty, though, at his family's having survived when those of his two partners, except for Many Bells, had died. He knew that that was not his doing; that it was the spirits', but he felt guilty anyway.

Looking at his wife and son, he knew the trip to Tall Clouds's village would have to be made. That would be dangerous enough a journey, but far safer than the alternatives. It had to be done, and there was nothing he could do to make it otherwise.

Once the decision was made, Campbell was able to calm himself somewhat. The rage didn't go away, but it was at a manageable level. It would never leave him, he knew—until Bullock and his five cohorts were lying dead at his feet. But he would be able to function now, to do what was necessary to save his family and Many Bells. As long as he focused on that, he—and they—would be all right.

He quickly explained to the women what he had decided. Neither protested.

Campbell wanted to be on the trail as soon as possible, but as they sat there for the rest of the evening, he could see how tired and worn down Morning Sun, Many Bells, and Coyote Heart were. He decided that they would wait a day or so. He still had some meat left, and he would hunt some more. That would keep them going for a few days. With a day or two of rest, plus some warm, filling food, they should be able to move at a steady, if rather slow, pace.

Besides, there was more than a foot of new snow and more was falling. That would make their traveling all the more difficult, so they would wait.

Campbell used the time to make each adult a pair of crude snowshoes. He also hunted several times, bringing in two deer and another old, stringy elk. The women smoked the meat as well as they could under the circumstances. With the weather as cold as it was all the time now, the meat would stay frozen for a long time. The two women patched their clothes with the fresh deer and elk hides. It wasn't the best job they'd ever done, but it was the best they could do with the materials at hand.

Three mornings later, Campbell rigged up a travois to the mule. They put their meager supplies on it, as well as Coyote Heart—tightly wrapped in a blanket. Campbell nodded and marched off, heading northwest toward Nez Percé country a few hundred miles away. The snow had stopped the day before, but the wind had picked up, dropping the temperature. But the wind blew some of the snow out of their way as they struggled on.

The small, bedraggled group battled through the snow, slipped on ice, crossed creeks, some of which were running fast enough that they were not frozen over. They maneuvered through snow-clogged passes, up sharp inclines, and down steep slopes. They passed through forests of pine or aspen and through mountain valleys and dark, worrisome canyons.

They followed no trail other than one of Campbell's making. He knew the countryside somewhat, but not nearly as well as he wished. Though he kept them moving steadily toward their destination, there were times when his lack of knowledge about the land caused trouble. Twice they came to the edge of cliffs that offered nothing but a straight drop-off of several hundred feet, so they were forced to backtrack until they could find a way around the obstacle. Both times it meant miles and miles of extra travel, adding to the days spent on the trek.

Snowstorms, freezing rain, an avalanche, two rock slides, and mud all served to slow them even more, but they plodded on.

After a couple of weeks, their moccasins, coats,

and clothing became ragged and worn. Once again the women used what they had at hand to try to patch their outfits, hoping the garments would last long enough to get them home. There they could make new ones, with assistance from friends and family. Still, that did not help them now; their feet grew cold from the constant soaking of melted snow and ice, and they shivered as the wind blew through holes torn in their clothing by branches and rocks.

Having to husband his meager supply of powder and ball, Campbell curtailed his hunting early on, and by the time they were three weeks or so out, their food supply began to run low. It was just one more worrisome thing on this interminable trip. As were the fever and ague that all three adults and the child suffered intermittently on the trek. Wood for warming fires was sometimes scarce, and the mule suffered from a lack of forage.

As the tattered, threadbare procession edged into the fringes of Nez Percé country, Campbell began to wonder whether they would make it the last short distance to Tall Clouds's village. He could never be sure exactly where it would be at this time of year, so he would have to search it out. That would take more time, which they could ill afford to spare. All of them were suffering and exhausted, ailing and strongly dispirited.

Campbell continued to be periodically feverish, which sometimes left him unable to tell the difference between reality and fever-induced thoughts. More than once he had snapped out of the mild delirium to find that he was leading his small party in the wrong direction.

Finally he called a stop. It was snowing again, and seeing which way to go was difficult at best. After he had tended to the weakening mule, he sat and checked his shooting supplies while the women built a fire. With the flask Morning Sun had stolen from Bullock's men, they had enough powder, but he had only six rifle balls left. Not enough to withstand an attack by hostile Indians should they encounter any.

That was the strangest thing to Campbell—that in their entire journey they had not come across a band of enemy Indians. While it was winter, and most tribes were encamped until spring arrived, usually a few small war bands would be seen. But there had been none so far.

That made Campbell's mind up for him. "I'm gonna try'n get us some fresh meat," he announced to the two women, as he staggered to his feet. "We've got to have some or we'll nae make it the rest of the way."

Morning Sun nodded. "Are you well enough?" she asked in Nez Percé.

"Aye." He paused, then smiled grimly. "Or if I'm nae, I canna tell the difference." He hefted his rifle, made sure his snowshoes were on, and headed off, fighting the fuzziness in his head.

He eventually shot a mule deer, but it cost him four lead balls, leaving him only two. He shrugged. There was nothing he could do about it now. He tied some of the horsehair rope around the deer's neck and then began hauling it back toward his camp, aware of the pack of wolves that had mysteriously appeared and was striding in the same direction as he, forming a horseshoe behind him.

"Goddamn wolves," he muttered, hoping the animals would not start attacking the deer. If he got back to the camp, he figured he and the meat would be safe. But if the wolves gathered up enough courage to attack the carcass now, he would be in serious shape.

One wolf edged closer, then dashed in, teeth bared in anticipation.

Campbell heard the sudden change in tone of the animal's snarl, and he instinctively jerked the rope. The deer carcass leapt forward a little, just beyond the wolf's reach. The animal backed off, sinking onto its haunches, growling fiercely.

Campbell tried to speed up, but he had little energy left. However, the wolves did seem to be appraising the situation again, and he figured he had gained a few minutes' margin. It was sufficient, barely, but finally he was back in the little camp. He collapsed in a heap, breathing heavily. "Made those critters come, goddammit," he gasped, grinning fiercely.

The women listlessly started skinning and butchering the deer, as Campbell slid up until he was sitting with his back against a boulder. The fire was warm and comforting, and he dozed off with a chorus of wolf howls playing in the wind-slapped snow.

Morning Sun woke him gently after dark had fallen. He was weak and utterly exhausted. But the smell of the roasted meat filled his nostrils, perking him up a little. He smiled at her. "Thankee, Morning Sun," he said, taking the slice of bark on which the hot meat was piled. He ate greedily, then asked for more and downed that, too.

They spent three days there, gorging on meat, sleeping for hours and hours, drinking gallons of snow-melt. The time served to break their fevers and chills, rest them, and help them regain some of their strength.

Finally they moved on again, physically in better shape, though not improved spiritually. In addition to all the worries they had carried with them from the start, Campbell now was also constantly concerned about being attacked by hostile Indians. He would not be able to defend them with only two rifle balls, and though he had some strength back, it was not sufficient to turn back even a small war party.

Several times they spotted signs of a village in the distance. At each, Campbell would move forward alone, creeping up until he could determine whether it was the one he and the others sought. He was fairly certain that they would be welcomed in any of the Nez Percé villages, but he could not be sure. A lone white man, in his condition, with two bedraggled Nez Percé women, might be attacked, though the Nez Percé had never been known to have hurt a white man. So until they found Tall Clouds's village, they would avoid the others.

It was just over a month after they had begun their journey that Campbell lay atop a wooded ridge and looked over a village of familiar lodges. His relief was great, though tempered by the rage that still burned in him. He hurried down the hill to the two women and the child.

The small group headed over the hill, moving slowly toward the village. Each fell several times, slipping on the slick, ice-coated snow. Then they were on the flats and moving more swiftly toward the lodges set up amidst the pines along a rushing creek.

Before they were halfway between the hill and the village, they spotted half a dozen armed warriors galloping at them. The travelers stopped and pulled off their hoods so they could be seen. Then all three shouted their peaceful intentions.

It was but a few moments before the charging warriors recognized them and slowed their horses.

10

It took a few weeks of frequent eating and sleeping before Campbell was feeling normal physically. Spiritually he wasn't sure whether he would ever be his old self again. Too much had happened, he had suffered too many losses, had seen too many good people die to allow himself to think that life would return to the way it was two months ago.

He was saddened by those losses, and what they meant to him and Morning Sun. But he was comforted inside by the hate and thirst for revenge that glowed in his belly like the red coals of an oven.

Within a day of his arrival in the village, Campbell had explained what had happened to Tall Clouds, Talks of War, and the rest of the warriors. And he had let it be clearly known that he was going to get the men who did it. "If any of ye lads want to come wi' me, I'd be glad to have ye along. If ye dunna want to join me, I'll understand, and go on my own."

"I don't know about any of the others, but I'll

go," a warrior named Coyote Leggings said. He was Campbell's closest friend among the Nez Percé.

"I'll go, too," Hawk Strikes added.

"Good," Campbell said with a nod. "I plan to be on the trail by the day after tomorrow. Can ye lads be ready?"

"That's too short a time," Talks of War protested. "It's winter yet. We must prepare."

"And a storm is coming," Coyote Leggings appended. "A big one."

"Yes," Hawk Strikes interjected, "plus you haven't regained your strength yet. You need more time."

"Like hell I do. This chil' can go on, and'll do so as soon as possible," Campbell retorted.

But his friends had been correct. He wasn't himself, and he felt it the next day and the day after. Then the snowstorm hit, followed by a day of calmness and then another storm, and another, and another.

Campbell began to think he would never be able to leave the village. But the seemingly never-ending snow gave him time to think. Finally he realized it really would be foolish to leave now, in the depths of winter. He would be gone beaver in hardly any time at all. Especially in his still-weakened condition. Angry but fatalistic, he relaxed as much as he could and sat out the winter, trying to enjoy himself some. It was difficult, but with Morning Sun's help, and the presence of their healthy, growing son, Coyote Heart, he was almost content.

Occasionally he stoked the flames of his rage, making sure it did not burn itself out through too much comfort. He talked little of it, but there were times when he would speak to Coyote Leggings or Hawk Strikes or Stone Buffalo, another friend. They would listen, nod, agree, let him speak out. It was as it should be amongst friends.

He hunted with his friends—when the weather permitted—and helped out around the village however he could. He spent as much time as possible with Morning Sun and Coyote Heart, though he still wasn't quite certain how to act around his son. His upbringing had not been conducive to fostering a strong bond with a young son. On the other hand, he could see that the Nez Percé treated their children with the utmost respect and love. The conflicting emotions confused him, and he really had no inclination right now to sort the situation out. It wasn't that he didn't want to, it was just that his desire to avenge his slain partners was uppermost in his mind. Nothing—not his friends, his wife, or his son—was able to crowd that out.

He chafed and fretted as the harsh weather dragged on and on, forcing him to stifle his desire to be on the vengeance trail. It made him edgy and tense around everyone.

Finally, though, Campbell began to feel subtle changes in the air, and he knew that he did not have long to wait. Since he was eager to be on the move, he began making plans. That presented a new set of problems. He had no horses of his own, and no supplies.

Talks of War knew what his son-in-law was going through, but he said nothing for some time. Only when Campbell had called for a council of warriors did he speak up—after decisions had been made.

The decisions were not to Campbell's liking: The warriors would not go with him.

"But ye said ye would," Campbell protested, using English. "I thought ye were men of your word."

"We are," Tall Clouds said quietly in Nez Percé. "But the good of the band must come before one young man's thirst for vengeance."

"I have damn good reason for seeking revenge," Campbell snapped. "And ye damn well know it, too."

"Yes, we do know," the elderly chief said slowly. "Caleb and Ethan were our friends, too. And the others were of our band. We want those who took their spirits to pay for that. But now's not the time."

"Why the hell not?" Campbell said, growing more heated. "It's been months, and all we've done is sit here on our asses."

Tall Clouds nodded. "That's true. But the winter has been long and harsh. The Nimipu had much meat, but even our supplies were used heavily. The People need food, my friend. And soon. After we've made the spring hunt, when our bellies are filled and our children no longer cry from hunger, then will be the time to seek the black hearts."

Campbell knew quite well that Tall Clouds was exaggerating the tribe's desperateness for meat, but he also knew that the old man was telling the truth, that this was no time for the People to go chasing after ghosts.

Campbell was torn. He should stay and take

part in the hunt, paying the band back a little for all the help and comfort they had given him. But his heart, mind, and soul were in a winter camp down on Buffalo Fork. Or in hundreds of other camps on countless beaver streams throughout the mountains. Or at rendezvous, where he and Caleb Finch and Ethan Sharp had raised hell with the best of the mountain men, drinking and fighting, gambling and gorging. His heart really wasn't with Nez Percé hunters, no matter how good friends they were, waiting nervously for the hunt leaders to give the word to begin. No, the only hunt for him now was for the men who had so horribly altered his life.

Finally he nodded. "I understand, Tall Clouds," Campbell said quietly. "But I'll nae be going on the hunt wi' ye."

Coyote Leggings began to argue, but quickly shut up. He was a little upset because he really did want to join Campbell on his quest. The two slain white men had been good friends, and he thought it only proper that he help run the villains down and make them pay for their heinous actions. But his loyalty had to be with his People. He wished he could get Campbell to wait until after the hunt.

The rest of the warriors understood what was going on inside Campbell, and they accepted his decision. They all wished him well—and good fortune on his hunt—and then began filing out. Until only Campbell, Talks of War, Coyote Leggings, and Hawk Strikes remained sitting around Talks of War's fire.

"You sure you won't wait until after the spring hunt?" Coyote Leggings asked hopefully.

"I canna do that. I have to go after those bastards now. I've set here far too long already, I be thinkin'." He shook his head. "I should've gone after them right off. I'd have planted them by now, this chil's saying, and I could be here to join ye on the hunt."

"What're you going to do with Morning Sun and Coyote Heart while you're gone?" Hawk Strikes interjected.

Campbell shrugged, suddenly uncomfortable. He really did not want to talk about this in front of his friends, but it seemed there was no choice. "I was hoping ye'd watch o'er them for me, Father," he said, looking at Talks of War. "If that would nae be too much to ask of ye."

"It will be no trouble, my son," Talks of War said solemnly. The warrior was about forty, and in his full prime. His hair was long, thick, and lustrous, his muscles strong and supple. He was as fierce a warrior as Campbell had ever come across, but in camp he was often full of laughter.

"Thankee, Father," Campbell said sincerely.

"Is there no more I can do for you, my son?"

Campbell shrugged again. He was not about to ask for help in the form of horses, powder, ball, food supplies, and more. As it was, he had nothing but the mule, his saddle, and his weapons—though no means to use the latter.

"Are you sure?" Talks of War knew Campbell's pride. He would feel the same in Campbell's position. But he was not about to let his son-in-law go traipsing off after half a dozen proven killers with nothing. Still, he did not want to embarrass the young man unduly.

"Aye," Campbell said, but there was a definite note of doubt in his tone. He thought he could see what Talks of War was planning, and he appreciated both the reality of it and the way it was being handled.

"You have horses?" Talks of War asked in feigned surprise.

"Only one mule."

"That's no good. Powder and ball for your weapons?"

"Nae."

"Hmmm," Talks of War mused, rubbing his chin. "Supplies—meat, coffee?"

"I have a little meat put up. It'll keep me going until I can hunt some. Coffee . . . ?" he shrugged again. "Well, I reckon I can do wi'oot, if I need to."

"Have you forgotten, my son?" Talks of War said, acting as if he had just remembered something of great importance.

"Forgotten what?"

"That you let me have some meat and coffee and other supplies that one time when we were on a hunt?"

"Nae," Campbell said a little suspiciously.

"Oh, yes," Talks of War said brightly. "Of course you must remember. You did the same for Coyote Leggings and Hawk Strikes, as I recall. Right?" He winked at the two young warriors.

Both caught on right away. "Yes, yes, he did that," Coyote Leggings said immediately and with enthusiasm. "It was what, the summer before the last one?"

"Yes, that's when it was," Hawk Strikes agreed.

"We hadn't gotten to go on the spring hunt yet when Alex and our two other white-eye friends arrived. When they saw we were low on food, they did some hunting, and Alex gave most of his catch to us."

A slow smile spread across Campbell's face. "I did nae such thing, lads, and ye goddamn well know it." He paused a moment. "But if it'll make ye feel better to think of me in such kindhearted terms, well, then, who is this auld chil' to deny ye such a small pleasure?"

"That's better," Talks of War said, grinning. "And now it's time we paid you back for that help."

The two younger warriors nodded agreement.

"If ye think that's proper," Campbell said, acknowledging the gift.

"I do," Talks of War said with a firm nod. "And now I remember that you gave me several ponies last year—ponies you wanted me and your friends here to break and train for you. They're ready now."

"That's a crock of buffler shit, Talks of War," Campbell said, grateful to have his father-in-law offer him horses, but too pridefully reluctant to accept the offer straight out.

Talks of War shrugged and grinned some more. He pulled out a long-stemmed clay pipe, filled it, and lit it. "To call an elder a liar is bad manners," he said easily. "Is that what you're doing?"

"Nae, Father," Campbell said with a laugh. "I just could nae remember doon that."

"Well, you shall have your five ponies back when you're ready to leave," Talks of War said with finality, a cloud of pipe smoke obscuring his face.

Campbell nodded. He was happy, but ashamed at the same time. Still, he told himself that he had done enough things for Talks of War and the other Nez Percé that he was not exactly taking charity. He also knew that if he rejected Talks of War's generous offer, he would deeply insult his father-in-law. And probably his two friends as well. He could see no reason to do that.

Three days later he rode out of the village. It was barely a week into April, as far as he could figure.

He rode a splendid Appaloosa, one of those fine spotted horses bred so well by the Nez Percé. Four other horses—two Appaloosas and two paint mustangs—trailed behind him on ropes, as did the big mule. The two pintos and the mule were loaded with supplies.

Campbell was outfitted in new, fringed elkskin shirt and trousers. Simple, center-seam moccasins, lined with buffalo hair, were on his feet, and buckskin leggings covered the lower half of his pant legs. A buttocks-long, hooded coat made of a thick wool blanket protected him from the elements, as did bear-fur mittens. Atop his head was a round, flat hat of otter fur.

Morning Sun had made the new garments, working diligently to finish so he could leave. She didn't want him to go, but she knew he had to. She was grateful that he had left her in her own village. Though she did not doubt his strength or toughness, or his abilities as a warrior, she worried about him tremendously. There were so many dangers out there. A man, by himself in that great wilderness, could not see everything. And if he found those he sought, he would be outnumbered six to one, not very good odds for even as brave a warrior as Alex.

Still, she prepared his things well. If he was going to leave—and there would be no stopping him, she knew—she wanted him as ready as he could be. With her efforts, he would be warm and protected from snow, rain, and hail; his food supplies were sufficient for a while, and all were loaded so that the packs would not shift and hurt the animals.

Campbell kissed Morning Sun and Coyote Heart goodbye and rode out. He felt good about himself, and was glad to finally be undertaking his mission. His rifle rode across the pommel of his saddle, through the small leather loop. He had two pistols in his leather belt, worn outside his coat, and another packed away. He also had a tomahawk and a big butcher knife.

11

Not knowing where else to start, and knowing it was much too early to make his way toward the rendezvous site at the confluence of the Wind and Popo Agie Rivers, Campbell headed for the place where the women had escaped from Bullock and his henchmen. He didn't expect to learn much there, but he held out the hope that he might be able to determine which way they had gone.

It did not take him nearly as long to make the trip back as it had to get to Tall Clouds's village. Then he had been burdened by two grieving women and a child, with only one animal. Now he was well supplied and well mounted. Plus he was alone, and did not have to worry about being slowed by women who were worn down by harsh treatment and grief.

Still, it was more than two weeks before he neared the area. He had thought not to go to where his winter camp had been, but then he decided he should. He needed to pay his respects to Finch and Sharp, and he wanted to make sure their eternal rest had not been upset by animals or men disturbing the graves.

With mixed feelings, Campbell rode into the old campsite. It seemed eerily quiet, as if all the animals and birds were avoiding the place. The wind blew steadily, as it always did, but for Campbell it had a mournful tone to its whistling. He shivered a little under his heavy blanket coat, but it was not from the cold temperatures. Rather, it was caused by the chill of death and spirits from the Afterworld.

Campbell dismounted and tied his horse and the pack animals to a tree. He stood a moment, breathing in the cold mountain air, his breath making clouds in front of his face. Despite the eeriness of the place, Campbell felt almost at peace. He pulled his rifle from the loop on the saddle and walked slowly toward the single grave.

The burial plot had not been disturbed, which was a relief for Campbell. He squatted next to the hump of rocks, holding his rifle across his thighs, trying to sort out the jumble of his thoughts. It took a few minutes, but finally things cleared for him. He was still full of grief and he was yet enraged by their needless deaths at the hands of men who were miles from being their equals.

"I've nae forgotten my vow to ye, ol' lads. Nae. I'll be on the trail of those fuckin' rat-humping devils by tomorrow, my friends. Aye. They'll regret having e'er tangled wi' the likes of the three of us." He meant every word of it, but a voice deep inside told him that fulfilling that promise would be a lot more difficult than making it.

He squatted there for a long time, reminiscing

about his times with Ethan Sharp and Caleb Finch. He was still amazed at how they had taken him on without knowing a thing about him. And they had taught him all the things he needed to survive in this harsh land. They had swiftly become more than friends, more even than partners. They had been like brothers to him, older brothers who watched over him and protected him by providing him the means to keep himself alive. It was an invaluable gift, and he would be forever in their debt.

The two mountain old-timers also had given him respect. Granted, he had earned it with hard work and courage, but they could've waited to dole out their respect until he had proven himself for a few more years. Many other men would have done so.

Now he hoped he could take all they had given him and use it to bring mountain justice to the men who had killed them. He had proven to be fearless in battle, resourceful, and a superb rifle shot, and few were better than he with a knife or tomahawk. He was big, as powerful as a bull buffalo, and as fiercely determined as a wolf pack on the hunt. Still, a kernel of doubt about himself remained. He wondered if he had really acquired the skills to do what was needed.

He smiled a little when he thought of how Finch and Sharp would have ribbed him if he had ever expressed such doubts in front of them. They would have been unmerciful. Indeed, he could hear Finch's slicing voice saying, "Goddamn, boy, if ye ain't the most worryin' ol' coon this chil's ary seen. Damn, ain't ye got no fuckin' balls a'tall?"

"Damn, but I'm gonna miss ye lads," Campbell said, chuckling a bit despite the tears that spilled down his cheeks and dripped on the still snow-covered graves.

He finally pushed himself up, shaking off the gloom somewhat. That was another thing his two partners would have ridden him about—seeing the gloomy side of things.

While Finch had been a rather dour man, he was still quick to laugh. In poor times, he would growl and stomp for a while, but then he would come to see something positive—or at least a way out of the trouble.

Ethan Sharp, on the other hand, had generally been an even-tempered sort, who reasoned ways out of trouble as often as not. Instead of letting gloom befall him, he took almost everything with equanimity, not getting too excited at the good things in life, so not despairing at the bad.

"Well, I'll nae disappoint ye, lads," Campbell said with a small grin. Yes, he would miss his two partners greatly, but he would show them that he had been worthy of their friendship, their trust, and their respect.

He strolled around the area. There was little evidence of its having been a comfortable winter camp. The snow where their lodges had been was a little less deep than elsewhere. There were a few corral rails still up, and two fire rings of stones could be seen. Other than that, what remained of the camp was buried by a half winter's worth of snow. Somehow, it seemed fitting that crisp, clean snow covered a place that held such a tale of violence and loss.

Campbell went to the animals and was set to mount his horse when he stopped. Darkness was less than two hours away, and he was tired. He decided he would spend the night here, getting a little extra rest and allowing the animals the same. It also seemed that staying here was somehow the right thing to do.

Still, he didn't want to spend the night where the main camp had been. He walked the animals into the trees a little way—opposite of where Bullock and his men had stayed—and found a spot that would do.

By the time he had unloaded his supplies, unsaddled his horse, tended the animals, gathered wood, and built a fire, it was dark. He put on coffee and a hunk of meat from a bear he had killed that afternoon. He finally sat—on the hair-side of the bear hide that had provided him the meat. He leaned against the trunk of a lodgepole pine and stretched out his long legs. While he waited for his meal to get done, he pulled out his pipe, filled it, and puffed a while.

After eating, he leaned back with another pipeful of tobacco and a third cup of coffee. Those things were prized. Meat he could get most anywhere, but coffee and tobacco were hard to come by out here once a man ran out of them. He was certain that Talks of War had dug far deeper into his store of both than he should have, and Campbell was quite grateful for his father-in-law's generosity.

He spread out his buffalo sleeping robe and wrapped himself in its comforting warmth, with his rifle inside. He was asleep in moments.

Campbell awoke with a renewed sense of determination. He had a hasty meal of bear meat and coffee. Eager to be moving, he hurriedly saddled his horse and loaded the supplies. He took a few minutes to stop at the grave of his two friends, then mounted his horse and trotted away down the wavering trail he had plodded along a lifetime ago. This time, however, there was no uncertainty, no wrenching sense of loss or of overwhelming grief, just an age-ripened rage that would be quenched only by the blood of each and every one of Bullock's men.

He rode at a steady clip, one that would cover ground swiftly but not wear down the animals. He rode proudly, unafraid, at one time becoming aware that all senses—honed by his several years in the mountains—were working well; that is, without conscious thought. His subconscious simply took in the many bits of information to be read on the ground and in the air, and then interpreted them. It was as it should be.

His first stop was where he had found Morning Sun, Coyote Heart, and Many Bells. He spent a few minutes at the site where they all had camped after they had been reunited. That was all he needed to tell him that no one else had been there in the intervening months.

His next stop was where Morning Sun and Many Bells had escaped from Bullock's men. He took a considerable amount of time there. He didn't expect to find much, if anything, but he thought it wise to give the place as thorough a search as he could.

He prowled around, growing more frustrated by the moment. Like his old camp, everything had been pretty well covered by snow. He found a couple of bones, which he assumed were either White Hawk's or Spotted Calf's, or maybe both, judging by their size. He shook his head in shame and rage. Using his tomahawk, knife, and hands, he hacked a small hole in the ground at the base of a tree and buried the bones.

He squatted there for a few moments after he had covered the pitiful things. "I'm nae sure such a burial is right by your ways, or e'en if it'll do ye much good in the Hereafter, but 'tis better, I be thinking, than letting all your earthly remains lie here for the animals and elements."

He began searching the camp again, but it was obvious that he would find no clues there about the men he hunted, or where they had gone. Within minutes, he had tightened his saddle, climbed aboard, and ridden out.

Not sure of where to go now, he followed the thin trail out of Bullock's old camp for a while. After spending the night several miles away, he awoke in the morning and decided he had nowhere specific to go. Whatever trace Bullock and his men might have left of their travel was long ago obliterated by snow and wind. So when he rode out that day, he began meandering. He figured he would make his way slowly down to where the rendezvous would be held in the summer.

He rode slowly, not seeing any reason to rush, other than the fact that he was eager to get this business over with. His eyes scanned from side to side, to the sky and the ground, hoping he might spot something that would tell him which way to go.

Over the next several days, he found a few camps where what little sign remained told Campbell that Bullock had stayed there. But after a week, even those faded, and he rode on, angry and frustrated.

Three weeks and two days after he had left the camp where Finch and Sharp had died, he sensed that there was something ahead of him. He instantly grew more alert, and he stopped, trying to pick up a sound, a smell, something in the air that would tell him what—or who—was out there.

But he heard nothing. He wasn't sure if his senses were playing a trick on him or if the sounds of his animals shuffling, snorting, and clomping hooves on the snow to get at a piece of grass had masked any sound.

He pushed on again, moving extremely slowly. He did not want a group of cutthroats like Bullock's men riding up on him unexpectedly. A half-mile farther on, he again had the feeling that someone or something was out there. He stopped and listened once more, and was rewarded when he caught a whiff of smoke. It wasn't from a cookfire, he knew, though there was something mighty familiar about it to him. He couldn't place it, though.

His instincts told him to be wary, because whatever was making that smell was not going to be good. He hoped it was a camp with Bullock and his men, but he doubted that. They had had months to roam since their attack on his old camp. They might have decided to winter up somewhere, but Campbell thought that was unlikely, considering that a couple of the camps they had used were in better places than this.

He proceeded cautiously. The smell of the foul smoke got stronger with each yard he covered. Then he saw a thin streamer of it coiling up over the trees. Whatever it was, he decided, was almost burned out, judging by the smoke. The smell would linger for a long time.

Campbell spotted a tiny gap between the bushes and trees to his right, and he pulled off the path. He forced his horse and the pack animals through the dense foliage until he found a small area that was almost clear. He dismounted, loosened his saddle, and tied the animals off.

Taking his rifle, he set off on foot, back through the vegetation to the trail. There he walked in the direction he had been going, staying right along the fringe of the trees.

A couple hundred yards later, he heard the squawking and snarling of scavengers. He moved more slowly, shoulders tense. He spotted a clearing ahead, on the left of the meandering dirt track he and others had grandly called a trail. He could see turkey buzzards circling over it, and he knew that whatever had caught his attention would be in that clearing.

He crossed the three-foot-wide trail and headed into the brush, then angled toward the clearing he had seen, moving carefully through the thickets. At the edge of the clearing, he stopped and stood behind a thick screen of antelope brush.

Campbell stood there for some time, silently watching. What he saw was a trappers' camp that had been left in the same condition as his and his partners' had been. From where he stood, he was certain the damage had been done days ago, even though some of the ruins were still smoldering. Yet he wanted to be as certain as possible that whoever had done this was gone. While he figured it had been Bullock's men, it could as easily have been a band of Indians, and he wanted no run-in with hostile warriors. If it had been Bullock's men, he didn't want to trap them out in the open when he would be so outnumbered. He would prefer to pick his time and place to take them on.

He figured after a while that he was alone, and he finally ventured out, rifle ready. He quickly found a few signs that it was Bullock's band of cutthroats who had ravaged the place.

He also found the bodies of five mountaineers. Scavengers had been at the corpses. He thought he recognized two of them, but he couldn't be sure. Not that it mattered to him. They were fellow trappers, and as such they deserved a better fate than this. They also warranted a decent burial.

Campbell went back and got his animals. He unloaded them, unsaddled his Appaloosa, and tended them.

Then he turned to the problem of hacking out a large grave for the five bodies. It was no easy task with only a tomahawk and a knife, and with the ground still frozen several inches deep. Almost four hours later, he decided that the six-foot-long, eight-foot-wide, and one-foot-deep hole would have to suffice. Darkness would be on him soon, and he wanted this to be done and over with.

He found a couple of old blankets—too threadbare to be worth Bullock's taking them—and lined the hole with one. Campbell dragged the stiff bodies over one at a time and rolled each one unceremoniously into the grave. He had spotted a few personal effects lying around the camp, which he figured had belonged to the men. He carried them over and placed them in the grave, then covered the men and their meager effects with the other worn blanket.

Finally he began shoving the dirt, snow, and ice into the hole. It didn't take very long, but finding and carrying rocks to place on the grave did. It was after dark by the time he dropped the last stone on the grave and stood there in silence a moment. Then he said quietly, "I dunna know who ye lads were, but ye were mountaineers and for that ye have my respect. And though ye be strangers to me, I'll pay yer respects to the verminous buggers who rubbed ye oot when I pay them back for doon the same thing to my partners. I wish ye well in the Hereafter, lads. May ye ne'er see starvin' times nor poor doons there."

He had picked out a spot earlier a little bit away from the smoldering ruins of the camp, and he went there now. With wood he had gathered before, he quickly started a fire and set meat and coffee to cooking.

He ate with little enthusiasm, realizing that he was far more bothered by his discovery than he had thought he would be. After all, these men meant nothing to him. Still, just knowing that Bullock and his band of cutthroats had done this to another group of mountain men cut him to the core. While most trappers were somewhat solitary and rather iconoclastic, Campbell had encountered none who was as malevolent as Bullock's horde.

He was also disturbed by the fact that he had found signs that there had been women and at least a few children here. Since he had found only adult male bodies, he assumed the women and children had been taken by the rogue mountain men. And that hit too close to home with him after what had happened to Dancing Feather, Spotted Calf, Otter, and White Hawk, and what had almost happened to his own wife and child. He had trouble believing that any man would do such things, and the thought infuriated him

He tried to shake off the gloom and reborn rage, but found it difficult to do. He finally turned in, but his slumber was not peaceful—visions of tortured women and children had him tossing in his sleep. It was still an hour or so before dawn when he got up, stoked the fire, and ate. He could see no reason for continuing to try to sleep when it was doing him no good. And there was no reason to stay here any longer. He had learned all he could here—which was, he admitted, virtually nothing—and he felt the need to be on the trail again.

The next day he saw signs of a traveler. Whoever was ahead of him was alone, it was obvious to Campbell. He stopped his horse, dismounted, and squatted to look at a few faint tracks in the snow. The traveler was on foot, and while the prints were of moccasins, Campbell was sure it was a white man.

He pulled himself back into the saddle and pushed on, increasing his speed a bit. He didn't know who was out there, but he deduced that it was not one of Bullock's men but rather a survivor, like himself, of Bullock's attack. He also figured that the man was wounded.

But he had not come upon anyone by the time darkness fell, so he shrugged and pulled off the trail. He made his camp, ate, and turned in. He slept better this night than the last, but not much. His dreams were still too disturbing for comfort.

By the next afternoon, he spotted a solitary figure hobbling along about a quarter of a mile ahead of him on a straight patch of the trail. Then the path curved, and the figure disappeared. Campbell broke into a trot and in seconds was closing in on the man.

The hobbling man heard the hooves behind him. He stopped and turned, raising a cheap trade musket.

Campbell halted less than ten feet from the traveler. He was a young man, Campbell saw, and appeared to present little threat to him despite the flintlock musket he held. The way the man was wavering, he wouldn't be able to hit anything.

"Easy, laddie," Campbell said calmly, holding out his hand, palm outward, "there's nae need for ye to be holding your weapon on me. I mean ye no harm."

The man just growled and thrust his musket out in a threatening manner. He had good reason to be wary of Campbell, who would have been the same under these circumstances.

"Now look, laddie," Campbell said evenly, "I mean ye no harm. And I think I can be of help to ye—if ye're willing to put away yon gun and talk to me a wee bit."

The man spit. "Go to hell, ya son of a bitch," he snapped. "Now ride on before I make gone beaver of ya."

"Don't be hasty, lad," Campbell said. "I saw your camp back yonder. That was your camp, weren't it?" When the man nodded tightly, Campbell said, "Judgin' from the sign, the vermin who set on ye were the same that killed my two partners a few months ago. Aye, left me for dead, they did, the rat-fuckin' villains."

"I ain't sure I believe ya."

Campbell shrugged. "It dunna matter what ye believe, lad. Ye're nae gonna get far in your condition."

"I'll git by."

"Ye'll be wolf bait in another day or so, lad."

"That ain't no concern of yourn."

Campbell shrugged. "I already told ye, lad, I can be of help to ye."

"How?" The man had not lessened his vigilance any.

"Ye plan to go after those murderous bastards, don't ye, lad?"

"You're goddamn right. And ain't you, nor the mountains, nor all of Bug's Boys gonna keep me from it."

"That's admirable, lad. Aye, surely 'tis. But ye'll nae get e'en close to accomplishin' it in your condition. Ye throw in wi' me, lad, and we'll make short work of those murderous scum. I figure I can take them alone. Aye, lad, I be one hard-ass critter. Killer of Blackfeet, friend of the Nez Percé."

"And full of buffler shit, I'm thinkin'." But the man relaxed some. After a moment's hesitation, he lowered his musket.

"Ye're nae the first to say such a thing aboot this auld Scotsman," Campbell said with a low chuckle. The joviality dropped suddenly. "But what I just said to ye, lad, be God's own truth."

"If you're sich a tough critter, why didn't ya stop those renegade bastards when they kilt your friends?" the man asked condescendingly.

"I made gone beaver of four of those ass-suckin' critters before another clubbed me down and stuck his knife in my chest."

"You don't look none the worse for it," the man said skeptically.

"I also have a wee touch of luck at times. When that son of a bitch stuck his knife in me, it hit a

couple of things, and it only ended up nicking me.
Then I got knocked oot. They left me for dead."
Campbell's face had grown considerably harder,
with lines of anger crossing it.

The man nodded. "Purty much the same thing
happened to me. I was wounded a heap worse'n
you was, but they left me for dead, too. I been tryin'
to follow after 'em ever since I come to."

Campbell nodded, then said, "I figure it was the
same villains that attacked our camp, but I have to
ask ye who attacked ye so I know for certain."

The man shrugged. "Don't know who they was.
I'd nary met 'em afore they showed up one day. The
leader said his name when they set to meat with us.
Soon's we was all comfortable, him and his men
attacked. I cain't remember his name."

"Lije Bullock?" Campbell asked.

"Goddamn, that was it."

" 'Twere the same who attacked me and my
friends. They left our camp aboot the same as they
left yours. Took e'erything they could and burned
the rest. Took the women and children wi' 'em, and
killed most of them wi'in a day or two."

The man nodded. He looked up at Campbell,
taking in the long-simmering rage stamped on his
face. He set the butt of his musket on the ground
and leaned wearily on the muzzle. "I believe ya, ol'
hoss. I can see it writ on your face. You're even
worse angry at 'em than I am."

"Aye, lad, I be terrible angry, and I'll nae rest till
those rat-fuckin' villains are gone beavers—at my
own hands."

"I'd be proud if'n you was to allow me to join

you on your venture, ol' hoss. I ain't in the best of shape right now, but I'll git well afore long. Then I'll be an asset to ya, I'm thinkin'."

"I reckon ye'll be a credit to the lads ye set your traps wi'." Campbell dismounted, walked the short distance separating him from the man, and held out his hand. As they shook, he said, "My name's Alex Campbell, lad."

"John Worthington."

"Ye look more than half done in, lad," Campbell said.

"I'll git by."

"Aye, I expect ye will at that. Well, there's nae likely place right around here to bed down for the night. Think ye can make it a bit farther—if ye're mounted?"

"Hell, hoss, you put me astride one of them Appaloosas of yourn and I can go till we reach the gates of hell."

Campbell chuckled just a bit. "I dunna think we'll need to go that far, John my lad. And I have nae desire to show up at Beelzebub's door for quite some years yet."

"Me neither, goddammit, but if that's what it takes to run them scum to ground, then, by Christ, ol' Scratch best watch his ass," Worthington said.

"Aye, he'd have himself a handful with us two coons, now wouldn't he?" He paused, rubbing a big hand over his red-stubbled jaw. "Well, ol' John, I reckon we better be getting a move on."

"I got no reason to loiter here, Alex. I'm ready to be on the trail."

Campbell gave Worthington a hand up onto one

of the other Appaloosas, and moments later they rode out, the animals walking slowly along. Worthington rode next to Campbell—the Scotsman had suggested it, though he didn't tell Worthington that it was because he wanted to keep an eye on him because of his wound.

They traveled for more than three hours before Campbell spotted a clearing through the trees left of the trail. They made their way through the aspens to the clearing some yards away.

When Worthington went to help him, Campbell said, "Ye go sit your ass down over at yon tree, lad, before I have to knock ye down."

"I'll rest when the chores is done," Worthington insisted.

"Ye'll rest now, lad. Ye be in bad enough shape. We dunna need ye getting worse by overdoon. There'll be many times ye'll be of help to me—once ye get well. Now go on and do as I say."

"Yes, sir," Worthington grumbled, but he was tremendously relieved. He would have worked till he dropped, for that was the kind of man he was. But he was weak and aching and his wound throbbed, and sitting down right now was like a gift from above.

It took an hour or so for Campbell to complete his chores. During that time, Worthington had regained a little strength. He rose and shuffled around, picking up wood for a fire. Campbell was ready to give him hell for it, but decided there was no need for that. He could understand Worthington's desire not to be a burden, and gathering firewood shouldn't be too strenuous, as long as he didn't overdo it.

Soon after finishing with the animals, Campbell had fresh deer meat and coffee going. He had questions he wanted to ask Worthington, but as he sat back against his saddle, he decided the silence between them was preferable right now. There would be time for questions after they ate.

13

It was still an hour or so before dark when they had finished eating. Worthington sat slackly; pain, exhaustion, and the horror of what had happened swamped over him.

Campbell went to Worthington's side and knelt. "I better look at your wounds, lad," he said. "Where are ye hurt?"

"The worst is here," Worthington said weakly, trying to tug open his bloody, filthy coat.

Campbell helped him and peeled the ends of the coat back. Underneath, Worthington's threadbare cloth shirt was covered with blood, mostly over the abdomen. Campbell sliced the shirt open to reveal an ugly, jagged knife wound perhaps seven inches long, slashing upward from just above the navel, then curling toward the ribs on his left side.

"Those unsaintly bastards did a hell of a job on ye, lad," Campbell said calmly.

"Looks bad, does it?"

"Aye, 'tis nae denying it, laddie boy. But ye seem a hardy sort, and I think there be some hope for ye."

"Really?" Worthington asked skeptically. He was fairly certain he was going to die soon, and was somewhat afraid to hold out the hope that he might actually recover.

"Aye, but I've nae done much in the way of doctorin', so I might be more harm to ye than your wound."

"You cain't frighten me with such buffler shit, ol' hoss," Worthington growled.

"Suit yoursel'," Campbell said with a grin. "To tell ye true, though, lad, there's nae much I can do for ye. I can sew that hole in your belly up and poultice it, but that's aboot it. The rest'll be up to ye."

"Well, git on with it, dammit. That wound ain't gonna close itself up any time soon."

Campbell shrugged. " 'Tis nae me who'll be feelin' the pain, lad."

"Goddamn, have you always been such a scaredy feller?" Worthington asked with a snort of derision. "Where the hell's the ol' hoss who regaled me with words of his toughness?"

"I left that lad back in a Blackfoot village," Campbell said. Then he laughed. "I hope ye be as tough as ye think ye are, lad."

"Why?"

"I dunna have anything to help dull the pain when I set into sewin' your pieces together."

Worthington blanched, but recovered quickly. He shrugged, and winced, but his voice was even when he said, "Then this ol' beaver'll jist have to grit his chompers and try'n bear up under it."

"That be the spirit. Aye." Campbell patted him

on the shoulder, and then stood. "I'll fetch a needle and sinew. Don't ye go nowhere while I be gone."

"Reckon I'm not of a mind to wander right now," Worthington said dryly.

Campbell got a long, curved needle, some sinew, and some yarrow root for a poultice. Morning Sun had insisted he bring some of the root to use for poultices in case he was wounded. He crushed some of it in an old pot and added a few chunks of ice, then set the pot on the fire. Then he returned to where Worthington lolled against a rotting log.

Campbell threaded the needle with a string of sinew and, without preliminary, went straight to sewing.

Worthington hissed with the first few jabs, but then settled down. It hurt, but it wasn't as bad as he had expected. And he found that if he fixed his eyes on the top of a crooked pine across the meadow, and paid no attention to the needle, he was all right.

When Campbell finished his surgery, he went to the fire. He couldn't remember what Morning Sun had said about the yarrow poultice, as far as how it was supposed to look or its consistency. He wasn't even sure that making it the way he had was correct. He usually let Morning Sun worry about such things, and when she had had to explain it to him—along with what seemed like a thousand other things—before he left the village, he wasn't paying much attention. He hoped it would work.

He slathered on the pasty, ill-looking stuff and then wrapped some old blanket material around Worthington's midsection as a bandage.

"Ye get some rest now, lad," Campbell said quietly.

"We leavin' in the mornin'?"

"Nae."

"You gonna ride out by yourself and leave me here?" There was no fear or worry in Worthington's voice. He just wanted to know so he could make plans for himself, if it came to that.

"Nae, lad. I'll nae leave ye here alone. I would nae do that to any man." He paused and grinned harshly. "Except for six fuckin' villains I know."

Worthington smiled and closed his eyes.

Worthington's recovery progressed rapidly, but it would be at least a couple of weeks before he was even remotely close to being his normal self again.

During that time, Campbell hunted and fretted. He did not show his irritation at the delay, which made Worthington wonder a little about him. As enraged as Campbell had been, it seemed to Worthington that the Scotsman would be pacing the camp when he was not hunting. But he seemed almost at peace. It was perplexing.

Worthington could not know, though, of the turmoil inside of Campbell; of the hate and sorrow that churned his innards until he was so tightly wound up that he thought he might explode at any minute.

The usually garrulous Campbell was rather close-mouthed, though Worthington had no way of knowing that such was out of the ordinary for the brawny Scotsman. Still, Campbell could not close himself off completely, especially when he knew he and Worthington would ride together for a while. So one evening, while they were sitting around the fire, he asked, "How'd ye come to be in the mountains, lad?"

Worthington spit out a piece of gristle and tossed away the small bone he had in his right hand. "I signed on with Matt Smith and his band of free trappers. As a pork eater," he said with a grimace. "I'd nary been out this way before. That were two years ago or so. After my first season, Matt and the others took me on as a trapper." He smiled sadly. "And I can tell ya, I was some glad to get out of doin' all them camp chores and sich."

"Ye must have proved yoursel' to those laddies while ye were still a swamper, or they'd nae have taken ye on for important business."

Worthington nodded. "Yep. There was this one time when we was set upon by some Utes up near the Pagosa Springs. What a hellacious fandango that was! Hell, I still didn't know my ass from a green stick, so I were kind of reluctant to join in. Till I saw one of those fat-ass Utes creepin' up about to brain one of the other boys. I jist run and jumped on that painted critter. About scared the shit right out of me, too."

"I know the feeling, lad," Campbell said dryly. "Aye, we've all been in that position. Sometimes more than once. Being scared is nae just for newcomers to these parts, lad."

"Ain't that a fact," Worthington said with a low chuckle.

"Did ye manage to finish that fractious critter off? Or'd ye just knock him ass o'er teacups and let someone else do the honors?"

"I did it," Worthington said with a touch of pride. Then he laughed. "Though fer a few minutes there, I thought that fat son of a bitch was gonna carve me a new asshole with that big ol' pig-sticker of his. Tell ya the truth, Alex, I did need some help. Ol' Matt, he seen what happened and come over to lend me a hand. Whapped that critter hard across the head with a goddamn log. I didn't have much trouble with him after that."

"I reckon ye didn't," Campbell said, chuckling a little. "Ye raise his hair?"

"Yep," Worthington responded with a tight grin. "Had it hangin' from my Dickert rifle, too, which those fuckin' villains took from me whilst I was layin' there next to dead."

"I suppose ye'd like to have it back, eh, lad?" Campbell asked.

"Goddamn right I would," Worthington snapped. "That's another thing Bullock and his scum have to pay fer. I worked goddamn hard to be able to git that rifle, and I'll be damned if I'm gonna let one of those asswipes keep it."

"Any reasonable man would think the same, lad."

Worthington nodded.

"Ye lose anything else important?" Campbell pried.

Worthington looked sharply at him, not sure what Campbell meant. Then he understood. "Sure," he said matter-of-factly, trying to disguise his grief.

"Five damn good friends. Plus the women and young'ns."

"Yours, too?"

"My woman, Raven's Wing, was took. I miss her, I reckon, but . . . Hell, I don't know." He sighed. "We was only together a short time, so's we didn't know each other all that well." He shrugged, not sure he had explained it very well.

"Still hurts ye, though, dunna, lad?" Campbell said. "E'en if just your pride."

"Yep," Worthington said after a moment's thought. He had suddenly realized the truth of what Campbell had said.

The two sat in silence for a bit. Each lit a pipe and puffed, gazing at the stars, immersed in his own mental wanderings.

Finally Worthington asked quietly, "So, what about you, Alex? How'd you come to be out here in these cold and dangerous mountains?" There was no hint of mockery in his voice. For John Worthington, the Rocky Mountains had several days ago turned cold and dangerous.

"Much the same way ye did, lad. Signed on wi' an ass-sucking scoundrel named Simon Beesley. A right bloody bastard he was. I killed one of his men for cheating at cards, and Beesley and the others left me oot on the Plains, thousands of miles from nowhere, it seemed. They expected me to either die or get killed, but as ye can plainly see, the wilds could nae put this auld chil' under."

"So what happened?" Worthington asked, interest piqued despite himself. He had asked the original question merely to restart the conversation, since he was getting bored. But now he found he was interested.

"Well, I wandered west, determined to become a trapper just like I wanted to from the start. I finally stumbled into the camp of two auld fellows. They took me on as a trapper—and for no reason that I could see. We become partners along the way somewhere." His voice had taken on a decided note of rage—and sadness.

"They the ones who was made gone beaver by Bullock and his bunch of scum?"

"Aye." Campbell paused a moment to make sure he did not weep any. That would have embarrassed him no end. When he was sure he would not, he went on. "Two finer men ye'll ne'er meet, boy. They were some now, those two." He almost managed a smile. "Full of piss and vinegar, and both had the hair of the bear on them. Aye, 'twas a fact. Generous in their own way. Good companions. Fine trappers, who knew all the best beaver streams in the mountains. And there's no one else I'd rather have at my side when hard doin's were afoot. We were together only aboot three years, but we faced off Blackfeet, Crow horse stealers, and every other kind of fractious Indians."

"They sound like good men," Worthington said. "The sort any ol' mountain hoss would be proud to call friend."

"Aye, that they were, lad. And it pains this chil's heart to know they were rubbed oot by the likes of Lije Bullock and his fuckin' scoundrels. And I've sworn on my only chil's head that I'll hunt them all down, e'en if it takes me to the end of my days, and repay them tenfold for what they did."

Worthington almost shivered at the chilling tones of Campbell's voice, which could very well have come from the depths of hell. He decided right then and there that he would not want to tangle with this tall, flaming-red-haired Scotsman. At least not in Campbell's present frame of mind.

"And I'll do it, too," Campbell tacked on, though it was not necessary.

"Well, I aim to help ye, hoss," Worthington said. He might not want to get into a ruckus with Campbell, but he had no qualms about fighting alongside him, especially for such a good cause. "Did ya ever see that Beesley feller agin?" he asked after a few seconds.

"Aye. I run into them by accident one day, him and his lads." He shrugged. "They dinna have much time to regret what they had done to me. I was of nae mind to let them live any longer to spread their pestilence to anyone else."

"All of 'em?"

"Aye. There was nae but three."

"All experienced mountaineers though, right?"

"Aye. What does that have to do wi' anything?"

Worthington shrugged. "It takes some doin' fer a man to take on three ol'-timers in the mountains like ye did and win. I'm impressed with ya, Alex."

" 'Twere nothing, lad. Really."

"Like hell it weren't." Worthington grinned harshly. "But I hope you'll act the same when we find Bullock and his bastards."

" 'Twill be a hundred times worse for those

villainous bastards," Campbell said tightly. "Aye, Bullock's men will nae get off as easily as Beesley's. I just killed those lads. Bullock's men, though, they'll be made to suffer before I make gone beaver oot of them."

Once again Worthington was glad Campbell was on his side.

Almost three weeks after they had made their small camp, Campbell decided it was time to ride on again. Worthington was not fully recovered, but Campbell just could not wait any longer. Worthington could straddle a horse and do some camp chores, so he would be no hindrance.

Worthington himself was getting itchy to be on the move. Like Campbell, he was not the kind of man to loll about. He made no objections when Campbell broached the idea of riding on soon.

Campbell allowed Worthington to ride the same Appaloosa he had before. The animal was sturdy and steady, and would give Worthington a reasonably comfortable ride. That would be important, since the last thing either of them needed was to have Worthington being jostled by a horse's harsh gait and tearing open the wound again.

They pulled out on a cool, misty morning accompanied by chilling wind and rain. Campbell hoped the dreariness of the day was not a sign of what was to follow on their quest.

14

Despite the time that had elapsed since Worthington's camp had been attacked, and despite the rain, Campbell found signs of Bullock and his men here and there. So he and his new companion followed, through passes, across meadows, and winding through forests of pine and aspen.

The going was slow, but there was no other choice. Shortly after they had left their camp, the single trail they had been on widened and widened until it was no longer a trail, but a mountain meadow. Numerous trails and false paths led out of the meadow, and Campbell and Worthington had to search each one before they found the one Bullock's men had taken.

Even then, though, the route wasn't much of a trail. It meandered, split, faded, and finally disappeared. From then on, it was a matter of constant searching, and then hoping that whatever way they went was the right way. More than once they had to double back and painstakingly search

for any kind of sign that would point them in the
right direction once again.

One time when they could not find any clue,
they had camped, and in the morning Campbell
randomly picked a direction. Campbell was
beginning to suspect he had chosen wrong when,
after five hours of traveling, he spotted the minutest
of signs. He breathed a sigh of relief, not letting
Worthington see it. He preferred to keep
Worthington in the dark about his own doubts.

So they plodded along, and Campbell fretted all
the more. The slower they went, the farther ahead
Bullock got. Campbell pushed himself and
Worthington harder, staying in the saddle as long as
he thought Worthington could take it. It meant he
had to do more of the camp chores, at least for the
first couple of weeks. By then Worthington had
regained most of his strength, and took a greater
share of the work.

They crossed the Snake River near where it
emptied into a large lake, and then continued in a
generally westward direction. A day later, they lost
the trail about halfway up the Teton Range. With an
annoyed shrug, Campbell led them higher, working
through another pass. He did not figure that Bullock
would have gotten this far into the range and then
have turned around. Bullock had no reason to
suspect anyone was on his trail. As far as he knew,
everyone in the camps he and his men had attacked
were dead. Campbell hoped he could pick up
Bullock's trail on the western side of the range.

In Pierre's Hole, Campbell decided to turn
south, heading toward the Snake River. Once again,

he was not certain Bullock had gone that way, but he thought it was likely. He was relieved when, two days later, he found a camp Bullock and his men had used just about the time he and Worthington had reached the eastern side of the mountains.

"We'll start pushin' harder tomorrow, won't we, Alex?" Worthington asked flatly when they were supping that night.

"Aye, lad. They're less than a week ahead of us, I be thinking, and they're in no hurry. Maybe we can catch them soon if we extend ourselves."

"Suits this chil'," Worthington said. He figured he and Campbell were close to their quarry now, and he wanted to go as fast as he could and get it over with.

"Then put an end to your gabbing, lad, and finish feedin'. If we're going to make tracks, we'd better hit the sleeping robes soon."

Campbell was up well before Worthington and had loaded the pack animals and saddled his Appaloosa before Worthington even stirred. Campbell had meat cooked and coffee hot by the time Worthington woke up.

"'Tis aboot time ye roused your lazy ass, lad," Campbell chided gently. "If I knew ye were to be such a lazy critter, I'd have left ye behind long ago."

"Christ, Alex," Worthington grumbled, "it ain't daylight yet. Hell, it's a least an hour till the sun comes up." He was still feeling some of the effects of his wound, and seemed to be more tired than he should be. It irritated him. He was not used to such doings, and he did not like to belittle himself in Campbell's eyes.

"Aye, 'tis true what ye say. But I dinna think ye were the kind to have to wait till the sun rose before ye got yoursel' moving."

"Ah, shet your trap, goddammit. I'm up, and I'll git to doin' the chores soon's I go piss and git me some coffee."

"The chores be all done, lad," Campbell said, hiding a smile. "Do ye think I was going to just sit around waiting for ye to wake up and help? Och, mon, I canna do such a thing. We need to be on the move, and I canna wait all day for the likes of ye."

Worthington fumed. "If you're gonna be such an asswipe about all this, then next time kick me awake soon's ya rouse yourself, ya son of a bitch."

Campbell broke into laughter. "Good Christ almighty, lad, but ye be a touchy one."

"Damn ya," Worthington said with a rueful grin. "Here I were thinkin' you was serious."

"Nae, lad. Had I been serious aboot this, ye would have known it for certain. I be an early riser, and 'tis nae unusual for me to be the first one up. And wi' your wound still paining ye of a time, I figured I could do us both the most good by getting the chores taken care of. This way you'll be fresh and can travel throughoot the day wi'oot trouble."

"I think you're jist giving me a pile of buffler shit because ya think I ain't up to what has to be done."

"If I thought that aboot ye, lad, ye'd nae be here with me now. Ye'd still be sitting back at that camp fussing o'er your wound by yoursel'."

"Then shet that flappin' hole and pass me some goddamn coffee," Worthington said with another grin as he squatted at the fire. He held his hands out to warm them by the flames. Though spring was here in full, it was still mighty cool most mornings.

They wolfed down meat, poured the dregs of the thick, acrid coffee over the fire, and left. It had been less than twenty minutes since Worthington had awoken.

As usual, Campbell was in the lead, and he set a good tempo. Throughout the day he occasionally looked back to check on Worthington, but he seemed to be having no problem in keeping pace, despite holding the rope that led to the pack animals and riding without a saddle. Because of the latter, he sat on a piece of thick, furry buffalo hide.

Campbell was fairly certain that Bullock was leading his men toward the Snake River, so he was not concerned about checking for signs. He just hoped he was right, or they would lose a lot of time having to backtrack.

They rode until past dark and made a quick camp. They took the time to fill up on meat and coffee and then turned in.

Campbell got a small bit of amusement the next morning when a grumbling Worthington rose only ten minutes or so after he did. But he did throw himself right into the work that had to be done. Campbell smiled. He had realized some days ago that Worthington was always a bear when he first got up. Not until he had some meat and coffee did he begin acting even remotely human.

That day was a repeat of the day before, as were

the next three. By then, Worthington was tiring some, though he refused to acknowledge it. Campbell could still see it on his face and in the way he held himself. Campbell also began to wonder if perhaps he had been hasty in choosing the direction to go. They had no indication that their quarry had been this way—no sign left by horses, no old camps, no discarded booty that had outlived its usefulness.

Most telling, though, was the fact that they had found no bodies. While Campbell could believe that Bullock and his men would haul along some Indian women, if they didn't cause any trouble, he could not believe they would keep any half-breed children all this time. It was not like them. And Campbell knew there had been six women and five children along—he had learned that while Worthington was recuperating. He had not wanted to say anything, but he had been surprised that they hadn't found any bodies, or even evidence of bodies, on the eastern side of the mountains. Especially of the children. Campbell figured that he had gotten off Bullock's track more often than he had suspected, and then lucked back into finding it. Or else Bullock had buried the remains. And that seemed most unlikely.

Campbell also was somewhat surprised that Worthington had not mentioned it. Since one of the women was his, he must have been worried about her. Campbell finally concluded that Worthington was well aware of the situation but was keeping silent about it, just as he would have done had he been in Worthington's position.

With nothing else to do, Campbell kept pushing

for the Snake River. It was as if something was forcing him onward.

But he and Worthington were still three-quarters of a mile from the river when something off to the side caught Campbell's attention. He stopped suddenly, and Worthington almost ran into him.

"What is it, Alex?"

Campbell shrugged. "I canna be sure, lad." He dismounted and flipped his reins toward Worthington. "Here, hold these. And keep your eyes peeled, lad."

"Don't you worry about me, you red-haired son of a bitch. I'll watch over things whilst you go roamin' 'round in the brush there chasin' after ghosts and sich."

Campbell ignored him. With rifle in hand he moved off, eyes carefully scanning the ground. He quickly began to doubt himself, thinking he had not really seen anything, that perhaps Worthington was right in saying he was chasing ghosts.

Then he caught a glint of something shiny. He swiftly moved toward it and knelt. With trembling fingers, he reached out and lifted the thin silver chain with the cameo attached to it. The last time he had seen the necklace, Dancing Feather was wearing it in the winter camp on Buffalo Fork. He rose slowly, the ornament dangling from his long, strong fingers.

He stood for a few moments, letting the anger subside to a reasonable level. Then he walked forward, moving by inches, eyes looking, searching. After three steps he squatted, and moved forward even more slowly. But his painstaking search soon bore fruit. He saw a familiar hoofprint at one spot, then a moccasin print he recognized. He sped up a little, and found more of the same signs.

Satisfied that he knew which way his quarry was heading, Campbell rose again, turning to face Worthington. He whistled once, and then waved Worthington toward him.

When Worthington trotted up, he asked, "You find somethin'?"

Campbell nodded. "Sign. It's a wee auld, but it be from them."

"How old?"

"Four days, maybe five."

"Which way're they headin'?" Worthington asked.

Campbell pointed in a generally westerly direction. "I expected they'd follow the Snake. Seems like they're doing so, but farther from it than I had figured. But from this sign, they're moving parallel to the river."

"Ain't that odd?" Worthington asked.

"Nae," Campbell responded as he mounted his horse. "Nae once ye think on it. No one'll try to ride right along the Snake. There be too many obstacles. Brush, mud, steep banks, cliffs, and all manner of other troublesome things. Oot here, ye'll miss all that, yet still be close enough to the river. Like I said, I expected them to get a little closer to the river before starting to follow it, but this is nae an unreasonable distance to do so."

"This fuckin' Bullock critter shines less and less with this ol' hoss with every passin' day," Worthington snarled.

"Aye, that unsaintly scoundrel has that trait. But it'll be his undoing soon." He clucked his Appaloosa into motion.

Campbell set a steady pace, but he would stop every half hour or so to look for sign. To his surprise, he found indications of Bullock's passage regularly, though he could find no sign that they were catching up to their quarry. That worried him only a little. Campbell figured that as long as they were moving swiftly they would catch up to Bullock's horde sooner or later. The former was preferable, since he was getting tired of the constant traveling and tracking. He wanted to be back in Tall Clouds's village, with Morning Sun and Coyote Heart.

Deciding they needed a little extra rest in anticipation of catching the renegades, Campbell called for a stop a few hours before dark.

"We ought to keep a-goin', Alex," Worthington complained. "We'll nary catch those stinkin' bastards like this."

"We'll catch them, lad. Don't ye worry aboot that. And I think 'twill be soon. When we do, we'll have to be at our best, since we'll be ootnumbered, lad. A wee bit of extra sleep won't throw us off much. Besides, we'll be that much more fresh in the morn so that we can make a longer day of it."

Worthington wasn't convinced, but he accepted it, since there was plenty of truth in what Campbell had said. Still, he sensed that they were getting close, and he was reluctant to be off the renegades' trail a moment longer than necessary.

The two men were quiet as they made their camp and did the chores. Both were testy and knew it was better to keep their silence lest they suddenly be at each other's throats.

As they were eating, Worthington suddenly threw the piece of deer meat he had been chewing on out into the afternoon sunlight. "Goddamn," he snapped, "I wish we could find us some fuckin' buffler. I am plumb tired of goddamn deer meat."

Campbell felt the same but couldn't see any reason to make such a show of his distaste. But he could certainly empathize with his new friend. It was another mystery to him. Usually buffalo were plentiful here, but they had seen only a few of the big shaggies, and those were some distance away.

Campbell steadfastly ate his deer meat. There was nothing wrong with it, of course, and he generally liked it. But it just could not compare with fresh buffalo cow. When he was done, he didn't even have the wherewithal to light his pipe. He simply rolled out his robes and went to sleep. He noticed that Worthington took to his bed right away, too.

15

With a sense that they were closing in on their quarry, Campbell and Worthington pushed themselves even harder. Following the course parallel to the Snake River, they stopped only to let the animals rest for five minutes or so every hour. In the early afternoon, they came across one of Bullock's old camps, and just before dark they found another.

Despite the ghosts that seemed to haunt the place, they decided to spend the night there. It was almost night, and by stopping now they would get a little extra rest, allowing them to push just as hard tomorrow.

They did just that, and they kept up that punishing pace for several more days. By then the animals were tiring, as were the men. And they seemed no closer to their prey than before. Both men were tense and irritable, so they kept their mouths shut for the most part.

They eventually came to a small trading post, and rode into it. It wasn't difficult to find the factor's quarters. The two tied their horses and then went inside.

A frock-coated clerk looked up from his paperwork, then stood, adjusting his spectacles. "What can I do for ye lads?" he asked.

Campbell smiled. He'd not heard a countryman's voice in a mighty long time. "Name's Alex Campbell. Ye might start wi' tellin' me the name of this place."

"Fort Hall," the clerk said, also smiling. "A tradin' post for the Hudson's Bay Company. I'm the chief clerk, Andrew MacGregor."

Campbell shook MacGregor's hand. "This be my friend, John Worthington," he said. Worthington and MacGregor shook hands.

"If ye're lookin' for work, lads, I'm afraid we have none for ye," MacGregor said apologetically.

"We dunna need any work, Mr. MacGregor," Campbell responded. "All we need is some information."

"And mayhap some supplies," Worthington added.

"I'm nae sure I can help ye wi' the information, but ask what ye will. The supplies'll be nae problem."

Campbell shrugged. "We have nae money to buy supplies, Mr. MacGregor," he said with remorse and a touch of shame.

" 'Tis regrettable, Mr. Campbell," MacGregor said. He did not sound sympathetic.

"We've nae reached starvin' times yet, Mr. MacGregor. And e'en if we do, we've both faced it before."

"Ah, Alex, I got . . ." Worthington started.

"Shut your trap, lad," Campbell snapped, slapping his palm out into the air in front of Worthington's face.

"But . . ."

Campbell turned a burning look on his companion. He said nothing, but Worthington silently cursed himself for having spoken up at all. He nodded.

Campbell looked back at MacGregor. "What we'd like to know, Mr. MacGregor, is whether a lad named Lije Bullock has been here recently. He'd likely have five men wi' him."

"I dunna know such a man," MacGregor said thoughtfully. "But there be strangers passin' through here all the time. Can ye tell me what he looks like?"

"Well," Campbell said, scratching the stubble on his chin, "he's some shorter than I am, but a wee bit taller than John here, and bulkier than him, too. He's got black hair, kind of curly. Usually clean-shaven, but I think he favors a mustache. He's got a scar across his nose, one from the corner of his lip around to his chin, and another o'er his right eyebrow."

"And he wears the goddamn ugliest hat this critter's ary seen," Worthington tossed in. "It ain't no color nature ary provided, and it looks like a herd of buffler ran over it and then wallered on top of it."

"Aye," Campbell interjected, "and the feather does nae look like it came from any bird I've e'er set eyes on."

MacGregor sat in his chair and leaned back. He closed his eyes, thinking. After perhaps a minute, his eyes opened. "Nae, lad, no one of that description has e'er passed through here. Certainly not recently."

"Ye sure?" Campbell asked, spirits sinking. He had been so certain that Bullock would have visited.

"Aye," MacGregor said. "I'd have remembered such a man."

Campbell nodded. "Ye have a place where travelers can find a wee bite?" he asked.

MacGregor looked at him suspiciously. "I thought ye had nae money," he said in accusatory tones.

"I have a few coins—aboot enough for a meal each for John and me," Campbell spat. "That's if ye dunna charge a king's ransom for some mealy bread and rancid meat." He glared at MacGregor.

The clerk did not seem to notice. "I'd suggest ye go back to your employer and tell him that the Hudson's Bay Company does nae get fooled so easily by the likes of ye."

"Ye've lost your reason, ye fuckin' worm," Campbell snapped. "John and me be free trappers, by God, and we be goddamn proud of it. Neither of us would stoop so low as to work for another."

"Especially a saggin'-tit company like the one hires on sich festerin' asswipes as you," Worthington said every bit as angrily as Campbell.

"It does nae matter," MacGregor said, unfazed "Ye'll be gettin' no help here, lads."

Worthington started heading onto the desk, going for MacGregor, but Campbell grabbed him and hauled him back. "Save your anger for Bullock and the others," he said. "This fuckin' scoundrel is nae worth your efforts."

"Ah, come on, Alex, I jist want to raise hair on that smug-faced chil'. I won't hurt him too much."

Campbell looked at MacGregor, and could see the fear in his eyes. He did not seem so proud now. "Nae, lad. But we can pass word around the mountains that the Hudson Bay Company is nae hospitable to free trappers. Or any other travelers, I'm thinkin'."

Worthington nodded. "I expect you're right, ol' hoss. And I expect the mountain boys'd like to know that this here Fort Hall place is bein' run by a goddamn clerk, 'stead of a factor."

"They would at that," Campbell agreed. "And a limp-dick clerk, too." He paused, shaking his head. "Well, auld beaver, let's be on our way." He and Worthington turned and walked out.

Once outside in the heat, Worthington turned on Campbell. "We should go back in there and make gone beaver out of that son of a bitch," he snarled. "Then go git us a meal and then supplies."

"We have no money. I told MacGregor that."

"I got a little cached away. Enough to keep us goin' fer a bit."

"Nae, lad, though I appreciate your offerin' to help. And if we harm MacGregor, we'll be in big trouble. Then we'd nae be able to go chasin' after Bullock."

"All right, goddammit," Worthington snapped after a bit, more annoyed than really angry. "We leave that shit-eatin' critter alone. But we ought to go git us a meal and some supplies before we pull out of here."

"I'd wager ye all the specie ye've cached away

that MacGregor's already sent someone scurrying o'er to the mess and to the supply house to warn them nae to deal wi' us in any way."

"We ain't seen no one come out of the clerk's," Worthington protested. "And we been standin' right here outside the door, so we sure as hell couldn't have missed anyone."

"Ye ne'er heard of a back door, lad?" Campbell challenged.

"Sure I have, goddammit, but we ain't seen no one come either side of the clerk's either."

"Are the buildings right up against the fort walls?"

"I don't think so," Worthington said, puzzled. "Why?"

"Because someone could have gone oot the back door of MacGregor's, moved along yon wall behind the buildings, and come oot from someplace else."

"You think that happened?" Worthington asked, cursing himself silently for not having seen such an obvious thing.

"Aye. I canna be sure, of course, but less than a minute after we walked oot the door, I saw a man hurryin' from behind yon building"—he pointed toward the far end of the fort—"and into what I ken is the dining room."

"Could've been anyone."

"Aye. But seconds later he came oot of there and hurried to the supply room. Him and the trader are standin' in the doorway, and he's pointin' in our direction."

"Goddamn if that don't suck wind," Worthington said, irritation growing.

"Aye, but we canna do anything aboot it."

"Shit. Well, then, I reckon we best be movin' on." Worthington looked at the door to the clerk's, wanting to go kill MacGregor.

"Nae, lad," Campbell said quietly. He lightly grabbed Worthington's shoulder and tugged. "Come on, now, John. 'Tis time we were gone—before we both make a foolish decision regarding Andrew MacGregor."

"You're one goddamn smug critter when you make sense, ain't ya?" Worthington groused.

"Aye." Campbell grinned tightly.

They rode out in a leisurely fashion, refusing to be hurried. In light of the potential danger, and to send a warning to anyone who might be foolish enough to get in their way, both men rode with rifle in hand, the butt resting on a thigh, barrel pointing up.

When they were a couple hundred yards outside the fort, heading back in the direction they had come from, Worthington rode up alongside Campbell. Both had slid their rifles away—Campbell in the loop on his saddle, Worthington in the makeshift buckskin scabbard hanging from his improvised saddle. During their journey, Worthington had fashioned a crude wooden saddle frame—basically an X for the front and for the back, with two pieces of wood on each side connecting them; the entire thing was held together with rawhide thongs that had been applied wet and had stiffened to ironlike hardness.

"Where away now, hoss?" Worthington asked.

"Hell, lad, I dunna know." Campbell stopped

and sat, pondering the question. "I was certain they would've stopped at the fort. But perhaps they cut off in another direction somewhere back up the way we come from."

"So that's the way we go, hoss," Worthington said flatly. There was no doubt in his voice.

"Aye, lad. But it's nae going to be easy to pick up their trail again. They could've moved off anywhere 'tween here and that last camp of theirs we found a few days back. That's plenty of ground to cover."

"Well, we ain't gonna cover none of it settin' here."

Campbell nodded, annoyed and angry.

"You ain't thinkin' of givin' up, are ya?" Worthington asked. The possibility worried and enraged Worthington. But one glance from Campbell's fury-twisted face disabused Worthington of that notion.

Campbell pulled out, riding hard. A mile or so on, he stopped. "I'll ride oot yon," he said, pointing away from the river. "Perhaps a mile. I'll cover the land from there to aboot here. I want ye to do the same wi' the area 'tween here and the river."

Worthington nodded, not having to be told what to look for. "Where do we meet?" he asked.

"Our last camp."

"Should we warn each other if we find sign?"

"Nae, lad," Campbell said after a moment's thought. "It might attract unwanted attention. And, since MacGregor would nae let us have any supplies, we better preserve our powder and ball."

Worthington nodded again and began turning to leave, but Campbell said, "Wait." Surprised, Worthington looked at him.

"Give me a couple of the animals, lad."

"Gladly."

A minute later, they headed in opposite directions, each trailing a few animals behind.

Once Campbell had put a little distance between himself and Worthington, he slowed until his horse was barely walking. He scrutinized the ground intently as he edged his way along, working in a zigzag, trying to cover as much area as he could in his painstaking search.

As the day wore on, and the heat became oppressive, Campbell grew more frustrated. He began to worry that perhaps he was missing the trail of his quarry, though he knew that he probably had not.

It was past dark when he pulled into their former camping spot. Worthington was there and had a fire going and meat and coffee cooking. As he came to help Campbell with the animals, Worthington said, "I were beginning to worry that you'd been set upon by savages."

"Nae, lad," Campbell said wearily.

"You saw no sign then?"

"Nae. Ye?"

"Nope." He paused. "But we'll find it tomorrow, Alex. We sure as hell will."

Campbell nodded into the darkness, unconvinced.

When they sat down to eat, Campbell asked, "What've we got left for supplies, lad?"

"Not a hell of a lot. Some jerky. Enough coffee to last us two, three days—if we use it sparingly."

Worthington sounded dejected. They had been out of cornmeal for more than a week, and were getting mighty low on tobacco—their only pleasure.

Campbell nodded. He had been in worse shape on the way back to Tall Clouds's village with Morning Sun, Coyote Heart, and Many Bells, so he was not too worried yet. He could get along without coffee, and tobacco, and cornmeal. Meat was another story. He figured there would be decent hunting, but with powder and ball running low, he and Worthington would have to be careful how they used it. He almost wished it was winter. That way they could hunt once a week, and the meat would freeze and keep its freshness. Now that it was almost summer, the meat would last a day, perhaps two, before it was too rancid to eat.

He sighed with annoyance and went back to eating, trying to savor the meat and coffee, but finding it hard to do.

16

Early the next morning Campbell found what he and Worthington had been so painstakingly seeking. Since they did not plan to meet until the end of the day, and he could not waste powder on a shot, Campbell decided to go find Worthington immediately.

He wheeled his horse and quirted it hard. The mule and two extra horses seemed reluctant to follow at such a rapid pace, but Campbell's Appaloosa was not to be denied. Despite his haste, it still took Campbell just over an hour to find his friend. Worthington spotted him riding while he was still some distance away, and got ready to fight before he realized who it was.

Campbell pounded to a stop. "Let's go, lad," he said.

"You found somethin'?"

"Aye." He quirted his horse again and thundered off, Worthington only a few paces behind him. They rode hard until they got to the spot where Campbell had found the sign. He stopped and loosened his saddle.

"What the hell're ya waitin' for?" Worthington demanded.

"The horses need a rest, plus feed and water. There be plenty of daylight left, we can afford an hour or so."

"But . . ."

"Dammit, lad, use your goddamn head, would ye. We dunna need to be put afoot. Besides, it's nae like we'll catch them in the next hour, or e'en day."

Worthington nodded tightly. He dismounted, and both men tended the animals, then sat in the shade of a tree, sipping water from a wood canteen. Neither saw any reason to talk.

Campbell closed his eyes and napped, his chin falling toward his chest. Seeing it, Worthington decided that wasn't such a bad idea, and did the same. When Campbell awoke, he checked the angle of the sun, and calculated that he had slept just over an hour. He looked over at Worthington, who was snoring loudly.

"Get up, lad," Campbell said, slapping Worthington on the arm with his hat. "Come on, damn ye, get moving."

Worthington came awake slowly, as he always did. "Wha . . . ?" he muttered, looking around dazedly.

"It's time we were ridin' again, lad. Plus ye're scarin' the horses with that devilish sound ye've been makin'."

"You sayin' I was snorin'?" Worthington demanded, trying to rub the dregs of sleep from his face with both hands.

"I suppose some'd call it snorin', lad," Campbell

said, fighting back a grin. "But there be many others who'd say ye was playin' Satan's squeezebox. With that damn auld mule yon brayin' an accompaniment, it sounded like a diseased moose fartin' in a cave where the sound was bouncin' all aboot. Only a hundred times louder."

"Ya know you ain't the most silent sleeper this chil's ary been near."

Campbell let a small grin crop up. "That may be, laddie, but at least my snorin' is melodious."

"Hah! As melodious as a bee-stung griz passin' a live goddamn bullfrog though his ass."

"Come on, lad, we have business to see to," Campbell said, growing serious again.

Worthington nodded. He swallowed a mouthful of water and rose, following Campbell to the horses. Half an hour later they moved slowly, looking for whatever sign Bullock and his men had left. By the end of the day, Campbell was encouraged.

"I dunna think we're too far behind those villains, lad," he said at the fire. "A day or two more than before we lost the trail by the fort."

"That may be, hoss, but things're gonna git a heap worse from here on out."

"Why's that, lad?"

"You ary been in these parts before?" Worthington asked.

"I canna say that I have."

"Another day or so the way we're headin' and we're gonna be in a land where there ain't shit but sand, sun, and goddamn fools."

" 'Tis that bad?"

"It's a fuckin' wasteland out there, hoss. No

water fer miles, except maybe an occasional waterhole somewhere—if they ain't dried up, and if you can find one that ain't poisoned with alkali. No trees, and not much grass neither. The animals avoid it when they can, and so do most Injins. They might be savages, but they ain't no fools. They know that hell is a place to stay away from."

Campbell nodded, accepting the information. "Well, lad, perhaps Bullock and his villains did nae go that way. What reason would they have for going into such a place?"

Worthington shrugged. "Who knows what those murderin' asswipes're thinkin'. But if ye turn north from there, a week's ride or so'll bring ya to Flathead—and then Nez Percé—territory. Shoshones're up that way, too. And Bannocks, Cayuse, and a heap of others."

"They might've headed that way to trade with some of those Indians," Campbell said more than asked.

"It's possible. It's just as possible they headed out there jist to make sure no one follered 'em."

"Who'd be following them?" Campbell asked, surprised.

"Hudson Bay boys fer one." Worthington felt good about having information that Campbell didn't. "Bullock must've knowed that tradin' post were there. I figure that's why he come this way before he reached it. But he'd want to know if mayhap someone from the fort had spotted them. I'm thinkin' Bullock and his murderous bastards have done what they done to us fer a spell, and I reckon they got enemies here. I'd make ye a wager that MacGregor, that goddamn asswipe, knows Bullock."

"Why did ye nae say something before?"

"Didn't think of it till now. Things at Fort Hall didn't seem right to me, but I jist started puzzlin' it out."

"And MacGregor said he did nae know Bullock so he could have company men find him," Campbell mused.

"That's my thinkin', hoss. I figure there's a reward out for Bullock and the others. A company reward."

Campbell nodded. "And ye know what, laddie?" he said tightly, "We played right into their hands. MacGregor did nae know why we were lookin' for Bullock. He might've thought we were cohorts of his."

"That'd explain his lack of hospitality. I ain't ary heard of the company treatin' visitors so poorly."

"Aye. But the real trouble, as I ken it, is that we have company lads on our trail—I'd bet my left nut on it. If MacGregor thought we were pals of Bullock, he'll have men followin' us, hopin' we'll lead them to Bullock. Hell, if we knew where he was, we'd nae have asked at the fort."

"Makes sense, hoss," Worthington said thoughtfully. He smiled grimly. "So now we take them boys on a little jaunt they weren't expectin'?"

"Aye, lad."

"It'll cost us time, Alex."

"Aye, that it will. But I'd rather waste time this way than have the company men find Bullock and his villains. I plan to deal wi' those murderous vermin by myself."

"Don't you try'n shove me out of this," Worthington said, eyes narrowed in anger.

"I'd nae do that to ye. I just dunna want anyone else gettin' to them before we do. And, ye know, if they do think we be Bullock's friends, those company lads're likely to make us gone beavers as soon as they find Bullock's camp. I've nae ridden all these miles only to be rubbed oot by some goddamn Britishers."

"That's somethin' this ol' hoss don't even have to think about before agreein' with."

Campbell fell silent, thinking. When his idea congealed, he explained it to Worthington, who agreed right away.

The next morning, they rode out as if everything were normal. Within a mile, though, they stopped amid a grove of trees. Taking his rifle, Campbell handed the reins of his horse to Worthington.

"*Vaya con Dios*, hoss," Worthington said. He clucked to his horse and rode off, moving unhurriedly.

Campbell nodded and slipped away. He found a tree that looked as if it could be easily climbed. He clambered up to a fork not too high off the ground and crouched there, waiting.

It was more than an hour and a half before Campbell heard horses coming. From his vantage point, he could see a fair distance back on the trail. The first man soon came into view. Campbell counted eight of them. They were riding lazily, and had some distance between them.

As the last one rode under his perch, Campbell jerked his rifle butt out and slammed the man hard on the side of the head. He didn't fall from the horse, but he was weaving. Campbell dropped out of the tree and in two steps had grabbed the horse's reins. He towed the animal into the brush and trees and tied it.

Campbell leaned his rifle against a tree, then grabbed the man and yanked him off the horse into the dirt. Hauling the man up, he kicked him toward another tree, and then shoved him down. The man sat, resting against the trunk.

"Well, lad," Campbell said as he squatted in front of the man, " 'Tis time ye and I had a wee parley."

The man looked woozily at him, trying to focus his eyes. It took some effort, but he finally managed. "Who the 'ell're you?" he asked.

"It dunna matter who I am, laddie. Just know that I'll cut your throat at the first hint of reluctance to do what I say."

"What do you want?"

"Does that pustulant swine MacGregor think I'm a friend of Bullock?"

" 'E does." The man was recovering a little— enough to understand the questions and make reasonably intelligent answers, but not enough to do much to help himself.

"Then he's a bigger fool than I had thought. I'm nae friend of that baby-killin' scum. I be followin' him for reasons of my own. Deep, personal reasons, not for some fuckin' company bounty money."

The man nodded, but Campbell could see that he had not believed a word of it.

"Bullock and his murderous vermin attacked my camp, killed my two partners, plus three children and a woman. Stole e'erything we had— horses, possibles, food stores, and a whole fall catch of plews. He left me for dead, but this auld Scotsman is nae so easy to kill. I've been trailin' him e'er since I recovered from my wound."

"You 'ave me sympathy," the man said in a harsh British accent.

"Ye make a poor liar, lad. Now I dunna care whether ye believe me or not. I've told ye the truth. But that dunna matter. I want ye to go to your friends oot there and tell them that if I catch any one of them on my trail again, I'll feed his privates to the wolves. And unless the company wants eight dead employees, whoe'er's leadin' this wee expedition should turn 'round and ride back."

"The men won't like that."

Campbell shrugged. "It makes nae difference to me whether I kill one Britisher or eight. And believe me, all of ye will die if ye continue on my trail. Now, if ye and the others e'er hear of me bein' rubbed oot, ye can trail Bullock from Fort Hall to the gates of hell for all I'll care. But if ye get in my way beforehand, ye'll be shakin' hands wi' the devil long before this chil' will."

"I'll tell 'em, but those chaps'll not be scared off by a chap like you."

"Then they'll be sorry bastards—and soon dead. Now stand up."

When the man had done so, Campbell grabbed his two pistols and jammed them in his own belt. "Your powder horn and the rest," he ordered. He slung the things over his shoulder. "Tobacco?"

The man hesitated a moment, then said, "No."

"I told ye before that ye're a poor liar. Now hand it o'er." The man scowled, but did as he was told. Campbell shoved it into his possible sack.

The Englishman took that moment to try to hit Campbell, who easily fended off the punch. He smashed a big fist into the man's abdomen, knocking the breath out of him.

Campbell shoved him down to the ground and then knelt. "I have nae quarrel with ye or any of your fellows. I could prove to ye that I be determined in my search and that I'll nae be denied a chance to make Bullock pay for what he did. I can take an ear, if ye'd like. Or perhaps your nose. Or e'en perhaps your piddling wee privates?" He grinned viciously at the man's sudden fear.

"But I'm nae going to do that, lad," Campbell said, "since I dunna have a quarrel with your people. Just remember all I've said, lad."

Campbell rose, spun, and walked to the man's horse. He climbed onto it, smiling, since now Worthington would have his own saddle. And rifle, since there was a good Lehman in the scabbard.

"You're taking me 'orse?" the man asked. "And me rifle?"

"Aye."

"But 'ow will I catch up to the others?"

"They canna have gotten far. Once ye get your breath back, ye'll be able to make good time." Campbell had been speaking calmly, but now his voice turned harsh. "And have nae doubt, lad, that I'll kill each and e'ery one of ye if ye dunna do what I said."

He spun and headed deeper into the trees. He would give the company men a wide berth. Once past them, he'd ride hard until he caught up to Worthington.

17

Campbell stood behind a large boulder on the side of the trail, waiting. It was late in the afternoon, and the sun was sinking fast. Campbell watched as one after another of the Hudson Bay men rode slowly by his hiding spot. He had suspected that they would not heed his warning, so about midday he had decided to turn back to check. They were out on the barren flats now, and it was every bit as desolate as Worthington had said it was.

Worthington had headed south with the animals, instead of almost due west. Campbell had gone west for another mile or so, wandering back and forth to create the impression that more than one man had gone this way. He figured that if the Hudson's Bay men got past him, they might get thrown off by this fake trail.

Then he rode hard eastward. He had earlier taken note of a mass of boulders, and he stopped there. The piles of stones offered enough cover for his horse, and one huge boulder sat right alongside the trail he and Worthington had created on the way out. The Hudson's Bay men would be certain to pass this way—if they were still following.

Campbell squatted behind the rock, waiting. He figured it would be another hour or so before they would show up, so he dozed. He finally stood when he heard someone coming. He watched two men pass, then four more, including the one he had accosted before, and he knew there were only two more.

As the last one edged past his boulder, Campbell stepped out, grabbed the man by the back of the shirt and jerked him down to the ground. As soon as the man landed, Campbell stomped on his stomach to keep him quiet. Then Campbell grabbed the horse's reins and moved the animal into the cover of the rocks. A moment later he came out and unceremoniously dragged the man back there, too.

Campbell tied the man's arms behind his back with a piece of horsehair rope. Propping him against a rock, Campbell squatted in front of him. "Your companion told ye of my warning?" he asked. When the confused man nodded, Campbell said, "And what I'd do if it was nae heeded."

"You're just as bloody goddamn crazy as 'Enry said you were, mate. Just who are you, anyway?"

"I be Alex Campbell, and a meaner fuckin' critter ye'll nae meet, lad."

"What're you going to do with me, you bloody arse?" The man did not seem concerned.

"Have ye take another warning back to your leader."

"I'll be bloody well damned before I'll be a messenger boy for the likes of you."

"We'll see aboot that, lad," Campbell said easily.

"I'll tell ye the same thing I told your friend: Quit followin' me. If ye dunna do so, ye and all the others wi' ye will die."

The man's eyes burned with rage, and he seemed defiant. He was not about to tell the others to quit. Not just because he had been surprised and trussed up.

Campbell shoved the man's hat off and grabbed a hank of his hair. When Campbell pulled his knife, the man's eyes widened in concern. "If ye make any noise, lad," Campbell said quietly, "ye'll be dead before ye finish. Ye got that?"

The man nodded, feeling Campbell's hand holding his hair. He saw Campbell move the knife toward him and felt a small tug at his head, but he wasn't worried. He felt no pain and figured that Campbell had simply cut off a lock of his hair, perhaps to scare him.

The man was quite shocked when Campbell moved back a little, holding a bloody knife in one hand and a section of hair dripping blood from the small piece of skin at the bottom in the other.

"What in the bloody 'ell did you do, mate?" the man asked, worry coating the words.

"Raised hair on ye," Campbell responded with a sneer. He looked at the gold-dollar-sized piece of head-skin from which droplets of blood still fell. "Now, I admit 'tis nae the best scalplock I've e'er taken, but I dinna want ye to be missing too much of your hair, seein' as how nature's graces have nae left ye all that much."

"You bloody bastard," the man hissed, still stunned.

When the man looked as if he planned to make a fight of it, Campbell popped his forehead with the heel of his hand. The man's head hit the rock, and he groaned a little.

While the Englishman was still groggy, Campbell went and cut a hunk of the man's saddle blanket. He went back and jammed the sweaty, foul rag into the man's mouth, then swiftly tied the gag in place with pieces of fringe yanked from his pants leg.

"Now, laddie," Campbell said, "I'll send ye back to the others. Ye'll take my wee message to them, now won't ye?" He got no response and asked more sharply, "Won't ye, lad?"

The man nodded, real fear in his eyes now. He had no idea of what this crazy man might do next. All he wanted right now was to get out of here without losing any more parts of his body.

"Good," Campbell said in feigned glee. He reached out and rubbed the Englishman's head, then recoiled in mock repentance. "Sorry, lad," he said without remorse. "I forgot ye had a wee sore spot on your head." He wiped the blood from his hand on the man's shirt.

With a smile, Campbell took the man's two pistols and shoved them in his own belt. "Ye'll nae be needing these, I'm thinkin'. Now, come on, 'tis time ye were on your way." He stood and hauled the Englishman up by his shirt, then shoved him toward his horse. Campbell bent, grabbed the man around the knees, and lifted him, though the man was not a small one. Campbell dumped him across the saddle, belly down. He undid the man's hands and rearranged the rope around his wrists. With the Englishman's arms out, Campbell wrapped the rope under the horse's belly and tied it to the man's legs.

He slapped the man's buttocks none too easily. "There, laddie, ye should be right comfortable till ye get back to your friends."

Campbell walked the Englishman's horse back toward the "trail," faced it in the right direction, and gave it a good smack on the rump. The animal leaped forward and ran. The Englishman flopped about like a hawk with one leg caught in a snare.

Campbell smiled, but he was still a little concerned. He hoped this threat worked. If it didn't, he was going to have to kill at least one of the Hudson's Bay men. He did not look forward to that, since they were not really enemies.

With a shrug, he pulled himself onto his horse. He crossed the "trail" and headed roughly southwest.

He glanced westward but saw no sign of the Hudson's Bay men. Now that they were all out in the open, more or less, he had to be careful not to be seen. It was not unthinkable that the Hudson's Bay men would top a ridge and have a view for quite some distance. Under the right circumstances he could be spotted. Especially if those men did heed his warning and were heading back this way. He pushed his horse a little, wanting to make some distance.

Campbell caught up to Worthington just before dark. Worthington had begun to wonder what had

happened to Campbell, thinking that perhaps he
had been captured or killed by the Hudson's Bay
employees. He was mighty relieved when he saw
Campbell trotting up, but he did not show it.

"So what happened?" Worthington asked when
they got back to riding.

Campbell explained it, grinning often. He
remained a bit concerned that the Hudson's Bay
men might be following, but he could still enjoy the
minor damage he had done to the one man.

They saw no more sign of the Hudson's Bay
men after that, but then they saw little sign of
anything. They began meandering, winding farther
and farther into the wasteland. This country was not
quite as desolate as it had first seemed, though it
was by no means hospitable. It was hot, arid, and
generally lacking in game or wood. There was more
than enough dust, wind, and heat, however, as well
as rocks and sage.

Almost a week after they had lost the Hudson's
Bay men, Campbell pulled to a stop. He looked out
over the rolling, ugly country. He never understood
how anyone could like such a sere, sun-saturated
country, though he knew some who did. He
preferred a land where it was cold and misty, with
rain and snow a-plenty. The emptiness didn't bother
him much, but all the rest did. He sighed.

"What's wrong, Alex?" Worthington asked. He
had moved up alongside Campbell.

"We're wastin' our time and energies oot here,
lad. We've lost those villains' trail, lad, there be no
way we'll e'er find it again in these goddamn
wastelands."

"So what do we do now, hoss?"

"I'm nae sure."

"You're not thinkin' of givin' up, are ya?" Worthington asked harshly.

"I'd as soon have my dick ripped off by a wounded griz as consider such a notion, lad. Ye've made that accusation once before. Don't e'er do it again."

"Ah, hell, Alex, you know I didn't mean nothin' by it," Worthington said unapologetically. He had meant it, in a way, though somehow not seriously. "It's jist somethin' for me to say at times like this since I cain't offer no ideas."

Campbell shrugged. "Then dunna say anything, lad." He paused, looking around some more. Then he added slowly, "Aboot the only thing I can think of to do now, my friend, is to head for rendezvous. 'Tis almost certain Bullock's vermin will be there to sell their stolen plunder."

"Why would they do sich a thing?"

"Why wouldn't they?" Campbell countered. "As far as they're concerned, there's no one alive to know of what they've done."

Worthington nodded. "I'd forgotten about that. But still, they've got plews that're marked by your people and mine. And they got plunder that some of the boys down to rendezvous will know. They'll question that, won't they?"

"Doubt it, lad. All they need to do is tell the traders that they bought those plews from us. Or that they bought them from some Indians who must've stolen them from us, and maybe killed us, too. Same with our plunder."

"Makes sense, I reckon."

"Besides, there's many of those traders at rendezvous who'd nae take one step oot of their way to save their own dear mum. Nae, I dunna think many of those lads'll ask any questions."

"Shit," Worthington snapped with a shake of his head.

"Dunna take it badly, lad. It means they'll almost certainly be at the rendezvous. And probably drunker than lords, too. Aye, and that'll make our job a wee bit easier."

Worthington smiled a little. "Yep, I reckon it would at that. Well, ol' hoss, what say we head south."

"Aye, that'd suit this chil'."

Not being in much of a hurry now, and knowing they had plenty of time—if Campbell's calculations as to the month and day were anywhere near accurate—they rode slowly, trying to spare the horses. In this arid land, the animals had it tough enough without being run into the ground for no good reason.

In just over a week they were at the Snake River. They took several days traveling up and down the shore trying to find a reasonable place to cross. They found no really good place, so they settled on one that looked a little less hazardous than the rest.

Campbell and Worthington made camp, though it was only afternoon. They wanted the horses rested and strong for the assault on the river. The men needed a break, too, so they took advantage of the

plentiful game along the river, and the cold water it
provided. For the thousandth time, Campbell
wished he had some coffee.

The river crossing went far better than they had
expected. They lost the last of their fast-dwindling
supply of jerked meat, and almost lost the mule, but
that was the worst of it.

Wet and cold from the water, Campbell and
Worthington unloaded their supplies and unsaddled
their horses. Then they started a small fire and set
some of yesterday's fresh meat to cooking. Both
stripped, hanging their sopping buckskin and cloth
garments from trees and bushes.

Once they had eaten, both men dozed a while.
Campbell woke an hour or so later, ate, and then
dressed in his now-dry clothes. He lightly kicked.
Worthington in the ribs, waking him, and then went
to load the horses. He was done with that and had
saddled his horse by the time Worthington strolled
over to take care of his mount.

They left minutes later, refreshed and with a
renewed sense of expectation. They roughly
followed the river, which ran generally southwest.
As before, they put a little distance between
themselves and the water, though not nearly as
much as previously.

Campbell picked campsites carefully.
Worthington kidded him about it, jokingly telling
Campbell that he was growing soft. He was
generally glad of Campbell's finickiness, though he
began to have some doubts about it the morning he
was awakened by a Blackfoot arrow that plunked
into his left calf.

18

As usual, Campbell was the first up, and something caught his attention. He was standing next to the mule, ready to load the supplies, when he stopped, trying to determine what small signal had registered in his mind.

He never did find out what it was. He just instinctively ducked behind the mule, rolled once, grabbed his rifle, and rolled again, stopping behind a tree. As he did, he had the fleeting thought that if there was really nothing out there, he was going to look like one prime fool. Of course, there was no one to see him, since Worthington was still sleeping.

The next thing Campbell knew, Worthington yelped as he came awake with an arrow in his leg. Campbell stayed put where he was behind the tree. He could see nothing out there in the brush, but he knew they were there. Problem was, he didn't know who they were, though it was plain that they were not friendly; and he didn't know how many of them there were.

Campbell was aware that Worthington was

scrambling for cover, though he wasn't watching his friend. His eyes were still scanning the brush. He was finally rewarded by seeing an unnatural movement behind a bush. Raising his rifle, he sighted on where he expected an Indian to be crouched. Then he fired.

As he swiftly reloaded his rifle with practiced efficiency, he wasn't sure he had hit the warrior—if indeed there had been one there—but there was no more movement behind the bush.

An eeriness fell over the camp. There was no sound other than the background noise of the river and an occasional grunt from Worthington as he tried to work the arrow out of his leg. There was virtually no movement either. It was as if the entire area had died.

"Ye all right, lad?" Campbell called out, not looking at Worthington.

"Yes, goddammit," Worthington snapped. "I'd be even better if I could get this fuckin' arrow out of my goddamn leg."

"Leave it there, ye goddamn fool," Campbell retorted. "Ye know what a war arrow will do to ye."

"But I cain't goddamn move with it."

"So break the damn thing off, laddie."

Worthington did so, annoyed at himself for not having thought of it. More annoyed that it had happened to begin with.

Campbell crouched there, waiting. He figured that sooner or later the Indians would do something. He would prefer that they did it sooner and got it over with. He also hoped that they would charge rather than continue lurking in the brush.

It didn't seem as if he would get the latter wish, though. So all he and Worthington could do right now was wait the hostiles out—for however long that might be.

However, it didn't turn out to be very long. Since Campbell was right there by the horses, he figured that if an attack was to come, it most likely would be here. He didn't know of any Indians who wouldn't try to get the horses first.

Still, he was a little surprised when the attack came. He had no idea one of the warriors was so close. Once again he sensed something and reacted instinctively. A second later, a stone-headed tomahawk cracked into the tree trunk inches from his head.

Campbell jerked his left elbow up and caught the Indian in the groin, but only partially. It gave him barely enough time to straighten in a rush and smash his rifle, held in both hands widely separated, into the Indian's face.

Blood spurted from the warrior's shattered nose and mouth. Campbell jerked the rifle back and then slammed it forward again, hitting almost the same spot. The warrior staggered back two paces.

Campbell swung his rifle around and fired it. Since the barrel was only a foot from the warrior's torso, the heavy lead ball created something of a mess when it exploded out the Indian's back. Sparks of gunpowder flickered on his buckskin war shirt.

Without making any effort, Campbell noted that the warrior was a Blackfoot as the Indian fell. Campbell swung around, anticipating another attack. It did not come, so Campbell dropped to one knee and began reloading his rifle again.

He wasn't finished when another Blackfoot popped up, this one in front of him. The warrior's lance darted forward, seeking a home in Campbell's chest. But the mountain man managed to twist at the waist and half fall back. The lance tip tore through the shoulder of his shirt and just nicked the flesh underneath.

Campbell tried to grab the lance, but the Blackfoot was too fast for him, jerking it out of the way. Then the warrior spun and slammed the war shield strapped to his left arm into Campbell's face, knocking him on his back.

Campbell spit out a piece of buffalo fur from the shield, and then scooted backward on his buttocks. The lance stabbed into the ground between his legs, but not too close to anything vital. He swiftly rolled, catching the lance between his knees. As he continued to roll, the weapon was jerked out of the Blackfoot's hands.

Campbell came up to his knees, grabbing the lance. He had no time to do anything much with it except to thrust it out as it was—butt end first. The charging Blackfoot ran into it, but managed to blunt its force a little with his shield.

That gave Campbell enough time to stand, spin the lance, and shove it hard at the warrior again. Though the Blackfoot got his shield in the way again, Campbell had so much power behind the thrust that he drove it through the shield and then completely through the warrior.

As the Blackfoot fell, Campbell let the lance go with him. Before he had time to draw a breath, another warrior plowed into him from behind, knocking the wind out of him and slamming him to the ground.

"Jesus Christ," Campbell thought. He didn't think he could speak, since he still could not breathe yet. He continued to fight, though, bucking and jerking, trying to keep the warrior from getting a solid grip on him.

Campbell began weakening as he vainly struggled to draw in some breath. He choked and gargled a few times, and felt the Blackfoot really begin to overpower him. Then he heard a familiar voice:

"Git off my pal there, ya ass-suckin' savage, ya."

The Blackfoot looked up and around over his shoulder, surprised. And got his head shattered by the butt of Worthington's old musket, which the mountain man was wielding like a club.

Campbell shoved the body off him and rose. "Thankee, lad," he said almost cheerily. "How're ye farin'?"

"Killed one of these goddamn devils over thataway, then come over here to save your miserable hide."

"I was doin' all right."

"I'll remember that the next time you're lyin' there gettin' humped by some Injin who's gonna ram his knife up your ass as soon as he's through pleasurin' himself."

Campbell suddenly reached out, grabbed a fistful of Worthington's shirt and jerked him forward and to the side a little.

Worthington had no time to react, he simply stumbled a few steps, trying to mouth a protest.

Then he heard a shot. He came to a stop on one knee and looked a little worriedly over his left shoulder.

Campbell had caught a movement and, before his eyes and brain really registered that it was another Blackfoot charging at Worthington's back, he had jerked Worthington out of the way, pulled one of his pistols, cocked it and fired.

Even the blast of the .50-caliber weapon could not stop the warrior from plowing into him. The weight of the large Blackfoot's body plus its momentum shoved Campbell back a few steps. But then Campbell got his feet set, and the warrior slid off him and to the ground, dead.

"I'd say we're aboot e'en, laddie, wouldn't ye?" Campbell said with a bemused smile.

Worthington rose, reluctant to admit the fact. "Hell, I think that savage was just hurryin' over here to surrender so's we didn't kill him like all his pals here."

"Ye can believe what ye will, lad, but he was aboot to split ye from asshole to crown." Campbell laughed a moment, then grew serious. "How be your leg?"

"I'll live," Worthington said with some anger. The wound was bad enough as a wound, but he was angry more because it was hampering his movement.

"We better take to the brush, lad, and make sure there be no more of these rat's-ass scoundrels aboot."

"Would be wise, I reckon," Worthington admitted. He had been about to suggest the same thing anyway.

They split up, each going a different way, silent now.

Campbell didn't figure there were any more

Blackfeet around. If any of the war band were still alive, they most likely were long gone, but he and Worthington had to be sure.

The two mountain men met again near the horses, from where they had started their search. "Anything, lad?" Campbell asked.

"Nothin' but five prime Blackfoot ponies." His grin was bright, almost blinding.

Campbell nodded, also grinning. This was good news. For one thing, it meant that it was highly probable that they had taken care of all the Blackfeet. A war band of five seemed about right. For another thing, they now had five more ponies—animals they could trade in at the rendezvous for supplies. Those supplies could be used to continue their search for Bullock and his men, or, if they found Bullock and took care of his murderous crew, he and Worthington could use them to start a trapping expedition. Though neither man had said anything about it, both understood that they would be partners from now on.

"Well, let's go bring those ponies in," Campbell said, "before they wander off."

They did so, with Campbell becoming more concerned about Worthington's leg. His friend was limping a lot by now, and seemed to be wincing with every step.

Once the ponies were tied alongside their own animals, Campbell said to Worthington, "Go sit your ass down, laddie. I'll go see if these savages have anything on them that might be of use to us."

There was little—a bit of powder from one, a small bag of corn from another, some tobacco from each. And, among the meager supplies the Indians had with them, a bag of coffee beans. "Ah," he muttered, "a wee bit of paradise."

With a grin, Campbell returned to the fire, which Worthington had built up. He got their small coffeepot and filled it with water. Then he placed a flat piece of buckskin on a rock, poured a small handful of coffee beans onto it, closed it, and pulverized the beans with the blunt end of his tomahawk. He poured the pounded-up result into the water. With the coffee set close to the fire to boil, Campbell glanced at Worthington and said, " 'Tis time I looked at your leg, lad."

"It'll heal up jist fine by itself," Worthington said grumpily. "You jist let it be."

"Have ye gotten scared after this wee tiff wi' the Blackfeet?"

"Hell, no," Worthington responded indignantly.

"Well, it canna be the doctorin' I gave ye before, lad. Ye be a livin' testament to the quality of my services in such matters."

"You're a goddamn butcher," Worthington said unconvincingly. He was not about to tell Campbell that he was really afraid the wound would prove to be worse than either of them thought.

"Well, that be too bad, laddie, for I'm going to look at that leg whether ye like it or not. And if ye give me any trouble in the doin' of it, I'll beat ye into submitting to it." He sounded almost as if the thought gave him pleasure.

"Jesus Christ, but if you ain't a pain in my ass, ya Scotch bastard," Worthington growled. Then he sighed, "Well, get to it, damn ya, afore I change my mind."

"As if that wee thing'd stop me," Campbell said

with a laugh. He knelt and sliced Worthington's pant leg open. "Oh, my God," he breathed.

"What is it, Alex?" Worthington asked, scared down to his toes.

"Ye've got an arrow in your leg, lad." He continued to look down, hiding his grin.

Worthington waited for more. When he realized after only a couple of seconds that there was no more, he snapped, "That's it? You make that horrified remark jist to tell me I got an arrer in my leg? Like you're tellin' me somethin' I ain't already aware of?"

Campbell looked up, still grinning. "Got your mind off whate'er was eatin' at ye, didn't I?"

"Goddammit, get on with it," Worthington growled, though a grin tugged at his mouth.

Campbell looked down at the wound. It didn't really look all that bad, though the arrow would have to come out. He wiggled the shaft of the arrow, which Worthington had broken off two inches above his calf. It was in there pretty tightly. "This is nae going to be fun, lad," Campbell said seriously. "Getting that arrow oot of there will take some doin'."

"Goddamn if you can't find some damnfool excuses for stickin' a knife in me."

"Och, ye chicken-hearted son of a bitch." Campbell found a stick and handed it to Worthington. "Chew on that, lad." He pulled out his knife and stuck it in the coals. While it heated, he inspected the wound more closely, plotting out how he would go in and dig out the arrowhead, which he was beginning to suspect had entered the bone.

Campbell pulled the knife from the fire and waved it in the air to cool it. Then he hunched over, face close to the wound. Without grace, he jammed the blade into the wound right down to the bone, and then sliced raggedly first one way, then the other.

At the first touch of the knife, Worthington had braced himself, but he was still not prepared for the searing pain of the blade as it ripped deep into his flesh. He gnawed on the stick in his mouth until his jaws and teeth ached; sweat beads popped out on his forehead and upper lip.

"Hang on, laddie," Campbell said quietly, as he pulled the knife out and dropped it. He spread the gaping edges of the wound with one hand and with the other probed for the head of the arrow. His index finger finally encountered it, and he lightly traced the flint downward. It was indeed in the bone, but not as far as he had worried it would be.

"Just another second, lad," he said, sweating a little himself. With his thumb and index and middle fingers, he grasped the arrow shaft just behind the arrowhead. Suddenly he yanked.

Campbell heaved a sigh of relief as the arrow pulled free. Dropping it, Campbell swiftly sewed the wound up as best as he could. It was a rough and ragged job, but he got it done, then wrapped the wound in a piece of buckskin sliced from a Blackfoot's shirt.

Campbell rose, noting that Worthington had passed out. Campbell nodded and went to have some of the coffee he craved.

19

"It's aboot time ye woke up, ye lazy bastard," Campbell said rather cheerily. He squatted at the fire looking across it at his friend.

Worthington sat up, a blanket falling down his front. His face was pinched with pain and befuddlement. He looked around as if he could not remember where he was or how he had gotten there.

Campbell poured a tin mug of coffee and carried it over to Worthington. He knelt and handed his confused friend the cup. "There be a dance startin' soon, laddie. Think ye'll be ready for it?"

Worthington sipped some coffee as the light of recognition began to filter back into his eyes. "What the hell'd you do to me, you son of a bitch?" he asked in accusatory tones.

"Ye dunna remember?"

Worthington shook his head. "All I remember is a fight with the Blackfoot and . . . the arrow in my leg. You cut it out, didn't ya?"

"Aye."

"Then what?"

"Ye could nae take the pain, so ye decided ye'd sleep for a wee bit."

"How long?" Worthington asked.

"Most of the day. I swear to ye I ne'er saw anyone sleep as much as ye. Ye be one lazy goddamn critter, ye know, lad."

"Ah, go to hell, damn ya, and let Satan hisself tickle your ass."

"Have ye been there and enjoyed such a thing?" Campbell asked innocently.

"Damn, you're exasperatin'," Worthington snapped. He drained the coffee. "There any more?" he asked.

"Aye. Go on and get yoursel' some." He was grinning, though. He took the cup and returned to the fire to fill it, and one for himself.

"How's my wound look, Alex?" Worthington asked, concern edging into his voice.

"Nae too bad. It'll take a wee bit of time for ye to be healing, but ye should be fine."

"I damn sure hope so. I'd be a hell of a lot more certain if'n it was someone else who had done the doctorin' on me, though."

"Ye got yoursel' the finest doctorin' in the Rocky Mountains, lad," Campbell said, the boast feigned.

"More like finest torturin'," Worthington snorted. "You get your trainin' from the Blackfeet or somethin'?"

"Comanche," Campbell responded, sounding blasé. Turning more serious, he added, "I dinna have anythin' to poultice ye with, lad. I sewed ye up as best I could, but I canna do much more—unless ye want me to put heat to it."

"About as much as I'd like to be humped by a rabid wolf," Worthington spat.

"Then ye'll have to leave your recovery to chance. I canna do anythin' more for ye, so ye'll not have to suffer from my ministrations. Ye better hope, though, that the spirits be good ones for the next several days."

"I don't need no goat-humpin' spirits no more'n I need a butcherin' savage like you."

"Now, now, lad," Campbell said, "such harmful words are nae gonna put ye in the good graces of the spirits. Or me." He took Worthington's now-empty cup. "Ye better get yoursel' some more rest, lad. 'Tis the best way for ye to build up your strength."

"We need to git on the trail, Alex," Worthington insisted. "I can ride, don't you worry about that."

" 'Twill be dark before too long, lad. There be no need to leave here. We'll give ye a few days to get yoursel' back to normal. Then we'll ride like hell for the rendezvous. There be time yet to get there."

"I don't want ye holdin' up our chasin' after Bullock because of me, goddammit," Worthington snapped.

"How far would we get in the couple hours before dark? We'd have to load the animals, saddle the horses, and all that shit first. Then move a few miles down the trail and undo all we just did. Now, I dunna know what ye think aboot that, lad, but it dunna make any sense to this chil' of the Highlands."

Worthington hated to admit it, but that made a whole lot of sense. "Then we leave at first daylight?" he asked insistently.

JOHN LEGG / 180

"The way ye sleep?" Campbell asked incredulously. "Hell, by the time ye raise your lazy ass from your robes, it'll be past noon. But no matter, we'll see how your leg is whene'er ye get yoursel' up."

"Now, I tol' you I . . ."

"Shut your yap, laddie," Campbell commanded, no longer joking. "A couple days to let ye heal up is nae going to hurt us that much after all the time we've spent on that villain's trail. I'd rather we did that than to be on the move with ye still painin' and not up to your usual irritatin' self and see oursel's be attacked by more goddamn Blackfeet."

Worthington nodded and lay back down. Just before Campbell rose, Worthington grabbed his wrist and pushed himself up onto an elbow. "I'm obliged for all you've done fer me, Alex," he said quietly. "I jist didn't want ya sittin' here worryin' about me when we could be on the trail."

"I've nae done anythin' extraordinary, lad. Ye'd have done the same for me, had I been the one who was arrow shot. So don't ye worry none, lad. Ye'll be up to snuff in no time, and we'll push on to rendezvous."

"You'll keep on trackin' Bullock and his murderous scum even if they ain't down to rendezvous?" Worthington asked with a yawn.

"Aye, lad," Campbell said fiercely. "There be no place those fuckin' worms can go that I will nae find them. There's nae any Indians they can stay with, nor any town they can go to that I will nae track them down." His eyes burned with the unnatural light of obsession. "Those villains can ride straight through the gates of hell and into Beelzebub's sitting room, I'll be there sooner or later."

"I'm glad to hear ya say that, ol' hoss," Worthington said wearily. The pain was getting to him, tiring him. He rested his head back down. "Because I'll be right at your side. And if'n ya had said no to that, I'd go on my own."

"I know ye would, lad. Now get your rest."

Campbell rose and went to the fire. He wasn't too worried. Worthington's wound when Campbell had first found him had been much worse, and he saw no signs now that this wound would put Worthington in any danger.

He was not so certain of that the next morning. Worthington's leg had swollen up, and the American was somewhat feverish. Still, neither man could see much to be concerned about yet. Both simply figured that it would take several days for Worthington to get sufficiently healed to move on, instead of the two or three that Campbell had first thought.

Worthington seemed alert in the afternoon, so Campbell decided to take the opportunity to hunt, since they were almost out of meat. He made sure Worthington's rifle and the old musket—seemingly none the worse for wear after being used to bash in that one Blackfoot's skull—and his pistols were near to hand. Then he headed out.

He rode past the spot where, just after he had finished his primitive surgery on Worthington, he had carted the Blackfoot corpses and dropped them.

He had scalped them first, for reasons he did not understand. It simply had seemed the proper thing for him to do at the time.

Scavengers of various sorts had been at the bodies, but they were still mostly recognizable. Campbell figured that would not be true in another day or so. Not that he cared. Like every mountaineer, he hated the Blackfeet. The feeling was reciprocated, and whenever the two sides came together there was bloodshed—and, as often as not, death.

Campbell returned a couple of hours later, a deer carcass across the steady mule he had had all along. Before he tended the animals, he checked on Worthington. He was sleeping but seemed less flushed. Nodding, Campbell went back, unsaddled his horse, and took care of it. Then he pulled the deer carcass off the mule and dropped it on the ground. He gave the patient, long-eared beast a cursory going over and then tied it with the horses.

Campbell dragged the deer over to the fire and unhurriedly began to butcher it. For himself, he spitted several good-size chunks of meat on a sharpened green stick and propped it over the fire. He got their small pot, filled it with water, and cut in some small pieces of meat. He figured that if Worthington's fever continued, feeding him some broth might be the best way of getting some nourishment into him.

He finally leaned back against a log, stretching out his legs, waiting. His eyes closed in tiredness. And a picture of Morning Sun suddenly popped into his mind. He had used his rage and determination to find Bullock to keep his wife out of his mind since he had left Tall Clouds's village. He had not wanted to think of her while he was gone, concerned that his resolve would waver.

But now here she was, so real that he started to reach out for her. His eyes opened, and he realized he was alone, in his and Worthington's camp, with his friend lying wounded a few feet away. There was no Morning Sun, no Coyote Heart. Just him, his wounded partner, and a lot of anger and despair.

"I'll be back wi' ye soon, Morning Sun," he whispered, wondering if the wind would carry his words to his woman.

Then he forced thoughts of Morning Sun out of his mind. It was not easy, but he felt it necessary. He thought he would lose his reason if he continued to have thoughts and visions of her.

Instead of getting better, Worthington steadily worsened. By the end of a week, he was delirious more often than not. On those rare occasions when he was awake and reasonably sane, Campbell would pour broth into him and try to get him to eat bits of whatever meat was handy. It was late spring, and with the heat, meat didn't last more than a day or two. So he hunted as often as he could, hoping every time he rode out that Worthington would be safe while he was gone.

Not knowing what else to do for the wound, he cleaned it with water every day. Sometimes he bandaged it back up; other times he would leave it uncovered, hoping the air would help effect a cure.

None of that worked, and Campbell sat one day, at a loss. Then he remembered that many of the mountaineers used chewed tobacco as a poultice for wounds. He was not fond of chewing on tobacco, but for the sake of his wounded friend, he would do so.

For the next four days, twice a day, he faithfully chewed some tobacco and then slapped the gross wad on Worthington's wound. He regretted doing so, in a way, since his supply of tobacco was growing woefully short, and he liked his pipe of an evening. Even more annoying was the fact that the coffee was fast running out, too, and that increased the irritation that had grown out of his concern for his friend's health.

It was evident after four days of tobacco poultices that the treatment was not working. Worthington's condition was worse than ever. His leg had taken on an unsavory look and odor.

The next time Worthington was awake—and alert—Campbell sat next to him. "Your wound is festered to hell and back, lad," he said quietly, voice touched with sadness.

"What's that mean, hoss?" Worthington asked, pretty certain that he knew and fearing the words.

"It means the leg has to come off if ye're to have a chance to live," Campbell said bluntly.

"No, goddammit," Worthington snapped. "I'd ruther die afore lettin' you take my leg."

"At least ye'd still be alive, lad."

"Buffler shit. What the hell kind of man would I be then, hoss? A fuckin' one-legged goddamn crimple of no use to anyone."

"That's nae so, lad," Campbell said soothingly. "Have ye e'er heard of a lad named Pete Smith?"

"Cain't say as I have. Why? What's that got to do with me?"

"I've heard the same thing happened to him. Took an Indian arrow in the leg. All his friends were too weak-willed to do what was needed—takin' the leg. So he did it himsel'."

"Christ, Alex, don't feed me sich lies about sich a thing," Worthington retorted.

"Well, lad, I dunna know if those stories are true, but I've met the lad mysel'. Down at the rendezvous. Two years ago, I think. And I'll tell ye the truth, lad—there nae was anyone who raised more hell there than that wooden-legged son of a bitch. Damn, he was a wild one. That peg-leg of his dinna slow him down a bit."

"I still think you're talkin' nonsense, hoss, but if it'll make ya feel any better, go on and do it. I don't reckon it can be any worse'n what I been through already."

"Ye willing to let this auld Highland chil' do the butcherin'?" Campbell asked, feigning surprise.

"Hell, there ain't no one else around here, though I reckon I could do what ol' Smith did."

"That's your choice," Campbell said with almost a straight face. "I'll nae get in the way if ye'd rather do it yoursel'."

"After all the hackin' you've done on me already, I might's well let you keep on with it." Now that he had made up his mind—hoping he was still sane—he felt more comfortable with the idea. Not that he liked it any more, but he at least felt as if he might be able to get by in life.

"Ye rest a bit, lad," Campbell said with a nod.

"I'll get what's needed." There really wasn't much he had to do. He took Worthington's tomahawk and put it in the fire to heat. He pulled out his own 'hawk and honed it some. He did the same with his knife. That was about all the preparation there was to be made. He knelt next to Worthington.

"It time?" Worthington asked worriedly. His face was flushed again and he was getting restless.

"Almost, lad."

20

Without warning, Campbell brought the tomahawk up and then instantly down, chopping through flesh, muscle, arteries, and bone, just above the knee.

So swift had it been that Worthington had time for only one short scream before the shock slammed into him and relieved him of his consciousness.

Campbell was unaware of that. He had simply grabbed the other 'hawk, which was red hot, and jammed it against the spurting arteries and freshly cut flesh, cauterizing them. Tossing the weapon aside, he grabbed his knife and trimmed off the few remaining ragged pieces of flesh from the stump.

Sweating more heavily now, Campbell grabbed a piece of blanket he had taken from a fallen warrior, wrapped it around the stump, and tied it in place with pieces of fringe from his pants.

At last he sat back and picked up the weapons he had used. He still knelt where he was as he cleaned them off. Finally he rose and went around the fire for some coffee. He had done all he could do for his friend. Now it was out of his hands.

He wondered, though, what would happen. There was a good chance that Worthington would die despite his own desperate efforts to help.

And what if Worthington lived? It would be weeks, perhaps, before he would be able to move, before he could even begin trying to sport a peg leg. In such a case, Worthington would slow down the search for Bullock considerably.

Not liking any of his options, Campbell decided that he would wait here for two weeks and then see what the situation was. If Worthington had not died in that time, Campbell thought he would rig up a litter or travois for Worthington to travel in. That would slow him some, but he thought he could still make it to rendezvous before the mountain festival broke up.

Once at the rendezvous, Campbell hoped he would have the opportunity to finish his business. If not, he concluded, he would foist Worthington off on someone he could trust, someone heading back east to the Settlements. Then he would resume his search for Bullock.

All these plans, however, did not lessen his irritation at the situation, his rage at Bullock's men, and his worry for his new friend. He had not become as close to Worthington as he had been with Caleb Finch and Ethan Sharp, nor would Worthington ever get to be as much of a friend as his two slain partners had been. But there was a strong friendship beginning. The two men had just started getting comfortable with each other when

Worthington was wounded. Campbell would hate to have Worthington die on him now.

The more he thought about it, the more he realized it was because he wasn't sure he could bear up under the death of another friend less than six months after Finch and Sharp had been killed. That might be selfish, but he could not help himself.

One day short of his self-imposed time limit, Campbell awoke to find that Worthington had died during the night.

Campbell squatted next to the body for some time. There were no tears—either of anger or of rage—just an almost numbing sense of loss. Worthington had seemed to be getting better, and Campbell's hopes had risen. Even when Worthington's condition worsened a couple of days ago, Campbell wasn't really too concerned. Now he sat here next to his new friend's body, wondering if he had done all he could to help him.

There were no answers for that, he well knew, but the thoughts plagued him anyway.

Campbell finally sighed and rose. He went to the fire, and without enthusiasm ate some meat and had the last of the coffee. It was all tasteless to him, but he needed the nourishment.

Done with his meal, he picked out a spot and began digging a grave. It seemed to him, as he hacked at the dirt with Worthington's tomahawk, tossing the soil aside with his hands, that he had done this far too many times in much too short a time. At least this one was easier to dig because the ground was soft.

Still, it was an onerous task, and he did not want to do it again, really, in the foreseeable future, except the six for Bullock and his men. On the other hand, he had no intention whatsoever of digging graves for them once he had dispatched them.

Campbell wrapped his friend in his buffalo sleeping robe and then laid him in the hole. He put in the old musket; he had decided that he would keep the rifle he had taken from the Hudson's Bay man. With the quarry he was following, there was a good chance he would need it.

He added Worthington's saddle and whatever other personal items of his friend's he could find. He had buried Worthington's leg—shortly after having cut it off. He exhumed it and placed it in the grave in the approximate position it would be in were it still attached. There wasn't a lot left to it at this point, seeing as how it had been gangrenous to start with and then buried for almost two weeks. But Campbell hoped it would allow Worthington to be a whole man once he got to the Afterworld.

Just before beginning to fill in the grave, he had an idea. He went to his supplies, got three of the Blackfoot scalps, and put them on Worthington's blanket-wrapped corpse.

"Maybe those'll bring ye some honors in the Hereafter, lad," he muttered, suddenly feeling foolish. "At least it canna do ye nae harm, I'm thinkin'."

Campbell finally began shoving soil into the hole by hand, since he had nothing else to use. It was hot, dirty, and unpleasant work, and he accomplished it with as much speed as he could dredge up from his tired body.

When he had finished and tamped the dirt down, he headed to the horse herd. He began to cull out the Appaloosa he had let Worthington use, but then decided against it. The Appaloosa would bring a much better price down at rendezvous than the other horses, and that might be important then. So he took a sturdy-looking Blackfoot pony, walked it over to the grave, and shot it once in the head with a pistol.

The animal dropped, but remained kicking for a little while in its death throes. Campbell stood there and watched dispassionately until the pony was still.

He turned, stone-faced, and began loading the small stash of supplies he had left onto the mule. Then he saddled his horse, moving faster now, eager to be away from this somber place. Finally he roped the horses and mule together. He mounted his Appaloosa and slid his rifle into the loop on the saddle. With the rope linking his remuda in hand, Campbell rode off.

He stopped once, when he had gotten a hundred yards away, and turned back in his saddle. "Farewell, my good friend. I'll pay your respects to Bullock and his men for ye."

When Campbell rode into the rendezvous site almost a month later, he saw right off that he had missed most of it. He was grateful, though, that at least some of the men were still there, reluctant to leave the comfort of the pleasant spot at the Wind and Popo Agie Rivers.

He had hoped to find Jim Bridger here. Bridger knew more about the mountains and the men who roamed them than anyone else. If anyone knew where Bullock and his men might be, it would be Bridger. But he had already gone. Campbell was almost as pleased to learn that Doc Newell was one of those still remaining. Newell had doctored him a couple years ago, after Campbell had escaped from the Blackfeet, who had held him for some months. It wasn't difficult to find Newell, who was a garrulous and well-liked man.

When Campbell plunked himself down at his fire, Newell grinned crookedly. "You're a mite late, hoss," he said. "You missed the best of the doin's."

"Looks like I missed it all. Was it a good time?" Campbell asked diffidently.

"It shined, boy. Plumb shined. Damn if it didn't."

"Wish I'd gotten here earlier," Campbell lamented. "I could do wi' a bit of frolickin'."

Newell had taken a look around and suddenly asked. "Where's Caleb and Ethan? It ain't like them not to be here, even if they are late." He wore a puzzled look. "Come to think of it, I ain't seed your Nay Percy friends either. What the hell's goin' on, boy?"

"Caleb and Ethan were rubbed oot," Campbell said bitterly.

"What?" Newell burst out. "I thought them two ol' beavers'd last till the Rocky Mountains was wore plumb down to pebbles."

"So did I," Campbell said, an uneasy combination of rage and sadness settling over him.

"What happened, boy? Blackfeet? Those goddamn red devils've been a pain in the ass of ary goddamn American since the day the first one of us come into these mountains."

" 'Twere nae goddamn Blackfeet, Doc. Nor any other Indians either." He paused, noting Newell's upraised eyebrows. " 'Twere fuckin' mountaineers."

"The hell you say," Newell snorted, not wanting to believe it.

"I'd nae lie to ye aboot such a thing, dammit," Campbell said flatly. " 'Tis why I'm here—lookin' for the murderous scum who rubbed my friends oot."

"Who were it?" Newell asked harshly.

"A putrefied bastard named Lije Bullock and his men. They said their camp was set upon by Crows and they had to run for their lives. We let them into our winter camp, told them we'd help them get on their feet. A couple days later, they attacked us for nae reason. There was a dozen of those ass-lickin' vermin against the three of us. We made gone beaver of more than half of them before we were laid low. Caleb and Ethan were killed. They left me for dead. Took e'erything we had—including the women and wee ones."

"You find any of them alive?" Newell asked, voice raspy. He knew that none of the beaver men who roamed these rugged, often-deadly mountains was a saint, but he had not come across anything like this before. He took it personally.

"Aye. My wife, Morning Sun, and son, Coyote Heart. Ethan's woman, Many Bells, too. I got them back to their village, wintered there to recover, and then started trailin' them."

"That were the proper thing, boy," Newell said with a nod of agreement.

Campbell shrugged. "Ye know Bullock?"

"Not too well, but some. He nary was a hoss this ol' chil' could take a shine to. I sure as shit ain't gone change my thinkin' to a more favorable way about that now, after what he's done. Damn. I am plumb goddamn ashamed to be a mountaineer after hearing of sich deviltry from white men. Caleb and Ethan were good men. Shined, they did. They was among the best beaver men in these here mountains. Right up there with Ol' Jim."

Campbell nodded, agreeing to it all. He finished off a mug of coffee. "Are Bullock and his fuckin' butchers here?"

"Nope. They was, but they pulled out a couple days ago. From what I hear, they had theyselves a considerable stash of plews."

"Ye know where they were headin'?" Campbell asked, furious at having been so close but still unsuccessful.

"Hell, boy, I cain't keep track of arybody in the mountains. I don't even know what direction them murderous critters went. But I reckon some of the other boys here might know. I'll spread the word of what those bastards done. Your amigos was well-liked among all the ol' mountain boys. That's a goddamn fact. But this Bullock bastard ain't. If there's arybody here who knows where he and his devilish critters went, they'll be happy to talk about it—especially once they hear what that goddamn villain done."

Campbell nodded. "When do we leave to spread the word?"

"You ain't goin' nowhere, boy," Newell said in a voice that made it obvious he would take no argument. "You set your ass right where you are and rest your bones. There's whiskey in the jug next to you. There's meat and coffee on the fire, as you can plainly see. I'll have some of the women come on over and see to your animals."

"I be going with ye, lad," Campbell said adamantly.

"Like hell you are," Newell said easily. "You look half dead yourself, hoss." He grinned a little. "As your doctor, I order you to set and rest. If you aim to head after them bastards, you'll need your wits and your strength."

Campbell knew Newell was right, so he reluctantly nodded. When Newell left, Campbell poured himself another cup of coffee and drank it down. It had been more than a month since he had had any, and it tasted pretty good, though it was thick and harsh. He sliced meat off a roasting antelope haunch and ate, slowly.

Then he remembered the whiskey. He grabbed the jug and just held it for a moment, trying to think of the last time he had drunk some. It was in winter camp with Finch and Sharp. He lifted the jug.

His eyes watered and he almost choked, but he sighed with satisfaction. "Aye, that be good," he muttered.

He went back to eating, alternating bits of meat with sips of whiskey. He soon felt sated, and then the weariness built up over six months or so began to spread over him. Without really thinking about it, he lay down and curled up on his side, cradling the jug in his arms. He fell asleep almost instantly.

When Campbell awoke, he was groggy, and it took some moments for him to remember where he was. He sat up then, blinking in the hot, brittle sunshine.

Newell was back across the fire, sitting cross-legged, letting two Shoshone toddlers clamber all over him.

"How's doin's, hoss?" Newell said.

Campbell shrugged. He wasn't concerned about how he felt, or anyone else either. "Ye learn anything?" he asked bluntly.

"Nope. Other than one of the traders—a mule's ass named Phil Mason—had some plews with your markin's on 'em. He was one of the last damned traders to pull out. Him and his wagons left a couple days ago."

Campbell nodded. "I'll be leaving oot as soon as I can get my animals ready."

"Best wait till mornin', hoss."

"Why would I do such a thing? I've been chasing those scrofulous bastards for a long time. Now that I'm closing in on them, I dunna want to waste another minute."

"Shit, hoss, it'll be dark in a couple hours. You won't make no more'n a mile, two, by the time you get your animals ready and sich. Stay here for the night, boy. You can leave out fresh in the mornin' with a full belly, a night's rest, and a heap of daylight ahead of you."

Campbell drew in a long breath and then let it

ease out. He knew Newell was right, but he really didn't want to admit it. Nor lose any more time. Still, it made too much sense. He nodded.

As they ate more meat, some of Newell's brigade drifted by and offered Campbell a word or two of encouragement or sympathy. Finally the stream of visitors ended, and Campbell asked, "Ye have any supplies I could buy from ye, Doc?"

"Not a heap of 'em I can spare, hoss," Newell said flatly. "Prices were more dear than usual this year."

"E'en worse than these bandits usually demand?"

"Hell, yes," Newell said with an angry shake of the head.

"Why?"

Newell shrugged. "Beaver trade's dyin', hoss, or so most of the goddamn traders tell me. Even Ol' Jim was sayin' sich before he left. But I ain't certain I believe sich booshwa. Still, even if it ain't true, the traders ain't buyin' beaver like they used to. Some of the boys are thinkin' of pullin' out of the trade. But most others're willin' to try riskin' a chance they can make another season or two out of it."

None of that meant much to Campbell right now. Once he had taken care of his business with Bullock he would worry about the future of the beaver trade. "Well, then, can ye sell me enough supplies to keep me goin' for a couple of days—till I can catch up to Mason. I'll get more goods from him."

Newell nodded.

21

It didn't take long for Campbell to load his supplies on the trusty mule, mount his horse, and ride on, his cavvyard trailing behind him. Newell hadn't given him much, though it should be sufficient for a few days.

He rode east, hoping to catch up with Mason's wagons, or any other supply train heading back to the States. But he figured that Mason was his best hope for finding where Bullock might have gone. Someone with his wagon train should know something of Bullock and his men.

He was confident Mason would take some of his ponies in trade for supplies. He was going to need them badly soon. What he had gotten from Newell was not going to last long.

He now almost regretted having all the animals. They were more trouble than they were worth, he frequently thought, though at least it was summer and there was plenty of grass for them. Still, just about every other hour Campbell considered letting the four Blackfoot ponies go to lessen his burden.

The only thing that kept him from doing so was the certainty that he could use them for supplies—or even as a bribe to put him on Bullock's trail.

Late one afternoon, a few days after leaving the rendezvous site near the confluence of the Wind and Popo Agie Rivers, he spotted a supply train in the distance. He picked up his pace and soon rode into a trader's camp. He saw no one he really recognized, so he hoped it was Mason's.

It was not difficult to figure out where the man in charge was. There was a good-size canvas tent set up in the center of the large box formed by the wagons. Campbell stopped in front of the tent and dismounted. Without warning, he walked inside and spotted a man of medium height, sallow complexion, and surly expression. The man was sitting at a wooden folding table. "Ye Phil Mason?" Campbell asked.

"Yeah. So?" Mason asked, surprised but recovering quickly.

Campbell thought Mason's attitude could use some improvement, but he didn't care right now. "Ye might have some plews of mine, laddie," he said flatly. "Do ye?"

"Git the fuck out of my quarters, asshole, before I have my men throw you out."

Campbell ignored the threat. "Answer my goddamn question, ye horse-faced piece of shit, or I'll tear your asshole oot and give it to ye for a necklace."

"You don't scare me, sonny," Mason said with a sneer.

Campbell grabbed him by the shirt and hauled

him half over the wobbly table. "I be of poor disposition and short of temper. I dinna come here to listen to your boastful buffalo shit. Now, I hear ye have some of my plews. Is that true?"

"Hell if I know, sonny," Mason said, not quite as cockily as before. "I bought me a heap of plews, and every damn one I got, I bought fair and square."

"Any of them have the markings FSC?"

"Might. I cain't be expected to keep track of every goddamn pelt comes in."

"They be mine. And my partners'. They were killed by the men who sold them to ye."

"That's your problem, boy. I bought 'em fair. I don't ask where them that brought 'em to me got 'em."

"Do ye know what happened to my partners?"

"Nope. Don't much give a damn either. And even if I did know, that wouldn't change nothin'."

"Aye, that'd be expected from the likes of ye," Campbell said flatly. He shoved Mason back into his chair, and stabbed the hunk of deer meat on Mason's plate with his knife. He took a bite and chewed slowly, realizing that Mason's men had gathered outside the open front of the tent.

"It may nae mean much to ye, laddie, what happened to my friends, but I'll tell ye anyway. Just so no one can say this chil' dinna give ye the whole of it."

Mason looked at him with distaste, but said nothing.

Campbell explained in short, quick sentences, rage and sadness coating each and every word.

When Campbell had finished, Mason shrugged,

"Still don't change anything, mister. I paid out good specie and a heap of costly goods for what plews I took in. Them other traders at rendezvous are cutthroats, dammit."

"Ye got any supplies left?" Campbell suddenly asked.

"Not a hell of a lot. I didn't cart wagons full of goods all the way out to the Wind River just to haul 'em back with me again." He paused, then asked, "You got the specie to pay?"

"I think we can work somethin' oot, lad."

"If you got no plews, there's nothin' to work out." Mason was confident in his reasoning.

"Horses?"

"I don't want no goddamn horses."

"Fuckin' worm," Campbell breathed. He was close to tearing the man's head off. He breathed deeply, trying to settle himself. "Ye know which way Bullock went?"

"Nope."

Campbell dropped the deer meat, grabbed Mason again and jerked downward. The trader's face slammed onto the tabletop. Campbell pulled him back up and said, "I see ye have difficulty answerin' questions, laddie boy. Perhaps ye'll change your mind aboot such things. Now, answer me."

"I don't know where they went," Mason said, the cockiness pretty well gone. "I bought some plews from 'em at the rendezvous. They rode with us a bit before pullin' ahead of us, still headin' east the last I saw 'em. That's all I know."

Campbell nodded. "I canna be sure ye're tellin'

me the truth, laddie, but bein' a reasonable man, I'll believe ye. Now, I have nae cash, but I think ye can spare a wee bit of supplies in exchange for a few good Blackfoot ponies."

Mason thought of protesting, but that idea vanished when he saw Campbell's cold blue eyes.

"I dunna need much from ye. A bit of tobacco, some beans, coffee, flour, a wee bit of powder, lead—and a couple jugs of whiskey."

"That's an awful lot, mister," Mason said uneasily.

Campbell nodded toward the outside to where the piles of beaver pelts and buffalo hides rested comfortably in the wagons. "It looks like ye've done well for yourself, Mason. Ye can afford the wee lot of things I've asked for." He released Mason again. "I'll be back at first light for those supplies. And dunna think of pullin' some damnfool business to get oot of it either, lad. I'd as soon make gone beaver of ye as look at your unsightly face."

Campbell spun and walked out, shoving his way through the small throng of men. Someone handed him his reins, and Campbell nodded thanks as he mounted the Appaloosa.

The man patted the horse's neck and said quietly, "Most of us heard what happened to your friends, mister. And we figger it's a damn good thing you're goin' after 'em."

"Thankee, lad," Campbell said as he rode off. He picked a spot across the camp from Mason's tent. He wearily began making his own small camp, taking care of the animals. Then he hobbled them well and set about gathering buffalo chips for a fire. When he got back from that, there was a fire going, and a shank of buffalo was roasting. Coffee was on, too, in a pot that wasn't his. He looked around but saw no one who appeared to be guilty of this minor, but appreciated, kindness.

Despite his tiredness, he had been out in this dangerous country too long to be caught unawares even while sleeping. He sensed something, and he rolled off his robes, then crouched in the night, allowing his eyes a little time to adjust to the feeble moonlight.

He caught a movement as someone slithered on his belly toward Campbell's robes. Campbell remained where he was, waiting, silent as the night itself.

Suddenly the dark figure half rose and brought a knife up, ready to plunge it into the sleeping Campbell's heart. Then he realized Campbell was not there, and he froze, fear squeezing his bowels.

Campbell stepped up behind him, unheard, and grabbed the man's lice-infested hair. "I dunna take kindly to cowardly sacks of shit sneakin' up on my robes in the dark thinkin' to make me gone beaver, lad," he said harshly.

"I wasn't plannin' to . . ."

"Ye make a worse liar than ye do an assassin, lad," Campbell said. His voice grated on the ears, as the frustration and rage of his long pursuit suddenly seemed to overwhelm him. "Now, who put ye up to this?"

"It was me own idea," the man said nervously.

"Even a fart-brained toad like ye has more sense than to tell me such nonsense, lad. Now who sent ye to rub me oot?"

"Mason," the man said in defeat.

"I canna say I'm surprised," Campbell commented dryly. "Now, just what shall I do with ye, lad?"

"I'd urge ya to let me go, mister," the man said hopefully.

"So ye can try again?"

"I won't do that, mister. My word."

"I canna say as your word carries much weight with this auld chil', lad. But I'll do it. But keep this in mind: If ye come after me again, I'll cut your bowels oot and tie them around your neck." Campbell let the man's hair go. "Now get oot of here, before I reconsider."

The man rose slowly, seemingly relieved. He took four steps before whirling and charging at Campbell, his knife raised.

The fight—if that's what it could be called—was over in seconds. Campbell blocked the man's knife arm, then smashed a forearm into the attacker's mouth, staggering him. A quick shift, twist, and jerk left the man with a broken arm. Campbell calmly scooped up the knife the attacker had dropped, knelt, and used it to tear a deep, ragged line from the man's diaphragm to his privates.

Campbell stood and dropped the knife on the man's gaping belly wound, which exposed a considerable amount of intestine. He realized that other men were standing around. "Any of ye lads want to claim this vermin?"

When no one stepped forward, Campbell added, "Then a couple of ye lads come and drag him away from the camp here."

"And bury him?" someone called out from the night.

"That be up to ye. I'd as soon leave his festerin' carcass for the wolves." With that he stretched out on his robes. Before the other men had dragged the body ten yards, Campbell was asleep again.

Mason gave Campbell no trouble in the morning when the Scotsman went for his supplies. That probably was due at least in part to the fact that most of Mason's men were obviously backing Campbell.

They did haggle a little. Campbell got more supplies than he had figured on, and Mason realized that the three—he had hoped to hold out for all four, but Campbell was not giving in—good Blackfoot ponies were a lot better payment than nothing at all. Besides, he figured he could sell them for a fair price back in the Settlements.

Campbell made sure he got more value than he would have gotten at the rendezvous. He was almost pleased at seeing the choler on Mason's face as he had to offer supplies at a price so low it would have been laughable if it didn't hurt his pride so much.

The man who had expressed sympathy the day before for Campbell's losses urged Campbell to take a half-dozen traps and accoutrements.

"Jist in case," the man said.

Campbell resisted the notion at first, but then decided that it made sense. If he managed to track

Bullock down soon, he could then head out for the fall beaver hunt. And he would have the traps at a much lower cost than he would have to pay if he bought them later. Then, if he couldn't find Bullock soon, he could always head into the mountains and trap so that he would have plews to trade next year to continue his quest.

"Thankee, mister . . . ?"

"Ben Wiseman," the man said. "And ain't no need for no 'mister' with it."

"I'm obliged for your help, Ben. I hope ye dunna git in trouble with Mason o'er it," he said pointedly, hoping that Mason would get the message.

Mason's face showed that he had.

With help from some of Mason's men, Campbell quickly packed his supplies on the animals and saddled his horse. With a last farewell to Wiseman and a last warning to Mason, he rode out, heading east.

But his search proved as fruitless on the broad, limitless plains as it had in the rugged mountains. It was a thoroughly frustrated Alex who rode into Independence, Missouri, a month after he had left Mason's wagon train. He had moved fast, seeing no reason to dally.

He traded in the other Blackfoot pony, plus one of the pintos he had gotten from Talks of War, for enough supplies to keep him going a while longer. He rode out again the next day. He had used his one night there to eat two big meals, put away half a jug of whiskey, and take his pleasure with a woman. While he loved Morning Sun deeply, he had not had a woman in a long time, and he was in need of one.

There was only one way for him to go now—
west. No one in Independence could recall seeing
Bullock or his men in quite some time, so Campbell
figured the renegades had probably returned to the
mountains. Campbell decided he would do the
same. He pushed himself hard, with the summer
winding down in a real hurry.

Once he got into the mountains, Campbell
headed in a direction that would bring him close to
the winter camp where Sharp and Finch had died.
He had no other idea of where to go.

Though he encountered several brigades of
mountain men on his journey, none had seen the
cutthroats. He continued to press on, even as fall
began sweeping over the mountains.

Still, knowing that winter would be on him
soon, Campbell decided that he might as well do
some trapping. And he would need a place to
winter. He would go back to hunting Bullock and
his men as soon as spring arrived. That was a quest
that might be delayed by winter, but would not be
stopped by anything short of his own death.

22

Winter finally forced Campbell to seek shelter to wait out the months of harsh weather. He found a cave low down on the eastern side of a steep slope in the Big Horns. The cave widened once he got through the narrow mouth and offered enough room for him to keep his several horses, the mule, and his single pack of beaver plews.

Pushed by the swiftly worsening weather, he hurriedly gathered what forage and firewood he could and stored it all in the cave as well. He shot game at every opportunity. Instead of trying to jerk the meat, he simply hoisted the carcasses by ropes up into the branches of the tall pines that were clustered on the rocky slope.

Finally he was ready to hunker down to wait for spring.

It was not an easy winter for him. He could bear the temperatures that would freeze a man to death in minutes; he could accept the snow that piled up in the surrounding lands; and he could ignore the wind that growled and hissed and threatened to come into the cave and get him.

What he couldn't bear were the haunting remembrances of Sharp, Finch, Worthington, Dancing Feather, Otter, Spotted Calf, and White Hawk. Painful memories of the way they had died ate at him, as did the fact that he was such a complete and abject failure. He had been chasing the phantoms of Bullock and his men for a year and was no closer to exacting vengeance than he had been on the day his camp had been attacked.

Making it all worse was the boredom, since the lack of meaningful work gave him far too much time to think. And that was when the memories came back to plague him. They wormed their way deep into his heart and soul and left him almost paralyzed with rage and self-loathing.

He tried to fend off the thoughts, but it was rare that he could. There just was not enough for him to do to keep his mind off such things. He cleaned and cared for his rifles and pistols frequently; his knife and tomahawk were so well honed he could have used either for shaving—had he had any interest in shaving. He had repaired his clothes as best he could with the materials at hand, had even made himself two new pairs of moccasins. He hunted occasionally, when the weather permitted, almost always using the crude snowshoes he had made.

Campbell had fashioned himself a new hat of a fox pelt he had taken during the late fall. He had braided himself two new horsehair ropes, made lead balls for his rifles and pistols, and put together a necklace of bear claws and teeth.

Beyond that—and the regular chores of caring for the animals and keeping the fire going and the fuel supply kept up—he had nothing to do. He wished more than once that he had found a book with Mason's men and brought it. He wasn't an accomplished reader, but he could have ciphered his way through a page or two of a good book each day. That would have gone a long way toward keeping his mind occupied.

But that was not an option, so he had to live with the raging of his thoughts, the pain of his memories—and the shame of his failure. And his thoughts of Morning Sun, too, which frequently came unbidden into his mind, reminding him all the more about his lack of success.

The dullness and monotony were broken only by the frequent storms, and one unusual event.

Campbell was sitting inside the cave when he heard voices. Since he was in one of his more foul and self-disgusted moods, he thought that he was just hearing things, that he had simply lost his reason after a couple of months of living in such loneliness and misery.

Then he realized that the words he heard were in Crow. He knew only a few words in that language, but he could recognize it. He thought it strange that when his mind had snapped the spirits would be speaking in Crow.

"Wait a goddamn minute," he whispered to himself. "That be a goddamn fool notion, Alex Campbell." He pushed himself up and slid toward the wall just inside the cave mouth, grabbing both rifles on the way. He rested one against the sooty rock wall.

The Crows were just about at the entryway now,

and Campbell figured they did not know anyone was inside. That would help, since it was almost certain he would be outnumbered.

The first warrior in hesitated a moment when he saw the fire, and Campbell slammed the butt of his rifle against the Crow's head. As the warrior fell, Campbell swung out toward the cave mouth and fired his rifle from the hip. The ball slammed through two Crows, killing the first, at least. Campbell wasn't sure about the second, but both staggered backward.

Just after they fell outside, three other warriors came boiling into the cave, one after the other. The first, a somewhat handsome young man, swung a stone-headed war club.

Campbell jerked his rifle up crossways and caught the war club on the barrel. He shoved the weapon away, then snapped the buttstock of the rifle around, smashing the Indian in the jaw with it.

Then the two other Crows barreled into him, slamming him to the ground on his back. His head hit a rock, rattling him a little. But he could not be concerned about that right now. He had more important things to worry about at the moment.

Such as two enraged Crows who were trying to pin him down so they could finish him off at their gruesome leisure.

He managed to jerk his head out of the way of another stone war club, but he was rapidly running out of time and maneuvering room. There wasn't a whole lot he could do, however, or so it seemed, except to continue to buck and jerk and hammer a warrior whenever he got the rare chance. It didn't seem to be doing him much good, though.

Then one of the warriors spit on his face, and all the past year's pent-up rage, frustration, fear, and worry burst inside him like a thunderbolt. He got an arm partially free and grabbed one warrior's genitals. He squeezed with all his formidable strength.

The Crow's eyes widened and he instinctively rose a little. Campbell used the leverage he gained having the arm entirely free to give the warrior a little impetus, throwing him off to the side.

The one still partly atop him growled something in Crow and tried to stab him in the face.

Campbell managed to block only part of it, and the blade caught his forehead just above the left eyebrow and skidded downward toward his ear.

" 'Twas nae nice of ye, laddie," he mumbled, rage still coursing through his veins like the flood-swollen Missouri. He hammered the warrior on the temple with a right fist strengthened by his fury. He did it again, and the Crow's eyes crossed a little.

"Fuck wi' this chil', will ye, ye goddamn ass-favorin' swine," Campbell roared. He rolled, dumping the Indian off him, then pushed up to his feet. "Well, 'twas a foolish thing for ye to do. I be Alexander Campbell, and I'll nae let the likes of ye put me under." He kicked the warrior in the face as he was trying to get up.

He spun and, wiping the blood off his face, headed for the one whose nuts he had squashed. The Crow was standing, looking tentative about it.

"Ye dunna look so goddamn devilish now, lad," Campbell spat.

The Crow responded in his own language.

Campbell didn't understand the words, but the general idea was clear on the Indian's face.

"I be tired of this here fracas, lad, and I aim to be endin' it. If ye know any prayers of your own gods ye'd like to be saying, ye had better get to it."

He had no idea of whether anything he had said was understood. Nor did he care a whit. He just moved up and pasted the warrior in the mouth. The Crow lurched backward and hit the wall.

Campbell could hear the other warrior getting to his feet. He ducked and grabbed the Crow in front of him by the crotch and throat and jerked him up onto his shoulders. He turned, lifted the warrior over his head, and then threw him.

The flying Crow hit his companion, and they both tumbled to the ground again.

Campbell stomped forward, feeling the rage burn in him, and it felt damn good, as if it belonged there. It was the first real chance he had had to release some of it since the attack on his camp, and he took pleasure in it.

Both Crows were nearly as tall as he was, though a little slimmer, so he easily yanked them up by their coats, one in each hand. "I dunna take kindly to such doin's, lads," he said with a vicious smile splitting his red beard and mustache. Campbell suddenly let go of their shirts and his hands jumped to their throats and squeezed.

It took only an instant for the two Crows to realize they were being strangled, and they fought back.

It was too late for them, though. With the strength of rage in him, Campbell slammed their heads together, without letting go of their throats. That took most of the fight out of them. Their struggles in the minute or so it took them to die were quite feeble.

Campbell dropped the two and turned his attention to the first one who had entered the cave, the one he had hit with his rifle butt. The Crow was sitting up, though he was quite groggy. Campbell went and squatted in front of him. "Were there only six in your war party?" he asked with signs. Then he wiped blood off his face again and cleaned his hand on his shirt.

It took a few moments for the warrior to answer, seeing as how he could barely think. Then he nodded.

"Where're your horses?" Campbell asked, again in sign.

"Bottom hill," the Crow answered in heavily accented English.

That was a little relief to Campbell. He had never considered himself very well versed in sign language, and it was always an effort to use it much. "What's your name, lad?"

"Brave Buffalo," he said rather arrogantly.

"What the hell're ye lads doon oot here in the winter tryin' to make war?" It was unlike the Crows, or any other Indians he knew, to venture forth in the winter without reason.

Brave Buffalo shrugged. This venture had seemed a good one when he and his friends had started out. "Wanted horses. Shoshones stupid. Don't watch 'em in winter."

"Ye dinna get far, did ye?"

Brave Buffalo shook his head and regretted it. "No," he said angrily. "Three days. We saw cave. Wanted to stay the night."

"Looks like the spirits were nae smilin' on ye this time, lad."

The Indian nodded. He straightened his back, and smoothed his face through will alone. He knew he was about to die, and he was going to do it with dignity, as befitted a Crow warrior.

"Ye can sing your death song, if ye want," Campbell said. For a few fleeting moments, he considered letting the Crow go. Then he realized that would be signing his own death warrant. This warrior would race back to his village and bring back a hundred warriors. Now, since this Crow and his friends had found him, even though by accident, he would have to die. "Just dunna be too loud aboot it."

Campbell got up and walked around the room, checking on the other warriors, as Brave Buffalo chanted a monotonous series of notes that to Campbell's ears sounded like bagpipes played by a drunken cow.

The other warriors were dead, so Campbell leaned against the wall, looking out the mouth of the cave. When Brave Buffalo stopped chanting, Campbell walked over to him and shot him in the forehead, not wanting him to suffer any more. Campbell was not a killer by nature, and now that the rage that had served him so well during the fight was subsiding, he did not feel so bloodthirsty.

Campbell stood there for a few moments, looking down at Brave Buffalo. Then he glanced at his horses and the mule. They had not liked any of this, right from the first, and they were made even more skittish by the gunsmoke and noise. He was glad he had built a makeshift corral for them. It was one of the things he had thought of to keep himself busy for a few days. He had cut logs and hauled them up into the cave. There he wedged them into rocks on either side of the cave wall until they were about chest high to him. It was troublesome to undo to get the animals outside when needed, but now he was glad he had done it.

Finally he took a look around at the carnage and shook his head. "Well, laddie," he said to himself, "now that ye've gone and created such a wee mess, what do ye do wi' the remains of it?"

He did not look forward to the work it would take, but he had to get the bodies out of here, and he had to dump them someplace where they wouldn't be found. At least not until spring, when he would be gone.

He reloaded his pistol and the one rifle, then headed outside and down the banked hill. The six ponies were indeed there. Campbell untied one and led it up the hill and into the cave. He placed one of the bodies across its back, tied the corpse down, and then led the pony back down the hill and tied it off. He repeated that process five times.

He took the logs of his corral down so he could get out his favored Appaloosa, then rebuilt the corral. He saddled the horse, walked it outside, and mounted it. At the bottom of the hill, he saw that a pack of wolves was already showing considerable interest in the tied-up ponies and their grisly cargo.

"Begone, ye servants of the devil," Campbell

growled at the wolves. He was in no mood to try to be nice to the snarling pack of carnivores. He gathered up the Crow ponies and rode off under the cold light of the full moon.

The spot he wanted to use was about a mile from the cave, and he made it in quick time, and with no trouble, though the wolves were following. He dismounted, tied the horses to rocks and trees, and then cut the ropes holding the bodies. One at a time he carried the corpses to the thin, deep crevasse he had discovered a month ago and dumped the bodies down it.

Then he pulled out, charging ahead and laughing as the wolves scattered.

Back at the cave, he unsaddled the Appaloosa and then tore down the corral wall. He hoped his animals were used to staying where they were and would not wander around while he was outside. He walked down the hill and then led the Crow ponies up it and inside the cave.

Once all the animals were inside, at the back, Campbell started rebuilding the corral, but then realized it would not work now. He found another spot to wedge the logs, some feet farther out, giving the animals enough room inside. His living space had been trimmed considerably, but he figured it was worth it.

23

Though Campbell frequently thought the winter would never end, it eventually did. Not all at once, of course, but in its usual gradual way, a step forward, several back, another step or two forward. A few days above freezing, followed by another raging snowstorm.

At the first sure sign that spring might actually be contemplating an arrival, Campbell began preparing to leave. There wasn't much for him to do, but eagerness and a desire for relief from his relentless nightmares, incessant loneliness, and insidious boredom were goading him strongly.

Before it was really safe—or wise—Campbell left his cave for the last time. He could not stand being in that cramped, stifling den another day. In addition, with the coming of the spring, even if that arrival was mostly in his mind, he discovered in himself a renewed determination to find Lije Bullock and his five men.

He turned generally west, trapping as he went. He missed Morning Sun something awful, and wanted to see her more than anything. More even than he wanted to track down Bullock right at the moment.

But several nights out, sitting in his lonely camp, he realized he could not bring himself to do that. The shame in knowing that more than a year had passed and he had not found the men who had killed his partners and a woman and children was too much for him to have to face up to in front of Morning Sun and her people.

Reluctantly he turned southwest, hoping to find some decent trapping grounds. Though he had taken almost a full pack in the fall hunt, it was far less than he was used to. He wondered if he was becoming a failure as a trapper, too. He had never seen pickings so slim.

It was several more weeks before Doc Newell's words popped up in his mind: "Beaver trade's dyin', hoss." Maybe, Campbell thought, the trade was dying because there were no more beaver, not because the traders had decided it. Then he decided that thought was so ludicrous as not to deserve any attention.

"Well, laddie," he said to himself one night, "either ye're nae the trapper ye thought ye were or these lands're trapped oot." He figured there would be better hunting up in Blackfoot country, but he had other things to do before he could try that. The only reason he was trapping now was to build up a cache of plews he could sell for supplies. And his trapping route, if that's what it could be called, was merely an excuse to try to find Bullock.

He headed in a direction that would eventually

bring him to where the Siskeedee-Agie and Horse Creek met. That was where the rendezvous would be held this year, and Campbell hoped to get there earlier than he had last year. If Bullock and his men were to be found there, they would certainly be there during the height of the trapper's annual fair.

During his travels, he encountered several brigades of mountain men. Some of the men he knew, others he didn't. But he stopped to talk with the men of each one, whether they were still traveling or settled in for the night. And at each he would do the same thing: Tell the men what had happened, and then ask if anyone had seen the murderous Lije Bullock and his fellow cutthroats.

None had, and Campbell began to wonder if perhaps Bullock had left the mountains. There was little sympathy for Bullock's crew from the mountain men he came across, not after Campbell told his tale, so it was possible that Bullock had gotten wind of Campbell's pursuit and had left for the Settlements. Not that Campbell figured Bullock was afraid of his being on his trail by himself, but if the renegade knew that most of the trappers in the mountains were down on him and would let Campbell know where he was if they saw him, that might be enough to do it.

Campbell continued on, growing ever more frustrated and angry. The beaver take was incredibly small, which irked him, though he no longer doubted his abilities as a trapper. He had learned from the brigades and free trappers he had met that it was the same all over. What really gnawed at him, though, was the steadily growing perception that

Bullock and his five men had vanished from the face of the earth.

Sitting at his fire one night, with summer nearing, out of coffee, tobacco, and whiskey, Campbell pondered his future. His rage had driven him completely for almost a year and a half now, and to no end. And having learned that no one had seen Bullock in the mountains in some time, he wondered if going to rendezvous would be worthwhile. He wondered if the renegades would even be there. It was beginning to seem like a faint hope.

There was a little more to it than that, though. He hated to admit it even to himself, but he really didn't want to go to the gathering. If he went to the rendezvous, there was the possibility that he would encounter Morning Sun and Tall Clouds's band of Nez Percé. And that was something he was not prepared to face.

Discouraged at his failure, he decided that he would try something different, go against the grain of what he had thought was the most likely thing.

Since summer was just about here and the few furs he was taking were so poor as to be worthless anyway, he turned northeast the next morning. Some weeks later, he arrived at Fort Union, the American Fur Company's large trading post on the Upper Missouri River.

Kenneth McKenzie, the head of the trading post—and the major force along the Upper Missouri—was cordial to Campbell, though of little help. Neither he nor any of his men had seen Bullock.

"I dunna think that lad's the kind to roam around lands where the Company, the Sioux, and the Rees might be."

"I expect ye're right," Campbell said. His slight euphoria at having met a fellow Scotsman had ebbed fast. "If the lad had any balls, he'd nae be doon what he has." Campbell pushed himself to his feet and held out his hand. "Well, Mister McKenzie, I thank ye for takin' the time to sit a few minutes with this auld Highland chil'. I know ye're a man with much to do."

" 'Tis always a pleasure to chat a wee bit with a countryman. Ye dinna take up much of my time, lad. And I'm sorry I could nae be of more help to ye in your quest."

"I'm beginnin' to think it's more like a chase after a wild goose, Mister McKenzie," Campbell said with a shake of his head. " 'Tis like the earth has swallowed those fuckin' critters up."

"Perhaps that's nae far from the truth, lad," McKenzie said thoughtfully. "Men like those are certain to run afoul of many Indians. Perhaps they've done so, and their bones are now rotting in the summer sun outside some Blackfoot village. Though after the infestation last year, there's nae many Blackfeet left."

"Infestation?"

"Aye. Smallpox swept o'er them like a wildfire last year. Word I get from my employees and others is that there's nae half the Blackfeet as there were the year before."

Campbell was not too bothered by that. He had no love for the Blackfeet anyway, and right now, considering his fruitless quest, he wouldn't care if every Blackfoot in the world had gone under. "Well," he said, " 'tis a possibility they might've been rubbed oot that way. But I'll nae give up my search for them till I know for certain that some auld chil'—red or white—has made wolf bait oot of him and his men."

"Ye surely carry the blood of your brave ancestors in ye, lad," McKenzie said, rather impressed at Campbell's determination, though not with his sanity.

"Aye," Campbell said cockily, the first time he had felt that way in a long time.

"Is there anythin' else I can do for ye, lad?"

"Aye. Ye can take some poor plews off my hands, plus six good Crow war ponies in exchange for some supplies."

"I can." McKenzie sat again. "But I must warn ye, lad, that the price for beaver has hit bottom. I canna give ye more than a dollar, maybe a dollar and a half per pound, if they're prime."

"That's mighty low," Campbell said, also sitting again.

McKenzie shrugged. "Ye'll nae find any better price. Not at another trading post, not at the rendezvous, and sure as hell not in Saint Louis or the other Settlements. No one e'en wants to buy beaver any more."

"Why?"

"Silk, lad. That's what they're makin' hats oot of now. No more beaver. Besides, from all the reports I've heard, from my own men and others, beaver are aboot played oot in the mountains."

"Seems that way," Campbell said with disgust. "Well, Mister McKenzie, what aboot the ponies?"

"I can give ye a fair price on them—if they're good."

"Prime war ponies, they be."

"I'll have one of my men see aboot that."

"I'm nae askin' for the moon, Mister McKenzie," Campbell said a little testily.

"Ye've cut me to the quick with such a statement, lad," McKenzie said, looking truly hurt. "Aye, 'tis true that I've a Scotsman's penny-pinching heart, but I'll nae take advantage of a fellow Scot."

Campbell knew McKenzie was lying through his teeth. He didn't really hold it against the fort factor, though it irritated the hell out of him. He figured that if he were treated even somewhat fairly he would have done all right for himself. He nodded. "Is there a place a visitor can get a meal and a bottle around here?" he asked.

"Aye, of course."

"And a woman?" Campbell asked hopefully.

"Aye. Talk to Mister Gregson. He'll show ye where to get all those things. The woman, I'm afraid," McKenzie added almost apologetically, "will be a Ree. That's all we have here."

Campbell shrugged. "I dunna care what she is. As long as she's got teats and a slit 'tween her legs and is nae gonna ask for all the foofaraw in the world, she'll do. I'm nae plannin' to marry the lass."

McKenzie laughed and nodded. "Good luck on your hunt, lad," he said, dismissing Campbell.

. . .

It didn't take long for Campbell to find Gregson. He was another Scot, a burly man with a large chest and belly, and a lot of head that once had been covered with bright red curls. The crimson beard and mustache were heavily flecked with white.

"Ye'll find a good meal o'er yon," Gregson said, pointing to one of the sturdy wood buildings. "The cook's name is Macintosh, and if he's in the right mood, lad, he might e'en make ye somethin' special. Somethin' to remind ye of the auld country."

"That'd be a welcome thing, Mister Gregson. And where would I round up some whiskey?"

"I'll see that some is brought to ye. We'll deduct it from what your plews and horses are worth."

Campbell nodded. "And a woman?"

"Ootside the fort, around toward the back yon." He pointed again. "A lad named Augustus Schmidt has several Indian lodges oot there with women in them. He's a thievin' knave, if ye ask me, lad, so be wary aboot him. I suggest ye ask for the one he calls Lisette. I dunna know her real name. She's nae half bad lookin' for a savage, she's mostly clean, and she's willin' to help ye along, if ye know what I mean. Unlike the rest of them, who just lay there like a sack of barley."

Campbell nodded again.

"And dunna pay that bastard Schmidt more than two dollars if ye want to stay the night wi' her."

"Thankee, Mister Gregson." Campbell headed for the dining room.

When the cook heard there was a visiting Scotsman awaiting dinner, Macintosh did, indeed, whip something special up for Campbell. And he personally brought it to Campbell's table. As he set the cock-a-leekie down, he said, "I'm sorry, lad, that I'm nae able to cook ye up some haggis. I make the best haggis west of the Mississippi River, lad. Aye."

"This'll do," Campbell said with a grin. "And I'm in your debt for your kindliness."

Macintosh beamed. "There be no debt here, laddie. Nae. But ye can fill my cup when ye manage to latch on to some whiskey."

"Gregson said he'll have some brought here for me. If ye're nae busy now, sit a wee bit, and we can chat. And when the bottle comes, we can toast to our homeland—and to your fine cookin'."

After polishing off the soup of chicken, leeks, and barley, and after more than a few toasts to Macintosh's culinary skills, Campbell headed toward the lodges outside the fort. He was not drunk, but for the first time in a long time he didn't feel too bad.

"Are ye Schmidt?" he asked a heavyset man sitting in a battered wood chair.

"Yah. Vhat you vant here?" His German accent was thick and harsh.

"What the hell do ye think I want, ye damn fool?" Campbell countered in jovial tones. "I'd like to sport wi' Lisette."

Campbell headed for the lodge Schmidt had pointed to. A Ree woman, attractive at this distance, waited outside, watching. She had a smile on her lips.

Campbell left Fort Union three days later. He had spent the first night with Lisette, but the next, he decided he would get drunk with Macintosh. He slept much of the next day, recovering from the debauchery. The addition of some of Macintosh's excellent cooking helped, and he finally strolled over to Lisette's lodge again.

"Ye mind if I spend the night wi' ye again?" he asked.

She didn't.

As Campbell rode westward, he found his mind turning more often to Morning Sun. He smiled at that a little, though the thoughts faded with time, replaced by a return of the abject disgust with himself for having failed to run down Bullock after all this time.

He encountered no trouble until he began working his way through Crow country. Despite his run-in with those warriors over the winter, he expected no trouble from them, really. The Crows were generally fairly disposed toward white trappers. Still, they had no qualms about attacking a lone white man with some fine horses and perhaps a pack or two of beaver pelts or other furs that could be traded in.

He was holed up along some creek in the Big Horns, trying to coax a beaver or two into his traps, when an arrow suddenly thumped into the meat of his shoulder above his left breast.

"Fuckin' devils," he muttered as he rolled away from his fire to sanctuary behind a tree, the arrow shaft breaking off as he did. He looked down at the wound and cursed again. He would have to cut the thing out himself. That didn't bother him nearly so much as the remembrance of what had happened to Worthington. He'd rather die here and now fighting Indians than die of gangrene poisoning.

He had thought at first that he had been attacked by Blackfeet, but the arrow had Crow markings. Angry, he decided he was not going to sit here and wait for the Indians to come to him. He would go find them. That was far riskier, but right now he didn't care.

He slipped through brush and around trees, as silent as the Crows were. He smiled grimly when he saw one behind a tree. The warrior had his bow nocked but not raised, and he was watching Campbell's camp intently.

Campbell leaned his rifle against a tree and pulled his tomahawk. He strode three large steps forward and then shattered the Crow's head. He wiped the 'hawk off on the warrior's shirt and slid it away. Retrieving his rifle, he pressed on.

He soon spotted another Crow. This one was also watching the camp, his bow loosely ready. Campbell crept forward, like a catamount stalking its prey. Suddenly he stopped and whirled—just in time to catch another arrow, less than two inches from the first.

"Shit," he snapped as he fell, but he kept his grip on his rifle. He jerked it halfway up and fired it.

The Crow who had shot him caught the lead ball in the throat, and it slammed him down.

Furious, Campbell stood and turned to face the other Crow he had seen. He snapped the arrow shaft off and tossed it aside. "Shoot or run, laddie," he roared. "And any else of ye lurkin' aboot in the bushes. Ye canna kill this Scottish chil'."

The Crow must have suddenly thought Campbell was crazy. He turned and ran. Campbell considered giving chase, but he knew he was too weak already. He had lost some blood and, if he went running around now, he would lose so much that he'd not be able to treat himself.

He walked into camp and reloaded his rifle. Then he sat and had a couple of very large swallows of whiskey. He got a fox pelt, a needle, sinew, and his knife and set them down where he could easily reach them. He folded the fur and shoved it between his teeth. Taking his knife, he blanked his mind to what he was about to do to himself.

24

Campbell was not conscious of time or pain. He simply plunged the knife blade into his flesh and created one large, jagged wound where there had been two smaller ones. Once that was done, pulling out the two broad arrowheads was simple.

He tossed them aside and picked up the needle, which was already threaded with sinew. He punched a hole in one side of the wound and then the other, dragging the sinew through. It made his skin jump and dance a little, like spittle on a hot rock. Campbell was not aware of that, either. He just continued his surgery with as much emotion as he would show while eating a dull meal.

When he was about halfway through sewing up the wound, Campbell stopped, letting the needle dangle from the sinew. He took up the bottle of whiskey and poured some in the wound, hissing at its bite. He was not sure it was going to work, but he figured it had to be better than what he had tried with Worthington. He set the jug down and resumed his stitchery.

When he was done, he tied the sinew and awkwardly sliced off the excess. He took a couple more large swigs of whiskey, set the jug down, and then passed out.

When he awoke, it was growing dark, and he had no idea of where he was. Not being able to remember sent a spark of fear through him and brought beads of sweat to his forehead. He went to push himself up, and the stomach-churning pain that ripped through his shoulder was a vivid reminder of where he was and why he was there.

He flopped back down to let the pain subside; then he managed to sit up without jarring the wound too much. Sitting with his back against a log, he had a dose of whiskey that served to settle him a bit. Only then did he chance standing. It worked, though with effort, and he felt woozy and as weak as a kitten.

He gathered some firewood, since he had little left. Then he set meat and coffee on the fire. He made sure the animals were all right and then went back and sat. After eating, he fell asleep where he was.

He felt fractionally better in the morning, and in the harsh, hot sunlight he inspected his wound. It looked all right as far as he could tell. It still hurt like hell, and it was tender to his tentative poke. He shrugged and poured a little more whiskey on it. Then he smiled tightly and drank his medicine.

After eating, he sat with a cup of coffee, puffing on his pipe. He knew he would have to stay put for a while to allow himself time to heal. He didn't much like the thought, but there was little he could do to change the situation. He decided after a bit that if he had to hunker down for a few weeks, there were many worse places than this one he could have been stuck in.

He finally rose and walked into the trees surrounding the small clearing where he had set his camp. The bodies of the Crows were still there, though wolves and coyotes had done a pretty fair job of tearing them apart. Campbell shrugged. Death was too common out here, always too close for him to worry about such things.

With a sigh of annoyance at his failure and his predicament, he returned to the camp and made what few improvements to it he could, since he was quite limited in strength and endurance.

It was several weeks before he felt he had recovered enough to travel. More than once during his convalescence he thought of pulling out, but reason took over and made him stay put. Finally, though, he knew he was sufficiently recovered.

Fall was inching its way into the high country as Campbell left his camp. As he rode, he trapped when and where he could. But many was the morning or evening that he checked his traps only to find them empty. The full import of the possibility of the beaver's being wiped out began to settle on him, and he wondered what he would do with his life— once he had taken care of Bullock. That was still uppermost in his mind.

But he was a man who needed productive work. The thought of going back to Morning Sun's village and living out the rest of his days there was seductive, but foolish. He would go mad there with no meaningful—for him—work.

He tried to put the worries about that out of his mind, but had little success. The sight of empty beaver traps day after day would not let him.

Dejected, sick of himself, concerned about the future, he finally gave up trapping and began searching for a place to winter up. Since it took less work to deal with a cave, he inspected all he saw, until he found one he was satisfied with.

This winter's haven was much like his previous one—on the eastern slope of a mountainside, out of the weather, not too far up. It was large enough for the horses, and even had a narrow passageway partway through it that led to a large, roughly round chamber. He herded the horses into that "room," and all he needed was two logs wedged between rocks in an X shape to keep them inside. It was much less work than the setup he had had last winter.

The cold months settled in fast, and Campbell found himself every bit as bored, frustrated, angry, and disgusted as he had been last year. There was not even the excitement of an Indian attack to break the monotony of his existence.

He realized in that cold, bleak winter that he could not avoid rendezvous forever. So he decided that he would head there when spring showed its face. He just had to see Morning Sun, even if it meant facing her disappointment and that of the other Nez Percé. Morning Sun's band had always been good friends with him, and he figured he could live down the shame, and perhaps even get some help from his father-in-law and some of his close Nez Percé friends.

That thought bolstered him a little, made the loneliness seem a bit less oppressive. And as he sensed that spring would be coming before long, he felt a little of his old vigor and humor returning. He felt comfortable, too, with the anger that still simmered inside, waiting for the day he would find Bullock and it would be unleashed.

With a feeling of expectation, Campbell began preparing to leave. Much of it was make-work, since there was almost nothing for him to prepare that hadn't been taken care of during the winter.

He rode out as soon as he thought it was reasonably safe. He should have known better, having been in the mountains five years now. He got caught in a hellacious snowstorm two days after leaving, and had to hunker down in the meager shelter of an aspen grove as the storm howled around him, threatening to flatten his horses and even carry him away to some unknown land.

But it passed—after three days—and he moved on. Again, he trapped as he went. Or rather, tried to trap. He didn't spend more than a day at any one place. If he was lucky, he might pull up a scraggly beaver or two. He took their pelts, since they were better than none at all, but even he began to wonder if anyone would pay him anything for such poor plews.

He considered forgoing the trapping and making his way to rendezvous by a circuitous route, looking for Bullock and his men. But he couldn't bring himself to do that. It had become too ingrained in him by now, but he did worry occasionally about what he would do with himself after taking care of his enemies.

The rendezvous along the Siskeedee-Agie near the mouth of Horse Creek was a mighty poor affair, Campbell quickly found out. When he first pulled into the elongated series of camps, he thought he had arrived too late. He had spent some time looking aimlessly for Bullock, trying to trap a little as he went along. But both efforts were almost equally futile. So when he hit the rendezvous, he thought he had lost track of time on the trail and missed it. And he cursed himself for it.

Then he spotted Black Harris, whom he knew, though not very well. Still, the old mountain curmudgeon was willing to set and jaw a while.

"I must've missed the best parts of this doin's, eh, Black?" Campbell said as he and Harris lounged on the grass, leaning against logs, sharing a jug of whiskey.

"Y'all ain't missed goddamn shit, boy," Harris growled. His face, blackened by powder burns years ago, glowered fiercely at Campbell. "This here is it." He sounded truly disgusted.

"Ye're joshin' me, right, lad?" Campbell said, puzzled.

"Joshin' my ass. This here's the worst goddamn poor-ass rend-ay-fuckin'-vous this ol' hoss has ary seen. Goddamn if it ain't. Hell, the fust one back in twenty-five was ten times better'n this sorry shit of a doin's."

Campbell looked around, a feeling of gloom settling over him. "Auld Doc Newell must've been right. When I saw him at rendezvous year before last, he said the beaver trade was dyin'."

"Hell, boy, the beaver trade ain't dyin'. It's goddamn gave up the ghost already. I don't think we'll ary see another doin's again. Not even some piss-poor fandango like this one."

"There anybody buyin' beaver?" Campbell asked drearily.

"Fontenelle and a few others have trade tents set up, but they ain't payin' shit fer plews. You'll be lucky if them thievin' bastards give ye a dollar a pound, boy."

"Och, that does nae shine wi' this chil'." Then Campbell shrugged. "But there's nae a thing we can do aboot it."

"That's a goddamn fact." Harris shifted his weight, settling his back on the ground and his neck against the log. He pulled his hat down over his eyes. "Leave the jug when ya go, hoss," he said, and then fell asleep.

Campbell sat for a few minutes, morosely sipping whiskey. What was the worst about this was that there was probably no chance that he would find Bullock and his men here. If they had even stopped at the rendezvous, they would have left almost as soon at they got here, looking for riper pastures. Still, he had to explore the possibility that they were here. He looked at Harris and shook his head. He should have asked the old mountaineer right away; now Harris was sleeping, and he would have to wait to ask.

Campbell finally pushed himself up, mounted

his horse, and rode on, just looking around to see who he could see. He did not spot Bridger or any of the others he knew fairly well, though there were a few familiar faces. There also was a group of missionaries. Campbell stopped and stared for a bit, surprised at seeing the faces of white women out here in this wilderness. It somehow did not seem right to him; the sight was just too out of place.

He did not see Tall Clouds's band of Nez Percé, either, which in some ways made him glad. He was still embarrassed to have to face the Nez Percé—and Morning Sun. But as poor and dreary as this rendezvous was, meeting Morning Sun and her people would have been even more depressing.

He made himself a little camp off to himself, and turned in for the night before darkness had even arrived. In the morning, he took his two packs of poor beaver plews over to the first trading tent he saw. He neither knew nor cared whose it was. He pulled the two packs—about a hundred pounds each—off the mule, one in each arm, and dropped them on the rickety counter.

The trader gave them a cursory look. "Them's some shitty plews, sonny," he announced.

"They be no worse than any others ye've seen at this doin's," Campbell said flatly. "What will ye give me for them?"

"One hundred twenty-five dollars, sonny. Not a cent more."

"Anyone e'er tell ye that ye're a thief, lad?" Campbell snapped. He figured it out as best he could in his head. "That's nae e'en seventy-five cents a pound, lad."

"Them plews ain't worth even what I'm offerin' ya, sonny. I'm just makin' such a good offer out of the kindness of me heart."

"Ye dunna have a heart, ye thievin' sack of shit. And if by some chance ye still do, ye'll nae have it much longer if ye keep on insultin' me with such offers."

"You ain't gonna get no better anywhere else here," the trader said. It was pretty well true, and he could not help but gloat.

"Aye, 'tis probably true. But I'd rather throw these plews into the Siskeedee than sell them to a mercenary bastard like ye." Campbell grabbed the packs and turned toward the mule.

"Goddamn, but if you ain't something," the trader said. "Come on, sonny, put 'em back down. We can deal. I'll give ya a hundred fifty. And, I'm tellin' ya, sonny, they ain't worth that. I'll lose cash by makin' ya that deal."

Campbell believed him, but he had to give it a try. "Two hundred," he said hopefully.

The trader shook his head. "I can't, sonny."

Campbell nodded, disgusted and disheartened.

"You want supplies or cash?"

"Supplies, I suppose."

By the time Campbell left the trader's tent, he had enough necessaries to last him barely a month. And just enough cash left over for a gallon of whiskey and, that afternoon, a roll in the robes with a flaccid, featureless Flathead woman.

With no cash, and no real desire to have a spree, even if this rendezvous had provided some, Campbell decided to leave. There was nothing to keep him here. He had checked all around, and no one had seen Bullock or any of his men.

That night he sat at his fire, sipping from his whiskey jug, wondering where to go. The decision was not difficult. Having checked most of the northern Rockies, he decided that it was time to try the southern Rockies. He could not see that it would be any more fruitless than his earlier searches.

He rode slowly, stopping to check every wisp of smoke in the distance, every old camp he came across, anything that might give him a hint as to whether Bullock and his men had been through here.

He fought off an attack by Utes one time, killing two and sending the third running. His only injury from that little ruckus was split skin over a knuckle where he had hit a warrior's tooth.

He soon began to realize that this search was as wasteful as all the others, and after his second run-in with Utes, he shrugged and headed for Taos down in Mexican country. He figured there was no harm in trying there, and he had always wanted to see the place, after hearing of it often enough from some of the mountaineers he had encountered, and his partners.

When he rode into the sleepy, dusty, brown adobe town, he was tired, frustrated, dispirited, and fully disgusted with himself for his inability to track down the killers and avenge his partners.

25

"Waugh!" Kit Carson grunted, sounding something like a grizzly with a stomach ailment. "Them're the worst goddamn doin's this chil's ary heared. Good goddamn, I could expect such a thing from the goddamn Blackfoot, but white men—and feller mountaineers at that—well, that goes against this ol' chil's grain." He downed his copper cup of whiskey and then refilled it.

" 'Tis the way I feel," Campbell said, "but there's nae much more I can do. I've searched nearly e'er piece of the Rocky Mountains and the prairies. The few times I found traces of them, they'd been gone a week or a month or more."

"You'll find 'em. I'll have arybody I know in the mountains lookin' for them critters," Carson said grandiosely.

"Auld Doc said the same, but I've nae heard a thing from him."

"Hell, you know Doc. He's always thinking of tomorrow, nary today. He probably jist forgot."

"Perhaps." Campbell paused. " 'Tis more than

that, though, Kit. Trappin' last season was the worst I e'er seen it, and many of the lads say the beaver trade is dead."

Carson nodded. "I expect it is, hoss, but I aim to make one more go at it." His eyes suddenly widened. "Say, hoss, why don't you come with us? Me and a bunch of the Taos boys're plannin' to leave in a couple days. Don't know how much luck we'll have, but what the hell, if our medicine is strong, beaver'll shine again."

Seeing Campbell's hesitation, Carson said, "We could have the lot of us lookin' out for this Bullock feller."

"Aye, that we could. But I dunna know it that'd do any good. If the beaver trade is as bad as we all think it is, there be nae reason for a man like Bullock to stay in the mountains. There's nae easy pickin's any more."

"So, what're ye gonna do, hoss? You got a woman and a chil' waitin' for ye up in Nay Percy lands. And you ain't had no luck in findin' those bastards."

"Ye sayin' I should give up my hunt and just ride on to Tall Clouds's village?"

Carson shrugged. "That's a choice you'll have to make, ol' hoss. But it seems to this chil' that you've spent three years searchin' for the fellers and ain't got anywhere. Mayhap goin' back to your wife and chil' might change your medicine."

Campbell thought about that for some moments, and realized Carson was right. And even if his luck didn't change, he'd still be back with Morning Sun and Coyote Heart, at least for a while. Then he could set out after Bullock again with renewed spirits. "Aye," he said very softly, then repeated it more loudly. "Aye, 'tis what I'll do." Then he stopped, looking crestfallen.

"Somethin' soured ye on that plan already, Alex?" Carson asked.

"I hate to say it, but I dunna have any specie for supplies to get me anywhere." He sighed. "Damn, I'll have to take a job here, if someone will hire me on." He looked positively ill at the prospect, for he would be unable to find anything but menial work, he figured, since he did not speak any Spanish.

"Hell, hoss, if that's all that's botherin' ye, there's no worry. I ain't the most frugal of fellers, but I'm not without some resources in Taos. I'll see that ye have supplies."

"I dunna know when—or e'en if—I can repay ye. Or whoe'er does the actual supplyin'."

"Don't worry about that, ol' hoss. It ain't like you need these supplies 'cause you're too goddamn lazy to go out and earn 'em. You been busy trackin' the bastards who killed your partners. You'll pay it back when ye can. I know that, and so does anyone else I'll talk to about 'em. You jist tell me when ye want 'em."

"Thankee, lad," Campbell said quietly. He was somewhat embarrassed by having to beg for supplies. Even if he really hadn't begged, he felt as if he had.

Campbell rode out a few days later, well-supplied, his string of horses and the one mule loaded but as eager as he to be moving. He headed north, wondering if he should look for the killers, but really wanting to—well, needing to—see Morning Sun first. The next morning he began moving faster, his sharply growing desire to see his wife and child pushing him on.

It took him just over a month, but he finally spotted Tall Clouds's village nestled among the trees and brush along a swift, cool stream. As he rode past the band's horse herd, several of the boys watching the animals stared at him. Then one turned his Appaloosa pony, slapped it hard with his leather quirt, and raced away.

Minutes later, a small group of warriors galloped hard out of the village and pulled up in front of Campbell, who stopped, and sat there uneasily. The warriors stared at the white man, in his tattered clothes and long red beard and mustache, as if they had seen a ghost.

"It *is* you," Coyote Leggings breathed. He was one of the most courageous and fierce warriors among all the Nez Percé, but right now he was scared right down to the core of his very soul. This was highly unusual, and he was not sure it boded well for him, or for his people. The spirits were fickle, and this could just be a trick of some kind. He managed to hide his fears, though it was not easy.

"Aye, 'tis me, lad," Campbell said, voice cracking from lack of use. "Alive as ye and the others."

"I . . ."

"I'm nae ghost, Coyote Leggings," Campbell said almost stiffly. "Nor a bad spirit come to haunt the People." He shook his head. "Just a long-lost critter hoping he still has a place at the council fire here." He paused. "And a place in Morning Sun's lodge."

"You'll always have a place at our council fire," Coyote Leggings said in English. He relaxed minutely. "As for the other . . . ?"

"Has Morning Sun taken another husband?" The thought cut to Campbell's insides like a sharp knife. He had never thought of that possibility, though if he had thought about it at all, it would have seemed logical from Morning Sun's standpoint.

"You'll have to ask her that," Coyote Leggings said, almost embarrassed.

Campbell nodded, another chill of worry digging deeper into his gut. "Then let's go."

They trotted to the village, and an impatient Campbell paid his respects to Tall Clouds, the civil chief of this band. The ancient warrior stood regally, a blanket held close around him. His immensely wrinkled face caught the sunlight in odd ways, giving him something of the look of an old oak tree. Wispy gray tendrils of hair whipped in the air. He accepted Campbell's homage gracefully, though Campbell was not sure the old man even knew who he was any longer.

Then Campbell was heading with firm step but knotted belly toward Morning Sun's lodge. Though he had cut the lodgepoles for it, and had brought in the buffalo hides that made it, the tipi was by the Nez Percé way Morning Sun's. He hoped she would welcome him into it.

She was not waiting outside, as she usually did, though she had to know he was there. He called for entrance, and the soft, melodious voice he remembered so well granted his simple request. The voice also stirred deep, powerful feelings inside him.

Campbell went inside and stopped. The scents, sights, sounds were so familiar it was as if he had never left. Oh, he was fully aware of a thick tenseness permeating the air in the lodge that had never been there before. And he was conscious of Morning Sun. Very conscious of Morning Sun. He was divided as to what to do. His heart told him to stride across that short, yet vast gulf between them, sweep her up in his arms, and reclaim his rights as a husband. His head told him to hold off, to wait, to let her have her say, to explain to her what had happened, where he had been, what he had done.

But it was Morning Sun who broke the dull silence. "Come, my husband," she said quietly. "Sit by the fire. Ye must be hungry."

Campbell knelt and placed his rifle down, then walked to the small fire and sat. Morning Sun served him a bowl of buffalo meat stew thickened with flour and spiced with wild turnips. She poured him a tin mug of coffee and set it next to him.

"Would it be too much for me to ask ye to sit, lass?" Campbell asked.

"Nae, 'twouldn't," Morning Sun answered in English, which was still understandable and still flavored with Campbell's Scottish, but seemed rusty. Then she did so.

Campbell set the bowl of stew down. He was hungry, but he had no appetite. "I ne'er did find the men who caused us all these troubles," he said softly, in shame. "Though 'tis nae for want of tryin'."

It was as if Morning Sun had not heard him. "I

thought ye were dead," she said in English. "I waited and waited for ye, but ye ne'er came back. No one had heard of ye, had seen ye. What was I to think?" She was weeping softly. "Why did ye nae come back?"

"I was ashamed to face ye—and all the others," Campbell said simply, though it was like a knife in the heart to him. "I had made a promise to make those bastards pay for what they'd done to Ethan and Caleb. And to all the others. But I was nae able to do it, lass." The words were thick with bitterness and self-loathing. "I ne'er e'en found them."

"Then why did ye nae come back, Alex?" Morning Sun asked plaintively. "After the first year or so. The People would've helped ye, ye know that."

"Aye, I suppose they would've. But things kept getting in the way."

"What kind of things?" Morning Sun asked, beginning to bring herself under control.

"They're nae important right now, lass." He paused, knowing he had to ask this next question, but not wanting to because of what the answer might be. He sighed and then asked, "Have ye gotten yourself a new man?" He seemed to himself to have stopped breathing.

"Sort of. Wooden Horn's been courtin' me. We had plans to marry."

"But ye'd nae gotten to do it?"

"Nae."

Now came the next most important question for Campbell, another one he was loath to ask. "And do I have any chance of bein' your husband again?"

Morning Sun smiled a little, though her face was

still drawn from crying. "I ne'er tossed your things oot of the lodge," she said. It meant she had not divorced him.

Campbell's relief was palpable, though he did not express it. "Do ye want me back, lass?" Campbell asked, still uncertain.

"Aye," Morning Sun said without hesitation. "I ne'er wanted ye to go away. 'Twasn't like ye'd run off on me for a Flathead or something."

Campbell nodded. "But I'm nae in your good graces, though, am I?" he asked astutely.

"Nae, Alex," Morning Sun said with the hint of a smile. " 'Twill be some time before I'm comfortable wi' ye again."

Campbell nodded once more. He didn't like that, but he would accept it. He had put Morning Sun through too much to ask her to put aside these feelings just like that.

"What aboot Wooden Horn?"

"He'll understand," Morning Sun said with a shrug. "If not . . ." She shrugged again, dismissing him as a factor in her life. "That's nae your concern, husband."

Campbell nodded.

Things remained tense between Campbell and Morning Sun for several days, and their talks occasionally erupted into arguments. But their reconciliation progressed with time. On Campbell's fifth night back, Morning Sun allowed him to share her robes, and by the end of the next night, things were pretty well patched up between them.

Campbell had more than half expected trouble with Wooden Horn, but none arose. Campbell did, however, avoid Wooden Horn as much as possible, not because he feared the young warrior, but because he did not want to add to Wooden Horn's embarrassment and humiliation. Word came to Campbell through Coyote Leggings and Hawk Strikes that Wooden Horn appreciated the gesture.

Once he and Morning Sun had readjusted to each other, Campbell began making plans to leave the village to resume his search for Bullock and the others. But Morning Sun objected.

"Lookin' for them is foolish," Morning Sun said. "They could be anywhere. E'en back in the Settlements. Or dead."

Campbell was furious at her. "I canna give up now, lass," he said adamantly. "I've promised to find them and make them pay for what they did. Swore to it on the grave of Ethan and Caleb—and on my son's head."

"I know, husband," Morning Sun said quietly. "But ye searched so long, wi'oot findin' them."

"Goddammit, I know that, lass," a frustrated Campbell growled.

"Aye. But ye're good at trackin'," Morning Sun said proudly, matter-of-factly. "If ye could nae find 'em, they're probably dead or have gone east."

He really could not mount an argument to that, though he could not accept that in his heart. Still, the flattery helped assuage his anger and his frustration, and with a little more, he finally agreed that he would end his search, and just take up trapping again. Campbell did not tell Morning Sun his concerns about that, not wanting to make her worry any more than necessary. He thought that sometime during the winter he might hit upon a plan for what he could do.

They rode out a couple days later, leaving Coyote Heart in the care of Coyote Leggings and his wife. As they pulled out, Campbell continued to harbor the hope that he would still find Bullock and his men.

So now there were just the two of them, Campbell trapping and hunting, Morning Sun making meat as they went along, stopping for a day here, a day there.

Morning Sun, who was no fool, could see how small the catch was and, since she cured the hides, knew how poor they were. She could also see on Campbell's face that he was concerned about this. She wondered what would happen after the winter. If things continued the way they were, they would not have enough of a catch for even enough supplies to go out for another season. But she did not let on that she was worried. He had enough troubling him.

As fall began to drain into winter, Campbell and Morning Sun ran into a trapping party led by Jim Bridger. Kit Carson was among the members.

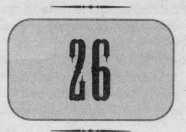

26

"Kit tol' me what happened to Ethan and Caleb," Bridger said when Campbell had sat at the fire and was sipping coffee. "It's a goddamn shame. Sinful."

"Aye, 'tis all that," Campbell said glumly. All his frustrations and rage were flooding back over him.

"You ever catch them boys?" Carson asked. "Damn, I cain't even remember who ya said they was. It's been such a piss-poor season that most other thoughts've gone straight out of my head. Sorry, hoss."

Campbell shrugged. He could not expect others to carry his burden for him. "Nae," Campbell said bitterly, "I ne'er did find them."

"Who was the shit-eaters who done it?" Bridger asked. "I know many of the boys in the mountains, as might be expected." Bridger was not bragging; he was simply stating a fact. "Mayhap I can help ya."

"The leader of the fuckin' villains is a lad named Lije Bullock. He's the only one who really counts."

"Jesus goddamn Christ," Bridger snapped, eyes

widening. "We run into that sack of shit a week ago or so. Him and his boys rode into my camp and set a spell. If we'd only known they was the ones . . ."

Campbell was suddenly alert. "Ye could nae remember them e'en when they were sittin' right here in your camp, Kit?" he asked, looking angrily at Carson.

"I weren't there at the time," Carson said almost as angrily. "I'd took a few of the boys off from the main party, lookin' to see if we could exploit some of the smaller beaver streams and sich. Me'n them hooked up with Ol' Jim again jist the day 'fore yesterday."

"Sorry, Kit," Campbell said not all that apologetically.

"Forget it, hoss," Carson said forgivingly. "Your mind's took up with more important matters."

Campbell nodded. "Which way did they go, Jim?" he asked, once again feeling urgency sitting on his shoulders.

"South. Southwest," Bridger said, chucking his chin in the proper direction. "Toward the Uintas."

Campbell nodded and rose. "Morning Sun, get the horses," he ordered. "We're leavin' oot."

"Whoa, hoss," Bridger said. "Don't go off half-cocked. You know, don't ya, that ya can't get all of 'em by yourself." It was more a statement than a question.

"Aye, 'tis somethin' I've thought of often o'er the past few years. I canna deny that."

"You ought to wait," Bridger cautioned.

"For what?" Campbell countered. "If I wait a wee time, are ye going to help me?"

"I got my boys here to think about, hoss. And my sponsors. We're expected to trap beaver, not go chasin' folks. And the way beaver ain't shinin' no more, we got our hands full jist tryin' to make a pack or two."

"I understand," Campbell said evenly. "I dinna expect ye to help me—for those very reasons."

Bridger nodded and stood. "Ye need anything, hoss?" he asked.

"Perhaps a wee bit of coffee and maybe some tobacco."

"We can do that for ya, hoss." He turned and issued some orders.

A few minutes later, Campbell and Morning Sun left, riding hard. They could not keep that pace up, so they soon slowed, but Campbell continued to feel as if he were being pushed by a giant unseen hand.

Eight days later, they came upon the camp Bullock and his men had used the night before. Though Campbell was excited, and eager to get after the culprits, he forced himself to stop for the night. The horses had been pushed hard, and he had not come all this way, gotten so close, only to fail because his horses faltered from lack of decent care. Besides, he could see that Morning Sun was tired. It showed in the dark rings under her eyes and the constant frown lines between her eyebrows. He was feeling pretty weary himself, but he had convinced himself to spend the night here because of the animals and because Morning Sun was so exhausted. He could have gone on for days without sleep, if need be. Or so he thought.

That evening, he tried to formulate a plan, but it was impossible, and he finally gave it up. He could make no plan until he knew where Bullock's men were, and even then it was doubtful.

In the morning, Campbell considered leaving Morning Sun here. The camp was comfortable, there was plenty of wood and water, and they had enough meat to last her a while. But he was divided. If he took her, she would almost certainly be in danger sooner or later. If he left her here, however, there might be a better chance of safety, but if danger reared its head, he might be miles away and of no help to her whatsoever.

He finally decided that he would take her with him. He reasoned that if they got into trouble together, he would at least have a chance to get them out of it. His decision had absolutely nothing to do with the fact that Morning Sun had somehow known what he was thinking and had told him in no uncertain terms that she was going with him. And when she spoke to him in that tone, with that look on her face, he knew better than to even consider arguing.

So they pulled out that morning, moving at a quick, steady pace. Campbell paid attention to nothing except the trail wandering between the trees. His eyes scanned the ground before him unceasingly, only occasionally lifting to take in the trail ahead, the trees, the sky, looking for any sign that Bullock and his men were ahead. He left everything else to Morning Sun.

By noon, Campbell had a splitting headache from concentrating so hard. He growled at himself and the pain, but pushed on. A few hours later, he spotted a cliff rising from a bed of pines. He stopped and stared at it, and within seconds he had decided he could climb it.

With a nod, he moved his Appaloosa into the trees toward the cliff. Towing the rest of the animals, Morning Sun followed him without hesitation. At the base of the cliff, Campbell pulled out his rifle and made a hasty sling for it. Slipping it across his back, he began his climb.

Below, Morning Sun watched him for a moment, a small smile lingering on her lips. Then she turned to start tending the horses and the loyal mule.

The climb was more difficult than Campbell had thought it would be, but when he got to the top, he had a view for miles. He could see the trail twisting through the trees like a hungry snake. It disappeared now and again, as if the snake had been chopped into chunks. To his right, the pine forests spread, crawling up and down all but the most precipitous mountainsides.

He sat on a rock, right at the edge of the world. He pulled off his hat, letting the wind cool the sweat from his head. Then he spotted movement, almost dead straight ahead. He tensed and stared intently, suddenly wishing he had a spyglass. He blinked several times in the brightness of the sun, but finally he caught movement again. It was a line of men, just coming out from a spot where the curl of the trail had hidden them behind the trees.

"Good Christ in heaven," he breathed, "it be them." He couldn't be absolutely certain at this distance, but he was sure enough. So sure that he was ready to run down the side of this cliff, but he forced himself to sit just a bit.

His eyes followed the trail Bullock and his men were taking, moving ahead of the riders. And then he swung his eyes to the left, and spotted a small, thin line of a trail that curled around and faded behind a long stretch of rocky ridges, not far from the main trail. He stood eagerly and tracked the path. With a little bit of work, he could be on that deer track in no time, and waiting on those heaped piles of boulders and cracked crags when his quarry came along, unsuspecting.

Campbell climbed down the cliff, moving as fast as he could without taking too many risks that would leave him with a broken neck. Morning Sun had seen him coming and hurriedly got the animals ready. She was set when he got to the bottom.

"They be oot there, lass," he said, voice a mixture of rage and excitement.

"Can we get to 'em?"

"Aye. I've seen a way that we can get ahead of them."

"I knew ye could do it, husband." She rested a palm on his cheek lightly for a moment. Then they left.

Pushing through the brush and forest was not as easy as Campbell had thought it was going to be, but he was mighty determined, so they moved pretty well through it all. Once they got on the slim little track, they moved faster. The trail was narrow, dank, and dark with the towering pines in places and sometimes cliffs, but it was wide enough to let the horses through without much trouble.

They made the end of the trail—and the rocky promontories—well before Bullock and his men. Knowing he had some time, Campbell prowled around the area a bit, and found a cave that wound into the heart of the mountain. Once inside, he realized it wasn't a true cave, but more a matter of the way gigantic boulders had fallen and created something of a haven.

"Bring the animals in, lass," Campbell ordered. "Then build us a wee good fire. A dry one. I dunna want smoke givin' us away."

"I know what I'm doon," Morning Sun said in annoyance. He should know by now what a good wife I am, she thought.

"Aye, I know that, lass. I canna help but be my own bossy self."

"Go aboot your work, Alex," Morning Sun said with a smile.

Once again Campbell slung his rifle across his back and began climbing. Since this was not an almost sheer cliff like the other, it was fairly easy to make it to the top. Within a minute, he had found an ideal spot. It gave him an unobstructed view of the main trail for three hundred yards in the direction from which Bullock would be coming and two hundred the other way. Rocks formed a natural window through which he could fire, and some scraggly bushes around it would help mask his gunsmoke for the few moments it would linger before the wind whipped it away. He sat and waited patiently.

Finally Bullock and his men hove into view down the trail. They rode easily, suspecting nothing.

Campbell grinned viciously at that. He had realized somewhere along the trail in the days since he had left Bridger's camp that he could not take them all on at the same time. He knew he was one hell of a fighter, but so were Bullock's men, and two or three of them likely would be a match for him in strength and stamina. So he had decided he would take care of them in ones or twos. And do so in ways that likely would create panic among them.

Campbell checked his rifle and priming, then stretched his long frame out on his belly and poked the rifle barrel through his window. Campbell drew a bead on Bullock, who was second in line, but then changed his mind. He wanted to save Bullock for last. He sighted on Floyd Willsey, as worthless a man as Campbell had ever met, aiming at the point where his spectacles met above the bridge of his nose.

" 'Tis time for ye to start payin' for the fuckin' evil ye done," Campbell muttered, remembering what Willsey had done to Otter. He held his breath and squeezed the trigger. The blast rocked his shoulder comfortably, but the smoke obscured his sight. As he had figured, the smoke was whisked away by the brisk wind in seconds.

With his field of vision cleared, he saw Willsey on the ground. The other men tried to control their prancing horses, and looked frantically around for where the shot had come from.

As he reloaded, Campbell considered firing once more and taking out another villain, but decided against it. That might be pushing his luck, and probably would send them scattering for cover. As it was, there had been one shot which had dropped one of their number stone cold dead. With no more gunfire, they would be left wondering just what had happened.

Within seconds, Bullock had his men and animals in control. Campbell could not hear what the renegade leader said, but he guessed that Bullock was telling his men to get to cover, make sure the horses were all right, and then start searching for whoever had fired the fatal shot. Campbell thought this would be interesting.

Campbell sat on his perch, hidden from the view of those down below, and watched as the five men hunted fruitlessly for him. At times he would squat-walk to one side or another to check on where one of Bullock's men was. None seemed to consider climbing the rocks to his aerie, and none got close to Morning Sun's haven. Campbell was also pleased to note that there was no smoke from the haven to give it away.

Bullock called off the search after about an hour. He angrily ranted and raved, an occasional harsh word drifting up to Campbell. The renegades stood by their horses, arguing. Campbell had no idea what that was about, but he didn't mind. He rather enjoyed seeing the consternation he had caused.

Finally two of the men dragged Willsey's body off the trail and into the brush. Campbell was a little surprised, thinking that they were going to bury him. Campbell didn't think Bullock's men had it in them.

He was pleased to see, though, that they did not go against their grain. They rode out, leaving Willsey where they had dumped him.

Campbell watched until they were out of sight a couple hundred yards away. Still, he sat, just in case it was a ploy—they might suddenly turn back and look for him again.

But such was not the case, and as the afternoon began fading rapidly, along with the temperature, Campbell scrambled down from the heights and made his way into the cave.

Morning Sun had deer meat and coffee ready, and Campbell grabbed some of both. "Ye should've seen it, lass," he said enthusiastically. "They dinna know whether to shit or go blind." He actually laughed, the first time he had really done so since the attack on the camp.

"Ye only killed one?" Morning Sun asked, surprised.

"Aye." He told her of his plan to throw terror into them.

"Not good," Morning Sun responded. "Dangerous."

"Aye, 'tis that. But I want those devils to suffer as much as possible. They dunna deserve quick and painless deaths after what they did to Ethan, Caleb, and the others."

Morning Sun nodded. That made sense to her. She worried about her husband, but she had great faith in him, too.

Campbell and Morning Sun stayed in the cave through the night, all the next day, and that night, too. Now that Campbell was right on Bullock's tail, he was confident he would not lose them. At the same time, he did not want to ride right up on them. He thought his action in killing Willsey was inspired. Not the killing itself, but the worry he figured it created in Bullock and his four remaining followers. Now Campbell knew he had to come up with something that would push that worry into fear. So he thought he would take an extra day in the cave to let the horses rest, and for him to think up something.

He still hadn't decided when they pulled out in the morning, but a germ of an idea had formed. Following Bullock was easy—there was only the one trail for the most part, plus they were making no effort to hide their tracks.

Campbell found out, though, that his quarry was traveling a lot faster than he had thought they would. That annoyed him, since he would have to hurry to close in on them again. But it also pleased him, because it meant they were indeed worried.

He held back a little, wanting them to start to relax, thinking the trouble had passed. Then Campbell figured he could give them another scare, making it all the worse.

Campbell and Morning Sun stayed at Bullock's old camps that night and the next. The following day, Campbell started out at a much faster clip, slowing only a little in the late afternoon when he saw signs that he was catching up to his quarry. He finally spotted a track leading off to his right. After a moment's indecision, he turned onto it. Morning Sun followed, unquestioningly.

After a mile or so, he found a small area partially cleared of trees. Other than the widely spaced pines, there was not much protection from the steady, chilling wind and the dropping temperatures.

It was almost dark by the time Campbell and Morning Sun stopped. The two of them tended the horses and the mule. When that was done, darkness had fallen.

"I hate to say this to ye, lass, but I dunna think it's wise for ye to go makin' a fire tonight."

"Aye," Morning Sun said with a nod.

Campbell shook his head. He was always surprised at her. She seemed to take everything in stride. She showed little signs of the tiredness Campbell knew she was feeling. Nor did she seem at all frustrated, though all he had done of late was to lead her here and there, dashing from one place to another. He was proud of her.

"What'll ye do now, Alex?" Morning Sun had

gotten over her ingrained sense of discomfort at looking directly at him. She had been taught since childhood that to look others in the eyes was impolite, and even disrespectful if a woman did so to her man. But Campbell was not like the Nez Percé men, and he preferred her to look at him. So she had diligently kept trying, submerging her concern over her behavior, until she could do it without too much uneasiness.

"I think I'll pay those murderous bastards a wee visit tonight," Campbell responded.

"Tonight?" Morning Sun didn't like the sound of that, but she repressed her feelings.

"Aye."

"But how'll ye . . . ?"

"Trust me, lass," Campbell said quietly, cupping her small chin in his big, callused hand. He bent and kissed her forehead, her nose, her lips. The last became more than just a simple kiss, and when he finally pulled away, he said, "But there be time for those doin's after a wee bit."

"Oh, you have somethin' else to do first?" Morning Sun asked, smiling.

"Aye, lass. Aye."

It was almost two hours later before he rode out of the camp into the pitch black of the night. Little moonlight managed to make its way down to this level through the trees and all, but Campbell just rode, letting the Appaloosa pick its own way along.

Once he hit the main trail, he sped up. Yet it was still three hours before he thought he spotted firelight in the distance. He slowed almost to a stop, looking for some place to pull off the trail. He finally found one. It wasn't the best spot, but he planned to be gone from here long before the dawn broke.

Campbell tied his Appaloosa to a tree, pulled his rifle from the saddle, slung it over his back, and moved ahead on foot. He was certain now that it was Bullock's camp just ahead.

He traveled through the pines and brush like a wraith—silent, fearless, deadly. He stopped behind a tree, looking out over the camp. It was difficult to see, since the fading fire threw very little light and the cold air made his breath frost in front of his face.

When he had assured himself that all the men in the camp were asleep, he slipped out from behind the tree, heading toward a man sleeping in a thick blanket a little farther from the fire than the others. The man was completely in the shadows, which would make Campbell's escape easier should one of the others wake.

Campbell knelt next to the sleeping man and ever so gently peeled the blanket away from his face. He didn't need more light than the faint orange glow from the fire to tell him that he had just found Ty Hubbard. He smiled, but if anyone had seen it, they would have been far more chilled than the air would have made them; it was not a pleasant sight.

Campbell stood, then straddled Hubbard, his shins on the ground. Suddenly he dropped his buttocks, which landed hard on Hubbard's stomach. At the same time, Campbell's left hand darted out and clamped on Hubbard's throat, squeezing into silence any shouts of alarm.

Bending over so his face was close to Hubbard's,

Campbell asked in a tight whisper, "Recognize me, ye fuckin' vermin?"

Hubbard's eyes widened, but he shook his head.

"I be one of the lads ye left behind in a ravaged camp to die after ye and the others had done your deviltry. Ye made a bad mistake when ye did nae finish me off, lad."

Hubbard tried to speak but could not, with Campbell's powerful hand clamped on his throat.

"Ye need nae protest, lad," Campbell said, still in a voice that sounded to Hubbard like the whispering of a cold wind over an Indian burial ground. "If ye do, ye'll only compound your sins by lyin'." He paused, almost enjoying the fear he saw on Hubbard's face. "Now, Mister Hubbard," he continued, "your time has come."

Hubbard tried to buck or kick or punch, but the lack of air, Campbell's weight, and the blanket confining his arms did not allow him to do much. He watched in terror as Campbell's right hand brought his big knife up. He thought he felt something pleasurable, and then realized that it was the sharp blade sliding across his throat, just above Campbell's fist.

Campbell was deliberate in his movements, not flinching when he sliced the carotid artery on one side of Hubbard's neck and a spurting gusher of blood splattered on his face and shirt. When he cut through the carotid on the other side, not nearly so much blood rushed out.

He sat there until Hubbard's body quit jerking. Then he let go of the throat, wiped his knife on Hubbard's clothes, and pushed back a little. He pulled the blanket up so it covered Hubbard's neck and nose. Only the dead, open eyes were exposed. Campbell rose, figuring that Bullock and his followers would be in for some surprise come morning.

Campbell slipped out of the camp as silently as he had entered it. In twenty minutes he was on his horse, and a few hours later he was back in Morning Sun's arms.

A week later, Campbell repeated the scene at another of Bullock's camps, more then a hundred miles away. It went just as smoothly and easily as the last time, as he slit Jed Moss's throat as nice as you could please.

Campbell let more than a week pass this time, allowing Bullock and his dwindling force to drink deep of the swill of fear, letting it ferment in their bellies and then slowly start escaping, like swamp gas. Then it was time to strike again.

During those eleven days, Campbell and Morning Sun had traveled about a day's ride behind their quarry, staying in their old camps so it lightened Morning Sun's workload at least a little.

When he decided it was time to strike again, Campbell set a much faster pace during the day, the horses eating up ground at a good clip. Relying on his instincts, he chose a place to pull off the trail. Working their way deep into the thinning forest, Campbell picked a spot where he felt Morning Sun would be safe while he took care of his deadly business.

Just before darkness fell, Campbell kissed

Morning Sun goodbye, mounted the Appaloosa, and headed to the main trail and turned southwest, following Bullock. It was night by then, but he still moved fairly swiftly.

Two hours later, Campbell spotted a fire, and he stopped. He sat there in the saddle, his rage burning no less hotly than the day Sharp and Finch had died at Bullock's hand. He considered slipping into Bullock's camp again as he had done before, but then he decided against it. He needed something different, to pierce the survivors with a new stab of fear.

He slid off the horse, reins in his left hand. His right hand patted the animal's nose to keep it quiet. Then he walked along, slowly but not fearfully, until he was a quarter of a mile past the camp, which was set off the trail a hundred yards or so.

At that point, Campbell jumped into the saddle and rode on, until he found a place he thought would suit his needs. He pulled into the trees about fifty yards and tied the animal off. Taking his rifle, a few strips of jerky, and his canteen, he went to the small stone tower that sat right on the trail. He climbed it and found a perch. He waited, sipping water, gnawing on jerky, and eventually napping.

Dawn came slowly. When it finally arrived. Campbell awoke, hopped down from his rock, and stretched his limbs. At this time of year in the high country, it was bitterly cold at night, and only barely warm during the day. Campbell was stiff from having sat in the cool night air, and wanted to be ready when Bullock and his two remaining cutthroats came riding by.

It was another hour before the three renegades

neared. Lying prone atop the small, blunt cliff, Campbell waited with anticipation. He watched as Bullock passed slowly by. Campbell had to fight to control the urge to blow the butcher's brains out here and now, but he managed. It was a little easier allowing Viktor Kleinholtz to pass by.

Campbell smiled grimly when he saw that Orval Creach was bringing up the rear and was quite a few yards behind. That suited Campbell's purposes fine. He could easily just shoot Creach, or jump on the man's horse and slit his throat, or any of a number of similarly easy things. But Campbell did not want that. Any of those things would create noise, and bring Bullock and Kleinholtz running. And that would not do—he wanted to continue inspiring fear in the survivors.

For that, there would have to be mystery. Creach must die quietly and be left where he could be found. Bullock and Kleinholtz would eventually realize their companion was not behind them and come back looking for him. What they would find was his body, slain by some phantom. Combined with the other deaths, it should raise Bullock's and Kleinholtz's fear to a new level.

He slid down the back of the mini-cliff and waited. Simplicity, Campbell had decided, would work best. When Creach came abreast of him, Campbell stepped out from behind the protection of the rock.

Creach's eyes widened in surprise, though he did not yet recognize Campbell. Hoping for just such a reaction, Campbell took advantage of Creach's astonishment. His left hand grabbed

Creach's reins near the bit. He took one long step forward and smashed Creach across the mouth and long, hooked nose with the barrel of his rifle.

Creach had not had time to react. One moment he was riding along, in no hurry to catch up to his companions; the next this apparition had appeared, and then he was weaving in the saddle.

Campbell dropped his rifle, grabbed a handful of Creach's rank shirt, and jerked him out of the saddle and into the dirt. The horse snuffled a little and stamped its hooves. Campbell took a moment to calm the animal down, and then let go of the reins. Bending, he hauled Creach to his feet and grabbed his own rifle. He shoved Creach forward, around the boulder.

Standing in front of the tall, scrawny cutthroat, whose back was against stone, Campbell asked, "Do ye remember me, laddie?" His voice was far colder than the temperature, yet his eyes burned with hate.

Creach shook his head, not sure he wanted to try talking with his mouth having been mashed the way it had.

"Ye dunna remember a winter camp up on Buffalo Fork several years ago? Where me and my partners gave ye assistance when ye said ye needed it?"

Creach's eyes widened again, this time in recognition. "But you . . ." he started, spraying some blood.

"Aye, ye vile sack of shit," Campbell growled. "Ye and the other murderous vermin left me for dead. Now it be time for ye to pay for what ye did."

"You're the one kilt Jed, Ty, and Floyd, ain't ya?" Creach asked, real fear growing in his gut.

"Aye. And now it be your turn." Campbell smashed his captive in the forehead with the heel of his hand. Creach's head banged against the rock. Before Creach could recover any, Campbell had pounded him five more times on the head and face.

By then, Creach could barely stand. His patchy beard and mustache were splattered with blood, and he was already beginning to color up.

Nearly blinded by rage, Campbell grabbed Creach's throat and squashed the life out of him, then let the body fall to the ground in a heap. Campbell stood looking down at the fresh corpse for a minute or so, letting the stoked flames of fury ebb. Then he grabbed Creach and dragged him out to the trail. Creach's horse stood nearby, seemingly unconcerned. Campbell brought the animal over and tied the reins to one of Creach's ankles.

Moments later, Campbell disappeared into the trees and made his way back toward where he had left Morning Sun, staying off the trail.

28

Campbell let Bullock and Kleinholtz sweat for a few days, knowing they would be nervous, afraid, wondering when and where the phantom would strike again.

As before, Campbell and Morning Sun followed at a respectful distance, using their old camps. He did note, however, that the two renegades were moving considerably faster than they had been. Light snow a couple of times did not slow them, either.

After several days, Campbell picked up his own pace, closing the distance. That night he and Morning Sun made their own camp less than a quarter of a mile behind Bullock's, but on the other side of the trail.

During the night, Campbell slipped into Bullock's camp. Resisting the urge to just kill the two villains and be done with it, he stole their rifles, and even managed to get one of their pistols. He left the camp and dropped the seized weapons into the stream, then went back to his own camp. He had no trouble sleeping.

Campbell woke before dawn.

Morning Sun did so, too. She knew what he was

planning, and she knew she could not talk him out
of it, even if she had wanted to, which she didn't
think she did. She had more than enough reason to
hate those men. She also had the utmost confidence
in her man. She rolled toward him.

They made love quickly, hotly, after which they
lay in each other's embrace for a short while. Then
Morning Sun rose, knowing that Campbell would
want to be on the move soon. She heated up the
coffee and put some meat over the fire.

"Ye have your rifle, just in case, lass?" Campbell
asked.

"Aye. But I'll nae need it."

"Don't be so certain."

"Ye'll do what needs doin' and then come back
here."

"Ye put a lot of faith in me, woman," Campbell
commented.

Morning Sun shrugged. She did not know how
to explain to him that she thought it was well
deserved; that in her eyes Campbell could do
nothing wrong.

"Well," Campbell said slowly after kissing her,
"ye be ready just in case."

"Aye." Morning Sun pulled away from him.
"Now go."

Leaving his coat behind—it was too bulky and
would only get in his way—he slung his rifle across
his back and rode off toward Bullock's camp. He
stopped in the cold predawn darkness on the "edge"
of the camp and tied the horse to a tree. He stood
and waited.

It was not long before dawn's frost-tinged

mistiness began creeping over the mountain country. Tendrils of vapor clung to tree branches briefly before floating onward at the gentle urging of the chill breeze. Campbell took a few steps forward into the cool, growing grayness, and stopped again. He stood, face as hard as the surrounding mountains, eyes colder than Satan's heart.

"Rise and shine, laddies," he called out, his remorseless voice eerie in the otherwise silent camp.

Bullock and Kleinholtz came awake fast, reaching for rifles that were not there. Rather than wonder what had happened to the weapons, both men rolled a few times in different directions, then came to their feet, hands heading for pistols in their belts.

"Ye lads dunna want to do that," Campbell said calmly, harshly. When the two renegades froze, Campbell added, "Now one at a time, ease those pistols oot and toss them away, back into the trees."

With rising anger, Bullock and Kleinholtz complied. They still did not know who was out there. It was still not very light, and the mist obscured their vision further. They were not sure if they were facing one man or a dozen, though only one had spoken.

Campbell took several steps forward, looking like a phantom as the mist swirled around him. He stopped a few feet from his longtime quarry.

"You!" Bullock said, eyes wide.

"Aye, lad, 'tis me. Come back from the grave to hunt ye down for your devilish doin's."

Bullock was fast regaining his equilibrium—and with it came his arrogance. "So what're you gonna do? Just shoot us?" he asked cockily.

"Nae," Campbell said tightly. "Such a thing'd be too easy."

A grin spread across Kleinholtz's broad, Germanic face. "I like dot idea," he said in his thickly accented English. "Yah. Anytime you're ready."

"I'm nae in any hurry, lad," Campbell said. "I've been trailin' ye lads for a long, long time, and now that I've got ye, I plan to exact my revenge at my own pace."

"You're mad as a goddamn hatter," Bullock said, grinning a little, "if you think you can take the two of us."

"I dunna think that'll be so difficult, lads," Campbell said easily. "Not when I've been in and oot of your camps for the past month or so wi'oot ye knowin' it."

"So that was ya all those times, eh?" Bullock mused. "I should've known as soon as I seen ya. You're pretty good, I gotta admit." A touch of fear came back over him, thinking of how easily Campbell had infiltrated his camps and done virtually what he had wanted.

"Aye, that I am, lad. What do ye think happened to your rifles? And one of your haggis-eating partner's pistols, eh?"

The fear in Bullock grew stronger, and even Kleinholtz—who was too dimwitted to be scared by much—felt some pangs of fright.

Campbell sneered. "Ye lads are nae very terrible if ye're nae ootnumberin' others by a long shot. It took twelve of ye to overcome me and my partners"—just the thought of Finch and Sharp brought the rage back to a full boil—"and ye still lost more than half your men. Ye've lost near all the others since, until only ye two fuckin' cowards're left. Soon, e'en ye two'll be in the depths of hell wi' your late, unlamented friends."

"I don't think so, hoss," Bullock said with a lot more confidence than he really felt.

"Yah," Kleinholtz added. "So, if you haff no objection, I say ve get this *tanz* started."

Campbell shrugged. He had waited long enough for his vengeance. He tugged his rifle off and set it down. Drawing his tomahawk in his right hand and his big knife in the other, Campbell nodded.

"Ach," Kleinholtz growled. He pulled out two knives.

Bullock said nothing, just drew a knife and a tomahawk.

Campbell charged, heading straight toward Bullock. The two renegades held their ground, only a few feet separating them. He surprised them when he suddenly dropped his left shoulder, threw himself down and forward, and rolled on the shoulder. He came up just beyond the two men, a bit nearer to Kleinholtz than to Bullock. As he smoothly came to his feet, he spun, tomahawk heading for Kleinholtz's head.

The big German barely managed to get one of his knives out, catching Campbell's 'hawk just behind the head. But Campbell jerked his weapon, and Kleinholtz's knife sailed off into the cold, brightening morning.

Campbell whirled the other way and fended off a hard chop from Bullock's tomahawk, and then all three backed off just a bit. They had each tested the other, and now took a moment to reassess.

Snow began falling heavily as Bullock and Kleinholtz moved apart, putting a little distance between them. They figured Campbell would not be able to defend himself as well if he were attacked from two sides.

Campbell knew what they were doing, but he did not care. His entire being was focused on the job he had to do here. Plus he had strong medicine now; Morning Sun had told him that, made sure of it in a way he could not understand. And he had the spirits of his Scottish warrior ancestors, as well as of Sharp and Finch, watching over him.

Bullock charged, and Campbell waited till the last moment to swing that way and face the assault. He surprised Bullock by not falling back—toward Kleinholtz. Thus, Kleinholtz had to move up.

Campbell suddenly jumped forward and sort of hopped, head-butting Bullock in the forehead and knocking him down. Then Campbell swung fast, dropping his knife and tomahawk. He grabbed Kleinholtz's descending knife arm in both hands, then jerked it down, around, and as far back up as he could. Holding the arm in an iron grip, Campbell swiftly hammered Kleinholtz in the nape of the neck with the back of his left elbow.

Kleinholtz groaned but did not fall, so Campbell pounded him again in the same spot. Kleinholtz's knees started to buckle, but Campbell wouldn't let him fall yet. Instead, he jerked the arm up some more and was rewarded with an audible snap as the upper arm broke and tendons tore. Campbell swung behind Kleinholtz, let go of the German's right arm, and grabbed the left. He tugged it up behind

Kleinholtz's back. Through brute strength, Campbell jerked the hulking German around.

Bullock, who was charging for all he was worth, could not stop himself, and his knife plunged deep into Kleinholtz's stomach. Not that he cared all that much.

Kleinholtz moaned again, even though he was still woozy from his other hurts.

Campbell let the German fall and punched Bullock in the face, knocking him back a step or two. Then Campbell jumped over Kleinholtz and scooped up his tomahawk. He rose and turned to meet Bullock's assault. Campbell ducked out of the way of Bullock's 'hawk and then lashed out in a sort of backhand with his own, up over Bullock's right arm. The sharp blade of the tomahawk whacked Bullock on the head and tore out a dollar-sized hunk of flesh and hair, exposing the bone.

Campbell stepped back, waiting, as Bullock fell. "Come on, lad, get up," he said, his voice a mixture of elation and cocksureness, laced with almost four years of rage and hatred. "Aye, I'll give ye that chance. I dunna think ye deserve to die that easily."

Bullock got up and turned to face Campbell. He looked hideous. Like all head wounds, this one was bleeding copiously. The blood had slathered across most of Bullock's face, and in the snowy grayness of the new morning, it gave him the look of a creature raised from hell.

"Ya shoulda kilt me when ya had a chance, ya fuckin' dick wart," Bullock growled, voice raspy. "Now I'm gonna do to you what I did to those stinkin' friends of yourn." He laughed, the sound as ghastly as his face. "They was whimperin' little shits, boy. Jist like you. And I'll . . ."

Campbell had had enough. He charged, swinging his tomahawk as his warrior forebears had wielded their battleaxes against the English.

Bullock suddenly had the feeling he was facing five or six men, each more formidable than the last. It was impossible to fend off the ones he imagined, let alone the one real one. He screamed, and again, and continued it.

Campbell swept in on Bullock like an eagle on a salmon, unstoppable, unrelenting in his ferocity, yet somehow in control—barely—of his rage. Rather than just kill Bullock right off with a fatal blow to the neck or head, Campbell managed to rein himself in enough to instead just hack off chunks of Bullock's flesh.

Finally Campbell stopped, panting. He was surprised that Bullock was still able to stand, since he looked more dead than alive. Bullock was covered in blood from hair-line to moccasins. Campbell slid his knife away.

Bullock was dead for all intents and purposes; the news just hadn't reached his brain yet for some reason.

Campbell straightened. "Goodbye, ye stinkin' vermin," he said. He stepped up and, with a good swipe, hacked Bullock's head off. The blood-spurting corpse toppled, and the head bounced several feet away.

Campbell turned and walked to Kleinholtz. The German was still alive, and was even trying to rise. "I dunna think ye're goin' anywhere but hell, laddie," Campbell said with a sneer. He kicked

Kleinholtz's good arm out from under him, and the German flopped back to the ground.

"There be many things I could do to ye, ye scum. But nothing I could do would be bad enough to match your evilness. Still, I'll give it a try."

Eyes burning with ferocity, Campbell drew his knife and knelt. With deliberate slowness, he emasculated and then disemboweled Kleinholtz. "That be for a wee girl ye defiled, ye festerin' sack of shit," Campbell said in a deadly flat voice.

With something akin to enjoyment, Campbell hacked Kleinholtz's head off, too. As he rose, he dropped his tomahawk and picked the head up by the hair. He walked over and also picked up Bullock's.

Spotting a tree with several small forks, he went there and dropped Kleinholtz's skull. He stuffed Bullock's head into one fork. "That be for ye, Caleb," he said. "Perhaps it'll nae do ye much good where ye be now, but 'tis to let ye know that I held true to my promise. And, since his hair be stuck to his head, I think it counts as raisin' his hair."

Campbell took Kleinholtz's head and jammed it into another small fork. "And that one be for ye, Ethan. The same applies, ye know. And now these unsaintly bastards'll ne'er reach the Hereafter."

He stepped back a few paces and stood in silence, not really seeing the wide-eyed heads glaring back at him. What he saw instead was Finch and Sharp, and he thought back to his first encounter with the two crusty trappers, and the many adventures they had had.

"May your eternal rest be always peaceful, my good friends," he said, explaining away the tears as just snow melting on his face. "I'll remember ye for all times. And if ye have nothin' against me, perhaps ye'll nae mind if we partner up again when I cross the divide."

Campbell almost jumped out of his skin when someone touched him on the arm. He turned his head and looked down at Morning Sun.

"Their spirits'll be at peace now," the woman said. "Aye, don't ye doubt it. They watch. And they say 'tis good what ye did."

Campbell nodded. "How aboot ye build up the fire a wee bit and we'll have us somethin' to eat."

Morning Sun handed Campbell his blanket coat and went to do as she had been bid. Campbell put the coat on and then gathered and cleaned his weapons.

They ate quietly. Campbell needed to be alone with his thoughts. He was sated with vengeance and somewhat proud of what he had done. Yet he was depressed and on edge.

After eating, Morning Sun asked, "What do we do now, husband?"

Campbell looked at her bright, beautiful face and suddenly realized there was life yet to be lived. He had done all he could for his slain partners and friends; now he had to get on with his life.

He shrugged. "Do what we always do at this time of year, lass," he said, "look for someplace to winter up." He paused, then added, "But ye know the beaver trade is nae gonna shine any more?" When she nodded, he continued. "It's all I know to do, and perhaps we'll have starvin' times before I can figure oot what to do to make my way."

"We faced starvin' times before," Morning Sun

said matter-of-factly. "Ye'll find a way for us," she added confidently.

Campbell smiled a little. An hour later, with the snow still falling heavily, Campbell and Morning Sun rode off.

John Legg is a full-time writer and newpaper editor who lives in Arizona with his family.

If you would like to be placed on John Legg's mailing list, in order to receive periodic newsletters and updates on new books, please send a postcard to:

John Legg
P.O. Box 39032
Phoenix, Arizona 85069

Please note on the postcard if you would like to receive a current list of Mr. Legg's books.

Thank you for your interest. Happy reading!